W9-CEG-167

THE MOTION OF PUPPETS

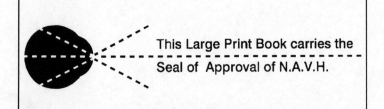

This Large Print Book carries the
Seal of Approval of N.A.V.H.

THE MOTION OF PUPPETS

KEITH DONOHUE

THORNDIKE PRESS
A part of Gale, Cengage Learning

GALE
CENGAGE Learning·

Farmington Hills, Mich • San Francisco • New York • Waterville, Maine
Meriden, Conn • Mason, Ohio • Chicago

BOCA RATON PUBLIC LIBRARY
BOCA RATON, FLORIDA

GALE
CENGAGE Learning

Copyright © 2016 by Keith Donohue.
Thorndike Press, a part of Gale, Cengage Learning.

ALL RIGHTS RESERVED
This is a work of fiction. All of the characters, organizations, and events portrayed in this novel are either products of the author's imagination or are used fictitiously.
Thorndike Press® Large Print Bill's Bookshelf.
The text of this Large Print edition is unabridged.
Other aspects of the book may vary from the original edition.
Set in 16 pt. Plantin.

LIBRARY OF CONGRESS CATALOGING-IN-PUBLICATION DATA

Names: Donohue, Keith, author.
Title: The motion of puppets / by Keith Donohue.
Description: Large print edition. | Waterville, Maine : Thorndike Press, 2017. |
    Series: Thorndike Press large print Bill's bookshelf
Identifiers: LCCN 2016046291| ISBN 9781410497307 (hardcover) | ISBN 1410497305
    (hardcover)
Subjects: LCSH: Large type books. | GSAFD: Occult fiction.
Classification: LCC PS3604.O5654 M68 2017 | DDC 813/.6—dc23
LC record available at https://lccn.loc.gov/2016046291

Published in 2017 by arrangement with Picador

Printed in Mexico
1 2 3 4 5 6 7 21 20 19 18 17

BOCA RATON PUBLIC LIBRARY
BOCA RATON, FLORIDA

For Bill and Luise Pugh

"Why did you glance back?
Why did you hesitate for that moment?"

— H.D. "EURIDYCE"

BOOK ONE

1

She fell in love with a puppet.

Because he was beautiful, because he was rare, because he could not be hers. Every time she passed the dusty display window of the tiny Quatre Mains storefront, she looked for him. Propped by hidden scaffolding, the puppet stood beneath a bell jar. Two black holes drilled for eyes on just the hint of a face. His smooth blank head was attached by a wooden hinge to his body, which had been hewn from a single piece of poplar, darkened by centuries, and his rudimentary joined limbs had been pierced at the hands and feet. A simple loop, worn and cracked, rose from the crown of his skull. No strings had been threaded through those holes in ages, but he was clearly a primitive marionette carved by an aboriginal Inuit craftsman long ago, the wood now riven by cracks that had opened along the grain. A thin scar ringed his chest, as though once long ago someone had been interrupted in cutting him in two. No bigger than one of her childhood dolls, just over a foot tall. The man out of time waited pensively for someone to rescue him from a glass prison. A skin of dust lay on the curve of the bell, and on a foxed paper label affixed to the bottom lip was inscribed in faded calligraphy: *poupée ancienne.*

He was the lord of all the other toys in the window, all now familiar as old friends to Kay. Six dolls flanked the man in the jar, three on each side. Brightly painted with frozen smiles and rouged cheeks, their bisque faces shone in the sunshine, and they stared straight ahead, focused on the same eternal spot. They had not been played with for nearly a century, artifacts of the Victorian and Edwardian eras, with thick brocaded gowns and traveling suits, fine nests of hair piled upon their heads. Two of them brandished folded parasols, the tips as sharp as spears. A brown bear in a tatted red fez and a vest embroidered in gold filigree balanced on an iron velocipede, the fur at his elbows and knees threadbare. A hand puppet slouched next to the bear, a sad hound she recognized from the early years of children's television, its extravagantly long ears dangling to the shelf below. A lurid Punch and

12

Judy, their garish faces bleached by the sun, grinned with their hideous mouths. Mr. Punch cocked his slapstick in hand, always ready to strike his wife. At a certain angle, she appeared to be raising her arms in defense. Odds and ends lay scattered in the shadows: a tiny troop of tin soldiers dressed in scarlet coats and bearskin hats, a pair of glass eyes with lapis lazuli irises, a half-size French horn with a lovely green patina winding through the twists and turns in the brass, and an articulated wooden snake poised to strike a heel stumbling through the grass. Behind the hodgepodge of trinkets, four black marionette horses hung from thick cords, disappearing into the rafters. In one corner of the window a cobweb, burdened with dust, stretched from wall to ceiling and below it lay the husks of two honeybees.

By all appearances, the Quatre Mains had been closed and abandoned. The display window never changed, not a thing out of place in the weeks since she and Theo came to Québec City and strolled to her first rehearsal. *Stop! Isn't this adorable,* she had said. No one ever entered or left. The door was always locked. No lights shone in the evenings or on those afternoons when thunderclouds rolled in and spat fat drops against the old storefronts lining the street. Giddy with the adventurous spirit of the newly married, Theo had once suggested that they simply break in to explore its hidden recesses. Because he had more time to go wandering away from his solitary work, he discovered that several of the antique and curio boutiques along this edge of the old part of town, the Vieux-Québec, had fallen on hard times and were similarly out of business, but his dire read of the situation did not stop her from dreaming. She wanted to hold the puppet in her hands. She wanted to take it. Not another soul was on the street, so she leaned in to look closer and pressed her hands against the dirty window. Light penetrated so far and no farther. She could only make out shapes and shadows, the promise of more. Her hot breath left a fog upon the glass, and when she saw what she had done, Kay grabbed the hem of her sleeve and wiped the patch of condensation. Ever so slightly, the wooden man in the bell jar turned his head to watch her, but she never saw him move, for she had hurried away, late again.

Kay had circled behind his desk and leaned over Theo, draping her slender arms over his shoulders, and clasping her hands against his heart, squeezing firmly until he raised his hands to hers. She kissed him lightly on the cheek, her long hair falling in front of his eyes, so that he felt encased by her until the moment he moved his hand and she unfolded herself and was away, always running late, trailing a string of good-byes as she departed the room, and the next sound was the door closing with a bang.

The silence after Kay left disturbed him more than the noise she made in preparing to go. For an hour, Theo had been trying to work on the translation, turning over in his mind the problems abandoned the night before, anxious to get to the solutions but waiting, waiting to be alone in the apartment so he could concentrate. He never began while she was present, not wanting to miss the opportunity to share a few words with her as she dressed or dallied over the eggs and toast they shared at three in the afternoon. Most days, she seemed barely aware that he hesitated for her, that he devoted his attentions, for she was also thinking ahead to her work, anticipating the moves that would be required of her during the show. She stretched her limbs and bent her body, and he watched from his chair, enthralled by her simple grace, turning over in his mind a particular phrase, the *mot juste,* the sound and sense of the French he struggled to turn into English. His mind in two places at once, with her and without her.

When they first came to this city, they contrived to spend as much time together as possible exploring the old French part of town. Most afternoons he would accompany her like a lovesick schoolboy, leaving their apartment on Dalhousie and winding their way to the warehouse where the company rehearsed, and he would sit with a coffee and the newspaper and watch the acts, week after week. The performers would meet there every afternoon to go over any changes to the show, and then head over to their outdoor performance space. Later, once the run of shows began, Theo would join the parade of visitors to the makeshift theater that had been set up for the season in a vacant lot underneath a highway overpass. It was a wonder to behold, the raised stage surrounded by fences and scaffolding, the arc lights and spots. Ropes hung down from the guardrails, and flying acrobats thrilled the audience by swinging out into the night sky. Small trailers served as dressing rooms, and at the back of the plaza sat a control center for all of the special effects. Most of the crowd would have to stand for the show — like groundlings at Shakespeare's Globe Theatre — but there were two portable bleachers for special guests and a small backstage area that was often crowded with performers making their entrances and exits. There he would watch from the wings night after night, anxious as she performed, until at last she excused him from the duty.

"You have work to do," Kay had told him. "You needn't make this journey every day. You will grow bored with it. Bored of me —"

"Never," he said.

She blushed and looked away. "You're sweet, but honestly. Work to do."

Theo wondered if she meant more by that, if she was not somehow glad to be gone, happy to be apart for those few hours. He uncapped his pen and laid it atop a blank page and then opened the text he had been engaged to translate. The French swarmed before his eyes like thousands of bees. *L'homme en mouvement,* a strange story about a very strange man, the nineteenth-century photographer Eadweard Muybridge, the man who studied the art of motion.

The manuscript was due to the publisher in eleven weeks, on the first of September, but Theo was only a third of the way through the translation, just at the point where Muybridge murders his wife's lover in a rage of jealousy. Muybridge had learned from their housekeeper that she had gone off to a cabin with her lover, so he loaded a pistol, left his offices in San Francisco, and raced to board the very last ferry north where he caught a train. From the end of the line, he hired a wagon to take him to the cabin far out in the country, goading the poor driver to whip the horses through the darkness. He knew his young wife was there with Harry Larkyns. When his wife's lover answered the door, Muybridge shot him through the heart. *Amour fou.* Theo considered the possibilities in English: love insane, fit of passion, fatal desire. What would drive a man to such an extreme act? Since the murder had been planned, could his behavior reasonably be called temporary insanity? If so, would not that be an equal madness guided by the same base emotion, the wayfaring heart, the obsessed mind? Crazy love, he decided, and satisfied with his choice, that was what he wrote: "He was moved by a crazy love for her. He would have done anything."

Theo well understood how love could sway reason. Kay was just impetuous enough to have raised a doubt or two before they were married, her secret life he could not know, her sudden flights. But she made him crazy for her in the end.

A boat's horn sounded on the Saint Lawrence just outside his window, and he used the distraction to rise from the desk and check out the scene below. Flying both the maple leaf flag and the provincial fleur-de-lis, the tour boat chugged to the dock, back from Tadoussac he was sure, where the travelers had gone in search of the whales that came down the seaway every summer — the humpbacks and fins, the minkes and even, it is said, the occasional enormous blue whale, to feed on the abundant schools of fishes and krill. He and Kay had made the trip on a rare day off, and she had been entranced by the white belugas moving like ghosts in the water. Settled in by the window, he watched the crew hop out and tie off the boat and then the passengers disembark, little windup dolls finding their legs as they struggled to the gangway. Framed in a Muybridge sequence, a study of the motion of landlubbers. One by one the people down below steadied themselves, and then they escaped the edge of the picture until they were all gone, and he felt uneasy like a god above whose world had been deserted.

In the heart of the Vieux-Québec, church bells rang evensong, and Theo looked at his wristwatch, surprised by how much time had elapsed since he wrote those last sentences. The work on his desk grumbled for attention, but he could not give it any. Maybe after dinner, once he cleared his head. He shoved his papers and books into his briefcase and shouldered it before stepping outside into the twilight. He loved the lonesomeness of the dusky hour when everything changed from brightness into darkness. Along the streets of the lower part of the old city, the Basse-Ville, the cars zipped by on their way home, and the Musée de la Civilisation had closed its doors for the evening. The street was emptied of pedestrians. They were out looking for a place for dinner perhaps, or headed for a drink and a show, and he envied the patterns of their typical days and the standard routine of their hours. Taking a shortcut to his favorite café on rue Saint-Paul, Theo followed the path Kay had just taken, past her favorite shops, slowing his pace to look in their windows, wondering what she might enjoy, calculating how much money he would have to earn to afford such treasures for her.

Across the street, a light snapped on at

20

the Quatre Mains, throwing a rectangle on the sidewalk. He was surprised by the sign of life in the little toy shop. Shrugging the strap on his bag higher on his shoulder, Theo headed across the narrow street to investigate. The dolls and puppets in the display stood out more sharply in the artificial glow, and he could make out the shelves of toys and the marionettes dangling from wires hung in the ceiling and a mélange of hand puppets propped on the hooks of a coatrack. He pressed his nose against the glass, fascinated by what had long been enshadowed. The room seemed alive with promise, and he tore himself away from the window to try the door, only to find it locked as ever. He knocked loudly.

"Hello, hello, anyone there?"

No reply. He banged on the glass and tried in French. *"Il y a quelqu'un? Allo."*

Nothing stirred inside. He listened for footsteps, made binoculars of his hands, and pressed close but saw nothing. Perhaps there was a back entrance off the alleyway. While he debated whether to check, he rattled the doorknob twice and called out again, his voice echoing off the storefront, embarrassingly strange in the street. A family of five passed by, parents of three small children, turning their heads in unison to

21

the disturbance he was making. The lights inside the store went out suddenly, and he found himself in the dark, pondering his next move. Backing into the street, he looked up to the second story of the building, but the windows were as bare and dusty as ever. There must be a rear door, he concluded, and gathering his wits, he crossed the street again, rueful over the missed opportunity for the gifts he might have bought for her. When he stepped inside the café, the boisterous crowd and sensuous aromas from the kitchen made him forget all else.

Sarant balanced her hands on the sphere and carefully raised her body, resting her weight on the fulcrum of her wrists and the bent angle of her forearms. The June air was hot and humid in the open plaza where the cirque held their free summer shows, honing them for the performances later that year. A moth fluttered inches from her face, but she did not break her concentration on her internal gyroscope. A bus rumbled along an overpass, but the people in the stands and the groundlings beneath them noticed nothing but the acrobats, the lights buzzing faintly, the swell of music from the hidden orchestra. Sarant pressed forward, arching her back and lifting and curving her legs, and then she pushed her arms against the sphere, extending and raising her whole body so that it appeared as a kind of question mark. Black as holes, her eyes focused on a spot above her forehead where she would soon put her toes, contorting her whole form. A low murmur of unease ran through the people closest to the stage, as they realized that the human body was not meant to bend that way. Her muscles twitched with the strain and she exhaled carefully, since one errant breath could upset her balance and send her tumbling. Out in the dark, weak applause grew into crescendo, and Sarant held the pose for a few moments longer before lowering her torso in one fluid motion. Then she swung her legs and straddled the metal ball, and leapt forward, landing perfectly on the flooring. Stuck it, like the gymnast she was. From her place in the chorus behind the acrobat, Kay could see the line of sweat along Sarant's backbone darkening her costume like a streak of blood. The applause trailed off, as she smiled and bowed. Kay wanted thunder — didn't they know how difficult this was? But, no, the audience saved their awe for the fliers who swooped from cabled rope attached to the bottom rails of the overpass, to the daredevils who raced across the ramps on their skates and bicycles and the ringmaster on his unicycle, for the climbers and the risk takers. The delicacy and grace of this interlude paled against the wow of motion that was the signature of the cirque.

Caught up in her grinding resentment, Kay nearly missed her cue. The eight of them, four on each side, rose together and shuffled forward to make the shape of an undulating lotus blossom with Sarant as the radiant center, and closing in on her, she seemed to disappear in their petaled embrace, slipping away through a trapdoor in the stage floor, gone when the flower unfolded. The trick never failed to draw an appreciative gasp from the crowd, the children in particular beholden and amazed. The spotlights snapped off so the petals could escape in darkness, while a new light shone on the group of men teetering on mountain bikes and skateboards on a platform that ran twelve feet overhead along the perimeter of the backstage. Kay had fourteen minutes to make her costume change for the final act.

Crammed together in the dressing room trailer, the acrobats and contortionists stripped off their leotards and found their more fanciful outfits, streaked on their face paint, wriggled into bustiers and head-dresses, a riot of feathers and spangles and bared skin. Reance, the master of ceremonies, weaved between the girls in their varied states of dishabille, stopping once to whisper a word in Sarant's tiny ear, a secret compliment that made her blush through the makeup. Squeezing between two half-naked women, he headed straight for Kay. She looked up at the faintly comical figure in front of her, his makeup craquelled on his skin, his old-fashioned pilot's cap and goggles perched atop his white hair, dividing it into tufts, his ridiculous sideburns and mustache, his long leather duster festooned with pocket watches and compasses and other dials dangling from chains. A steam punk Father Time, though she could never discern the symbolic importance of his character. The night pilot of all dreams, or some such metaphor. Truth be told, she understood little about the dramaturgy of the show, baroque as an opera, the plot a twist on a lovers' triangle, and a boy at the center of it all, caught in time, encased inside a dream of his future. To keep her mind on the performance, she rarely thought of the story. Little more than a way to showcase the acrobats and jugglers, the costumes and music and lights and dazzle of motion. Reance watched as Kay buttoned her blouse, and then he leaned in close enough for her to smell the garlic on his breath.

"Dinner?" he asked, lifting one bushy eyebrow, and she could not tell whether he was really flirting or just exaggerating for comic effect. Funny old lech. "Just a small party. Sarant has already said yes, and a select few others. But it wouldn't be the same without you."

In all of her weeks with the circus, Kay had been invisible, or perhaps she had not taken the other performers' notice into account. Every night Theo had been waiting by the dressing room trailer to walk her home, and she had made her good-byes. But now, she had been granted entrée into the inner circle. She pulled up the straps to her camisole and pretended to look for her shoes. "Yes, sounds fun," she said to the floor.

He laid a hand against her bare shoulder, the fingerless glove as startling as a snake. "I'm so glad you've agreed. Now, let's not miss another cue."

The crowd roared for the finale, a grand tumbling and vaulting parade of acrobats spilling down the platform thrust into their space, the lot of them, the fliers, contortionists, dancers, and clowns pouring out, an orchestrated boffo curtain call designed for maximum approval. The small boy, dreamer of the extravaganza, hopped from Reance's shoulder. Then they clasped hands and bowed; and the company bowed together to a chorus of bravos. The people beyond the footlights clapped till their hands hurt. At the peak of the sound, the lights were cut, and all the performers exited in the echoing darkness. She dipped into her locker and found the clothes she had stashed for a special occasion and quickly changed into a yellow sundress and her favorite shoes, a pair of pale blue heels. After the greasepaint had been wiped away, after the boas and spangles had been packed up for the night, Kay found the others queuing near the entrance gate. "Off to dinner with the cast," she quickly texted her brand-new husband. "Be home late. Don't wait up."

2

Theo woke up alone in the bed. The covers had fallen to the floor sometime in the night, and the sheets were twisted in a damp noose around his feet. For a fleeting moment, he thought Kay might have gotten out of bed early because of his restlessness, but her pillows lay plump and untouched. Or perhaps she came home late, and so as not to disturb him had gone to sleep on the sofa in the living room. His head ached. As he ran his fingertips across his brow, he replayed the night before, the beers and that plate of poutine heavy in his gut. Dreams of Muybridge racing through San Francisco to catch the last ferry, the wagon ride through the winding hills in the dark night to the cabin where his wife had gone to be with her lover. The last thing Theo remembered from his dream was the photographer knocking on the front door, pistol in hand.

"Kay," he called out, but no answer. He

struggled to his feet and stumbled out of the bedroom, repeating her name in the empty rooms. She wasn't on the sofa. She hadn't come home last night, or perhaps she had woken early and had gone out for a pair of hot coffees and those pastries he loved from the shop around the corner. With a fat yawn, he absentmindedly shuffled through last night's work, half his attention focused on the foyer, awaiting the sound of her return, the ding of the elevator, footsteps on the landing, the jangle of keys at the lock. The blank page offered no real distraction for his agitation, so he rose without writing a single word. He wandered from room to room, opening the shades to bring in the light, searching for where he had left his cell phone. A quick call to her would clear up the entire mystery. Chuckling at the memory, he found it at last behind a throw pillow on the sofa. He had been keeping vigil there before falling asleep to an old black-and-white movie and must have abandoned the phone on his half-awake trek to the bedroom. Right, she had sent him a text: *Be home late. Don't wait up.* But he had expected her for a while, and only reluctantly crawled into bed around midnight without her. He thumbed to her number.

When his call went straight to voice mail,

he hung up without leaving a message and then punched in a series of urgent texts, one after the other as soon as each was delivered:

Where are you?

Did you come home last night?

Call me.

No reply. He cursed the smartphone and all technology for its failure to bring him an instant answer. Either she had forgotten to turn on her phone, or it was powerless somewhere, in need of a charge. Just like the time when they were dating and she stood him up without a word. She could have called and explained, he would have understood. Her secretiveness had nearly ruined everything, and now he felt a mixture of annoyance and anxiety that weighed like a rock in his belly. Nothing to be done but wait, take a shower, make breakfast, keep busy.

Rubbing the beginnings of a beard, Theo thought of Muybridge and his magnificent nineteenth-century gray whiskers. Of course, he had married later in life, and his bride, despite having been once married and divorced already, was much younger. She must have been reminded of that difference in ages every time she saw that snowy beard. Perhaps that's why she strayed, looking for some vigor and excitement the older man could not provide. The same worries plagued Theo, though he and Kay were only a decade apart, but still. She should be more responsible, should know that he would worry, but he could hear her laughing it off when she came home. *You'll give yourself ulcers,* she'd say. *You fret too much. I just went out for croissants.*

But she had not returned by the time he finished taking a shower and dressing for the day. She had not returned when the coffee had gurgled through the machine, nor after he had finished his cold cereal. He badgered his phone for an update every few minutes, but she could not be reached. Late morning seeped into the apartment in a funk. The kitchen clock ticked like a metronome. Dust in the sunlight swirled like a lazy tempest. Through the open window, he could smell the exhaust of traffic below from cars on the street, boats on the water. A startling horn broke the reverie. The coffee had gone cold and sour. On the table, his books and papers threatened to fly away of their own accord, and his pen looked like a bloodied knife. The whole apartment felt like a crime scene. He could do nothing but wait.

If anything made their first months together difficult, it was his impatience and her independence. They had fought about it when Kay first landed the part to join the cirque for the summer.

"I'll be so busy with rehearsals and the show. You can stay in New York and work on your translation, and I'll find a sublet with some of the others in the cast," she had offered.

The suggestion poleaxed him, and the thought left him speechless. Kay sat next to him on the sofa, rested her head on his shoulder. "Of course, you could come up for the weekends. I'd miss you too much."

"I can't imagine being apart like that just when we are finally together."

"Be practical. I was only trying to save a little money."

Frantic at the thought of separation, he had juggled his schedule at the college in New York and used the advance from his publisher to find this place on Dalhousie, where he could work while she was off performing. The whole episode left him questioning how she prioritized their marriage and her career.

Shortly after noon, with still no word from Kay, he thought to call the stage manager at the warehouse rehearsal hall to see if they had any information on her whereabouts.

The number, fortunately, was posted on a sticky note next to the fridge, but unfortunately no one answered his call. Too early for the performers or crew to arrive and prepare for that evening's show. They would all be sleeping now, the upside-down world of theater people. He decided to go out and look for her, and, taking a page from his notebook, he scribbled a note saying to please call if she came home before he returned.

Bright June sunshine fell across his face as he stood outside their apartment considering the possibilities. She could be anywhere or nowhere at all. Injured and lying in a gutter or whisked off to a hospital. Or worse. He quickened his pace, following the familiar path between the apartment building and the warehouse, turning down rue Saint-Paul, past the cafés and antique shops, hurrying along the street till he reached the quayside farmers' market where they often went to shop in her free hours. Old Town stretched out over his left shoulder, the hotel Frontenac loomed like a castle on a mountain. He had to cross several busy streets before coming at last to the warehouse where the company had kept the enormous sets and contraptions that went into making their outdoor show a few blocks away. Now, it was largely empty, save for the few giant props that had not made it into the final version of the show. The large sliding doors at the front of the building were chained shut, so he went around to the side entrance, only to find that door locked as well. He banged his fist against the metal door, the echo empty and melancholic.

From deep inside the bowels, a shout worked its way forward, alternating in French and English, urging patience, *s'il vous plaît.* A deadbolt snapped, tumblers turned in a lock, and the door slowly swung open to reveal a rather sleepy-looking dwarf, who scowled in the sudden brightness. They considered each other for a moment in mutual suspicion. The little man rubbed the stubble on his chin.

"Go away," he said. "*Nous sommes fermés.* Come back at four." He began to close the door.

"Wait." Theo raised his voice. "I'm looking for my wife. She's with the show."

"No one is here. Cast and crew arrive at four o'clock. Tickets at five. Come back when the box office is open."

"I didn't mean to disturb you —"

"Well, you have a funny way. I was fast asleep."

"It's just that she didn't come home last night after the performance." He held up his phone. "And she's not answering my texts. I even tried to call, but no luck."

The doorman gave him a jagged grin. "Well, she wasn't with me, whoever she is."

"Pardon?" Theo looked over the little man's head into the cavernous room.

"I meant nothing by it. Just a bit of a fat morning, and you've caught me out of sorts."

"An acrobat with the show," he said. "Kay. Kay Harper. I'm her husband, Theo. I thought she might have spent the night here, with the other performers."

"Egon Picard," the little man said. "Assistant to the stage manager, and major domo of this empty building. Look, bub, if you want to come in and wait?" Egon widened the entryway, and then without a backward glance, he turned and led Theo through the dark passageway to a ramshackle office tucked into a far corner. A rumpled blanket covered the bottom of a small cot, and the room also held a tiny sink and a counter with a hot plate and an electric kettle. He produced a bottle of whiskey from a cabinet beneath the sink and two highball glasses, indicating with a gesture his offer of a drink. Theo nodded and inspected the room with a casual air.

Taped to the walls was a gallery of sepia pictures, nineteenth-century postcards of women in various stages of undress. In the one above the pillow, a fully clad gentleman reached beneath the skirts of a maid seeming to enjoy the experience. Another showed a woman with a riding crop resting against her bare bottom. Swinging on a trapeze, a third woman leaned back in all her glory above a trio of circus clowns just out of reach.

"That's quite a collection," Theo said. Ambling around the room, he paused to inspect the more provocative poses.

Handing one glass to Theo, Egon downed his own drink in a single swig. "My *spécialité*," he said. "I won my first beauty playing poker with a man from Fargo, North Dakota. Full house. Knaves over deuces to his hearts flush. And he had no money, so. Out of such chance comes obsession. Do they offend you, Mr. Harper? Do they scandalize you?" The little man was goading him, waggling his hairy eyebrows and leering.

Theo took a sip of his whiskey, the liquid burning pleasantly in the back of his throat. "Heavens, no. I just was admiring your eclectic tastes."

"Have you ever stopped to consider the fact that these women are all gone now, yet they live on in these pictures, captured in the flower of their youth and beauty?"

"The power and art of the photograph," Theo said. "To stop time. Do you know the work of Eadweard Muybridge? Stop-motion? He often used nudes to study the mechanics of how the body moves."

Egon poured another two fingers of Bush-mills in his glass. "I don't know any Muy-bridge. I know nothing about art. I speak of beauty, man. Youth and how it fades, even though a picture lasts forever."

The notion hung in the air between them, coaxing both to silent contemplation. Egon tilted back another dram of liquor, and Theo took the phone from his pocket to check for a missing message. He swiped and thumbed in his password, and his wife's image filled his screen. Dressed in a costume and wearing a wig from a now-forgotten show, Kay looked over her shoulder at him, caught in a moment between surprise and happiness. He showed the photograph to Egon. "Are you sure you don't remember her? She's in the balancing act with the contortionist, one of the flower girls. And she's in the tableaux, the tumbling finale." He thrust the phone closer.

Egon leaned in to take a good look. "Kay, Kay, Kay, Kay? Yes, I know that girl. Seems to me, yes, now that you showed me her picture, of course, I know her. Supporting cast. A voice in the chorus." With a wave, he dismissed the phone.

"So do you have any idea where she might be? Friends in the show? She texted me last night that some of the cast were going out after the performance. Not to wait up. But she never came home."

Wiping his eyes with the heels of his palms, Egon bore down on his clouded memories. "They all run together, these nights, but thinking it over, she may have been with a bunch of the actors. Sarant and some of the others, now I recall. She may be the girl arm in arm with Reance. You know him, the master of ceremonies? Old fart in a pair of goggles?" He caught the expression on Theo's face. "You mustn't be alarmed. There were a bunch of them going out together. Actors, you know. *Toujours gai, toujours jolie.* So he makes a play for each of them in time, but often as not, *pfft,* nothing comes of it."

"Where can I find this Reance?"

"Patience, *monsieur,* they have a call for tonight's performance at four o'clock. He'll show up."

■ ■ ■ ■

She should have never gone. At first, it was flattering to have been noticed and asked to join the party, and on the way over to the bar, they had been a jolly crew, Sarant and Reance, four others from the show. But Kay had too much to drink and that man had been pawing her at the table. Hand on her thigh to punctuate a joke. Brushing against her to reach another bottle of wine. Arm around the back of her chair and then leaning against her to tell a story. Whenever she dared to speak, Kay could feel his eyes upon her, rapt, attentive, darting with an unspoken question. She tried to shrug him off, change the subject, let someone else take the spotlight, but he persisted in flirting with her without saying a word. The empty glasses seemed to breed more glasses, and the bottles crowded the tabletop. All around them, couples finished their nightcaps, parties broke up and departed, leaving the place to the actors. At two, a weary waitress forced a check upon them, and they counted out the strange Canadian dollar coins to split the bill. The tipsy revelers staggered out and congregated on the sidewalk, caught between the desire to carry on with their fun and the flagging energy of a long night. Sarant and two of the other women called a taxi. The men wavered and waited under a crescent moon, Reance lurking at her side like a jackal.

"I think I'll walk," Kay said. "It isn't far. Clear my head."

"Let me escort you," Reance said. "So that you're safe."

"Not necessary," she answered quickly. "Besides, I go the other way. Our flat is in the Basse-Ville. There's nobody about, and I walk home alone nearly every night after the show."

"It's so late. I insist. I wouldn't feel right." He was playing the gallant, but just below the skin was a rogue.

"No, I insist. It was fun though. Thank you for asking me to join the party, but I will be perfectly fine." With a wave, she said her good-byes.

Muddled by the wine, Kay set off in the wrong direction and had gone down an unfamiliar side street before realizing her mistake. Rather than backtrack and risk bumping into her friends again, she circled around the block, past the empty businesses, the small hotels, and town houses drowsing with sleepers, feeling hopelessly lost in the tangle of alleyways. She thought of phoning Theo to come rescue her but did not want to wake him at such a late hour. She considered trying to hail a cab, but the few in town were almost always to be found on a main thoroughfare and rarely at this hour, so she walked on, the sound of her own footfall echoing against the stone houses. With each step, she invented someone following her, a madman, a killer, so she would stop and listen and laugh at her own foolish imagination.

For their honeymoon, Kay and Theo had rented a cabin near a lake in the Maine woods, and she had gone out in the middle of the night by herself to see the stars from the deck. The constellations were clear and crisp, but the pine trees had obscured Cassiopeia, so she walked along the driveway trying to find a better vantage spot. From the birches came a shudder, steps amid the falling leaves, and the shadow of a moose scared the wits out of her. She ran back inside as quickly as she could and stood on the other side of the closed door, panting and laughing at herself. When Theo heard her story, he had chided her for going out alone, and she seethed for half an hour about how overbearing he could be sometimes. But lovable, too, to be so concerned.

Without quite knowing how, she stumbled

onto rue Saint-Paul near the Marché du Vieux-Port, a landmark for her journey home. The familiar sight allayed her fears. Under the streetlights, the low-slung farmers' market appeared like a set of models from a miniature railroad, down to the smallest detail — the sign over the entrance, the empty pushcarts, and the covered stalls. If she drew closer, she felt they would be revealed as fakes, and so unsettled, she rushed past, averting her eyes, heading down Saint-Paul with grim determination. Kay was certain now that she was being followed, her pursuer matching her movements in perfect synchronicity. When she stopped, he stopped. Pick up the pace, slow, dawdle, speed up again. He was clever, for each time she turned around to confront him, she could find no one. In a curious way, she hoped it was Reance and not some random thug come to take her money, her life. Earlier when they were leaving the bar, Reance had pressed his hand against the small of her back at a precise juncture that signaled his desire. His hand felt hot and clammy through her thin dress. He had been flirting with her all night and now he was following her, she was sure. She jogged a few paces, past a tiny parking lot, the street narrowing.

Behind her, a hiss startled her, a cat chasing a rat, a snake in the cracks of the sidewalk, breath of air escaping from an anxious man. A single light snapped on and pooled on the sidewalk, a bright oasis in a desert of darkness. The two moments, the hiss and the light, followed as though one had caused the other, like the scrape of a match simultaneously producing the flame. Her heel caught in a crack in the pavement and snapped in two.

"Son of a bitch," she said, surprised at how loud her voice sounded. After trying to reattach the stem of her heel, she flung the broken piece in the gutter and carried both shoes, limping barefoot, realizing that the light was coming from inside the Quatre Mains. She flew to the storefront, escaping her assailer, and tried the knob to the perpetually locked door, a flutter in her heart as it turned.

Bells along the lintel rang cheerfully when she crossed the threshold, and even at the late hour, she expected to be welcomed to the shop by its proprietor, a kindly old soul: *May I help you?* But no one answered her hellos. The shop was crammed with toys, and all that had been hidden before was now revealed. She and Theo had never seen what lived in the shadows. Dead center was

43

a puppet theater, a sylvan scene decorating the proscenium, just the right size for a young child, and hiding behind the scenery were a handful of finger puppets — a porcupine, a moose, a beaver, a loon, a Mountie, and a damsel in distress. Along the wall next to the door was a long wooden counter with an antique cash register. She laid her bag and broken shoes atop a display case filled with tray after tray of parts for dolls, not just their costumes and accessories but glass eyes, arms, shoes, mittens, hair of every color from fiery red to coal black. A half-dozen marionettes hung on long ropes from the ceiling, twirling ever so slightly as she passed, Hansel and Gretel off to meet the witch, Alice and the Queen of Hearts. Along the other wall were rows of Pinocchios, Muppets on a hat rack, Indonesian shadow puppets, glove puppets, sock monkeys, and papier-mâché lions and tigers and bears. There were windups and cast-iron banks of old-time baseball players pitching and catching. A felted red rooster in a yellow beret. A flywheel monkey dressed in a green bellboy's cap and jacket. Clowns whose arms and legs jumped when you pulled a string. The creatures all seemed to be watching her as she roamed about the shop. In the peculiar quiet, she wondered where the owners were.

Behind the merchandise and around the corner, there was a staircase leading to what she assumed must be the living quarters. To the right, a beaded curtain hung like the entrance to a stage. She poked her head into the space, but the room was dark. In the half-light that spilled from the shop, she could make out a long rectangular table, odd tools, a vise and clamp. Parked on shelves and benches, toys in various states of disrepair. But no people. Nothing to indicate that the proprietors were alive and nearby. Where had they been all these weeks, and why was the abandoned shop suddenly open and empty at the dead of night? If she had seen the lights in the windows, perhaps the man who was following her would as well.

On her way to lock the front door, Kay suddenly remembered the puppet she adored, the ancient wooden man beneath the bell jar. She stole to the window, anxious as a lover, and discovered him waiting for her, as always. She held her breath to be so close. Ancient and beautiful, he seemed to contain a secret life. Gripping the glass handle at the top of the bell, she lifted, and just as she broke the seal between the jar and the wooden surface, the lights went out and she fell into the dark.

3

She was made of coiled wire under the skin, her limbs wound taut, as if one touch would spring the tensile energy of her body. Even her long dark hair was pulled back against her scalp, barely constrained. Only her face remained placid, expressionless, her eyes as still and black as a doll's. She tapped her foot as he spoke and rolled her wrists in intricate waves. Egon had detained her on the way into the warehouse, introducing her as Sarant, the Tibetan Knot.

"I'm worried," Theo said. "I haven't heard from her all day and that's so unlike Kay. I thought perhaps you could help me figure out what happened last night."

Sarant spoke with the disdain of a true star. "We went to dinner after the show, that's all. Don't ask me where. I cannot keep the names straight in this labyrinth of streets. Seven of us. Some drinks. Closed the place as a matter of fact, and then we each went our separate ways."

"But where did Kay go? She never came back to the apartment."

Biting her bottom lip, Sarant looked anxious to make her escape. "Look — Theo, is it? I don't know what happened to your wife. Those of us who don't live in the Basse-Ville called for a cab, and while we were waiting for it to arrive, she said she wanted to walk home. So she did."

"Nobody saw her home?"

"She's a big girl and said it wasn't far."

"All by herself?"

"At first, yes, but then Reance seemed worried about her walking alone in the middle of the night, so he took off after her. To catch her."

Popping between them, Egon rubbed his hands together. "So, your mystery is solved, *monsieur,* a tale old as the Neanderthal dragging a girl by the hair —"

The spring uncoiled and Sarant slapped him lightly on the crown of his head. "*Va chier.* Pay no attention to the little man, Theo. He is *osti d'épais* and knows nothing. None of us knows anything at all. I'm sure this will all be made clear when they show up. A logical explanation."

Before she could step away, she felt Theo's hand grasp her arm. "But you don't sus-

48

pect," he asked, "you have no reason to believe that there was anything between them?"

With the slightest twist of her wrist, Sarant freed herself. A wry smile creased her face, as if she was remembering some long-ago tryst. "In the history of men and women, anything is possible, as you are surely aware. But, that said, I don't remember your wife slobbering over Reance, if that's what you mean. Although he is a notorious roué and a sweet-talking man, and she was well in her cups. Maybe she just slept it off and has been nursing a hangover all day. You'll have to ask him. Or better yet, her." A fellow acrobat appeared at her side and rescued her, and they walked off, whispering and giggling, like two middle school gossips.

Egon pulled at Theo's shirtsleeve. An unlit cheroot hung from his lip. "Come, let us ambush the swain."

On the street in front of the warehouse with the smokers, they watched the others arrive from all directions. Puffing away on his little cigar, Egon nodded to the actors and crew while Theo scanned the faces in the crowd. They bore a playfulness and light, each and every one, as if painted by a single hand. Theo waited for Kay to show

49

up and pour out her explanations, but he did not care where she had been. He just wanted to see her again, safe and sound. *Where are you? Are you coming home?*

Exhausted by his long journey, Muybridge had composed himself, walked to the back entrance, and knocked on the door. He said, "I have a message for you from my wife" and then shot the man dead as soon as he opened his mouth. Theo wished he had a pistol in his belt. He pictured Kay and Reance innocently approaching, chatting intimately of the night before, without a clue, and he would take out the revolver and say "I have a message for you about my wife" and fire a bullet into the bastard's black heart.

The few show people Theo recognized as Kay's friends he stopped on the way in and asked if they had seen or heard from her, but each one seemed baffled by the question. His comrade Egon pressed the case, asking if they had seen Reance, had he said anything about coming in late? The clock sped past four, and neither one had shown up. Egon lit another cigar and sat on the stoop. In a little while, worn out from pacing the pavement, Theo joined him in the vigil.

"Women," Egon said, shaking his head.

"Am I right? I wish I had a woman to help me take care of the women in my life. A woman who understands women, a woman to explain women to me."

"But who would help you understand that woman?"

Pulling the cigar from his mouth, Egon considered the ash and the wet end. "I'm beginning to have serious misgivings about my whole plan."

"Do you really think she spent the night with Reance?"

A body threw its shadow across the place where they were sitting. "And who am I supposed to have slept with now?"

Squinting into the sunshine, Theo looked up to see a tall man above them, nattily dressed, a tweed coat and vest, a fob and watch chain disappearing into a small pocket. Theo struggled to his feet to confront him. "Reance?"

"At your service." He clicked his heels like a soldier and bowed his head. His face pinkened as he rose. His thin white hair had retreated toward the back of his scalp, and he wore a crazed mustache joined by two busy sideburns, giving the impression of a refugee from the Victorian era, a raja from the heyday of British East India.

On his feet, Egon spoke for his tongue-tied friend. "This man is making inquiries about a member of the company. Madam Harper, Kay Harper. And we have reason to believe that you were with her last night."

Through the white snake of his facial hair, Reance grinned at them. "It depends on what you mean by *with her*."

"What I'd like you to tell us," Theo said, "is if you know where she is right now."

"Good heavens. Why would I know such a thing? I just got here myself."

"You're late," Egon said. "And you needn't pretend. We have several witnesses who will swear that you were both at a dinner party together and that you followed her home last night."

Bending at the waist, Reance eased himself down so that he could be face-to-face with the little man. "Who may I ask is asking? Is this a detective?"

"Kay is my wife," Theo blurted out. "And I'd like to find out just where she is."

"Good sir, kind sir, I do not know anything at all about Kay's whereabouts. True, she was with a small party of lovelies that dined with me last night, but I assure you there was nothing improper, not a jot. You may ask Sarant or any of the others. Just a treat for the hardworking and unsung members of the company. And it is true, as well,

52

that our libations extended to the wee hours of the morn, but unfortunately there was never a moment when I was alone with any of the fair sex. After the party broke up, the women hopped in a taxi, and your wife, quite stubbornly and quite against my better judgment, decided to walk home, the night being fair and dry. She departed us, and my upbringing as a gentleman — call me old-fashioned — persuaded me otherwise. That is to say, she should not be unescorted at such a late hour. Sadly, however, I had waited too long to accompany her. She had mentioned a flat on Dalhousie, and so I set off, but could not find her. She had simply disappeared. And I have neither seen nor heard from her from that moment to this."

The thoroughness of his explanation silenced them. He was very good, this actor.

"And furthermore, I wandered about the Basse-Ville for a long while looking for Kay, until I myself was nearly lost, but then headed home for the night. Alone. My cats will verify. And because I was so worried, I could not sleep a wink till dawn and then woke late and am now tardy for the run-through of changes for tonight's show; and the director will have my hide. I'm sorry, Mr. Harper, about your wife, and I do hope you'll tell me what happened, or she will, when she shows up, but I really must be going. And as for you, Egon, my fine friend, we shall discuss your impertinence in private."

For a fleeting moment, Theo wished that Kay had been with Reance, so that at least she could be situated at a particular place in the world, but now she was adrift again, lost in the night. He checked his phone for the hundredth time that afternoon. He called her mother in Vermont and left a message asking her to call if she should hear from Kay, not to worry, just a miscommunication. He sent a mass text to all their mutual friends back in New York.

"I've got to get going," Egon said. "The show."

"Do you believe him?"

"He's an actor." He shrugged and showed him his palms. "That said, we're no closer to finding your wife than when you arrived. Perhaps you should think about contacting the police."

First, they took off her head. The big woman laid it out upon the table, where it rolled and wobbled before coming to a complete rest. Kay could see the rest of her body, straight as a corpse in a coffin, her

54

slender hands folded neatly across her chest. She was surprised by how small she had become. The big man above her grasped a long thin tool resembling a crochet hook and poked through the hole at the base of her cranium, but she did not feel any pain, only the sensation of discomfort she associated with a root canal. Instead of one tooth, it was her whole head. A whispering moan passed his lips as he gripped hold and tugged, pulling out a wad of cotton, and she felt a sudden rush of emptiness, a void where her brain had been. Taking a dollop of fine sawdust in his right hand, he held her empty skull upside down in the fingers of his left hand and filled the hollow to the brim. The giant then took kitchen shears and cut the length of her trunk from neck to navel and, reaching in with a forceps, removed what had become of her insides. He snipped her arms at the shoulders and her legs at the hips, sliced them lengthwise, and emptied those as well. Unstuffed, she thought of her wire-frame body as an empty suit of clothes, her arms and legs flat as pillowcases. It didn't hurt but was curiously fascinating. Using a small metal funnel, the hands poured more of the same sawdust into her hands and feet, and stuffed her torso with batting, pressing deep into the

55

corners and curves. Then, suddenly, he left, interrupted in his work. The lights in the workshop were turned off, and she was alone in five pieces with her head stuck on its side.

Ordinary time had no bearing in her state. She lay there for hours, days, perhaps longer, she could not tell. The room remained dark. The big hands did not come back. Disassembled, she had time to think. That she was missing from her job and home produced no anxiety, which is not to say that in her idleness she did not think of her husband, her poor mother. No, they occupied her mind for considerable stretches, but rather than worry over them or wonder what they must be thinking of her absence, she dwelt instead on the pleasant memories. With nothing better to do, with nothing at all to do, Kay flipped through her reminiscences like an old photograph album. Mother teaching her to tumble as a child. Mother in the morning come in from milking the cows, the sweet smell of hay and manure clinging to her clothes, the milk still warm from the udder. Mother's accident that left her in the wheelchair. Her father always with a pipe in hand in the short hours between supper and bed. Then her father gone for good, a grave, a headstone with his name. A boy she knew in Vermont, hair red as copper, who showed her how to hide behind a waterfall and sought to kiss her, but she wouldn't have him. Then a handsome man — her husband? — trying to teach her irregular verbs in French when she wanted nothing more than to go to bed with him and stay there. She did not miss these things. The thought did not make her sad. They were simply pages in a book that helped pass the hours or whatever it was that spun her world.

When the giants finally returned, it was a welcome relief. Had she eyelids, she would have blinked out of habit at the brightness, but the light felt good and warm. The big woman picked up her head and fitted it loosely to the trunk of her body, tacking the cloth in place on Kay's neck. Then, taking a heavy needle and braid of thread, she began to sew the pieces back together. After she had finished the arms and the legs and dressed her in a white blouse and simple jumper, the woman took two wooden dowels and attached them with loops of Velcro to Kay's wrists. The giantess picked her up with one hand circled completely around her waist and held her upright, her bare feet not quite touching the surface of the table. Kay had not stood in ages, and the change in perspective dizzied her and made her uneasy. Using the rods, the woman moved Kay's arms up and down, back and forth, and then rocked her hips so that she moved, she danced, she leapt for joy. Across the room, the male giant laughed and clapped his hands with delight, but his voice boomed like thunder, too loud to be understood. Both the man and woman were too big to take in fully. Like being too close to a mountain. Just their hands, larger than she, lined like maps of the planets, fingers as big as trees, nails as hard as antlers and horns. They played this way for a few moments, and Kay felt such unbridled exhilaration that she wanted to laugh, to shout, to sing, but she was mute as a stone. The giantess set her down gently on a different, smaller table, and in due course the lights went out again, and Kay waited. This time with less patience and more anticipation for them to come again.

Now that she was put back together, so to speak, Kay began to feel more like her old self. Old self in a new body. She reckoned her relative size from her surroundings. She judged her height as not more than twelve inches, her weight a few ounces, perhaps half a pound. At first her smallness startled her, but, like all change, she grew accustomed to it. Her head was made of wood and the rest of her was stuffed cloth. Her senses seemed intact, and she could hear her own words in her head, not just her thoughts but the sound of sentences and paragraphs, the very music of language, remembered songs and poems, the percussive surprise of laughter. But she could not speak. Her mouth was but a slash of paint.

There were others like her in the room. After a time she became acclimated to the darkness and could see the shapes around her. A pair of feet, the perfect globe of someone else's head. Once in a while, a stray sound broke the quiet, nothing more than a sigh from a dreamer anxious in her sleep, the drum of bored fingers, the creak of a stiff wooden joint. At regular intervals, she could smell food cooking and deduced the pattern of the days by the aromas. Eggs and coffee meant morning. Soup and cheese at midday, the richness of full dinners. She never felt the slightest hunger and was glad for the lack of appetite. Mostly the sameness of the days filled her with ennui. She longed for company, for the giants, not out of any lonesomeness but for the chance to play again, to feel the joy in movement. She was built for motion, and the stillness was the most difficult part of waiting for her life to begin again. When the overhead light came on in the middle of the night, suddenly and without warning, she felt the joy leap in the place where her heart used to be.

4

Forms, there are always many forms for these situations. The desk officer helped with the *Fiche descriptive outil profil* by asking Theo the questions and filling in the boxes. After the preliminaries and general description of the missing person, she moved on with the rest of the form.

"State of health? Any ongoing medical conditions?"

"She's fine. Fit. Nothing wrong with her. That's an odd question."

"You would be surprised. Many missing persons cases, it's the elderly. Alzheimer's, dementia, they wander off from home and get themselves quickly disoriented, and there's no bread crumb trail to follow. Their poor families find out, or the neighbor hears the cat crying through the night, they come to us to help find them. That's a tough one." The sergeant looked down at the form and translated the next question. "Does she go

61

to any medical specialist or have regular treatments? Therapy?"

"No," Theo said. "How many missing persons do you have?"

"I know of a dozen or so, outstanding, but, as I say, most are the old ones who are lost. Or runaways. Bad scene at home. Abuse. Maybe drugs. Does she take any drugs?"

Theo shook his head. Once upon a time, she had confessed to experimenting with an old boyfriend, but that was ancient history.

"When children are involved, we look at the parents. Sometimes they are split up, and Mom or Dad kidnaps the child from the other. Of course, she is no child, but perhaps a friend has heard from her? Can you give me a list of her contacts?"

Taking out his phone, he scrambled through his own lists for mutual friends, knowing that hers were different — and in her phone, wherever that may be. As he wrote them down, he asked if the missing were usually found.

"In many of the other kinds of cases, the missing aren't missing at all, just gone for a time. Run off with a lover for the weekend. Or on a bender. Gambling. The old folks wandering away. But unless something happened to them, they turn up fairly quickly."

"Is that why the police won't start looking until twenty-four hours have passed?"

"Mr. Harper" — she laughed — "you watch too many American police shows. No, we decide how to proceed on a case-by-case basis. If it seems a medical emergency, a matter of life and death, we start right away. If a minor is involved, of course, we spring to action. A likely *affaire de coeur,* perhaps we wait a bit. Do you think your wife might be having an affair?"

He hesitated with an answer, unsure as to whether or not to share his suspicion about Reance. It was only that, only a feeling and not based on any evidence. In fact, until this afternoon he had known of the man only by reputation. And Kay had been the same as always, or at least since they had come to Québec. He had no reason to doubt her. "No," he said at last.

"You're sure? Do you have a list of places she frequents?"

"Just home and the theater mostly. Some days we get a bite to eat in Old Town or go window-shopping, but no place she haunts. A jog along the boardwalk. But nothing frequent, unless of course you mean the same shop windows she stops at each time we pass by."

"We'll skip ahead to the final section,

then. Where she last was before her disappearance and the circumstances."

Theo told her the story that he had been told. The restaurant after the circus, drinks until two, Kay heading away alone from the group on her way home. Before that, she had been in the show, of course — there were hundreds of witnesses — and before that, they had been alone together in the apartment.

"And that is the last time you saw her, Mr. Harper?"

"The last time."

She did not miss a beat, perhaps because she was not looking at his face. "And we'll need a photograph of her. Recent."

"I don't have a photograph. Only what's on my phone."

"You can e-mail or text it to me, Mr. Harper. That's even better, and I can get it out to our officers to be on the lookout for her. In the meantime, you should go to the American consulate, if you please, tomorrow. We'll share this information with the QPP, the provincial police. Of course, we'll call you at once if we hear anything. That's all for now, unless you have any more questions for me?"

Standing to leave, he could not resist the fear in his heart. "But what about the other missing people? How many are never found?"

She lifted her gaze from the form and looked him straight in the eye. "This is Canada, Mr. Harper, not the US. There are about five or six hundred homicides annually for the whole country. Of course, there are accidents and so forth, but there's no reason to suspect foul play, no need to worry about murder."

He flinched at the word. Beads of perspiration broke out on his forehead, and he wondered how the police station had grown so hot, so suddenly. "What do I do now?"

"Go home. Get something to eat. Maybe ask a friend to keep you company. We'll be in touch."

A friend. He had no friends in Québec. All they had was each other. He rarely left the apartment but for meals or to see her to rehearsal occasionally. Once in a while, he went to use the library at the Literary & Historical Society, and there was a nice young woman at the reference desk, but he didn't even know her name.

He checked his phone again, nothing new. It was just before eight, so he hurried over to the cirque and found Egon loitering by the box office and asked if he could watch with him, bide the time. They sat out of

65

sight from the rest of the crowd. The show was drawing a full house every night since admission was free, part of a provincial scheme to draw more tourists to the Old City. The story, like the plot of an opera, was impossible for him to follow. It was about a boy confined to his bed, watching TV, listening to the radio, surrounded by computer screens and tablets and smartphones, something about the mediation of the imagination in the modern age, but really the setup was simply the scaffolding upon which to erect the electric dreams and flights of fancy, high-wire acts, tumblers and daredevil bicyclists, acrobats and contortionists. The circus played out on the scrim of his fantasies. In Kay's place, an understudy played the part of the second flower, the bohemian dancer in the tableaux, the fifth person to tumble and somersault down the gangway during the grand finale. He kept his eyes on that girl, expecting her to magically transform into his lost wife, and when she wasn't on stage, he watched the master of ceremonies, Reance, project a sigil on the sky to guide the boy, as he aped and mugged for the audience. The whole time, Theo wondered what the bastard had done with his wife.

After the encore, the crowds dispersed

into the night. Stray papers and forbidden cigarette butts littered the grounds, and the lights shone down on the empty sets. Always the saddest part of the performance, the aftermath dingy and sad, after the ball is over, after the dance is done. The artifice and glamor gone.

"What did the police have to say to you?" Egon asked. He pulled a flask from his back pocket, spun off the lid, and offered Theo the first drink.

"The usual bureaucracy," Theo said. "What you might expect, the filling of the forms, until the very end when the sergeant brought up the possibility of murder."

"Murder?" Egon took a swig. "Surely they can't think of such a thing yet. She's only been gone the day, and there's no body."

"No body," Theo said softly. All of the people were deserting the place. The high schoolers had just finished their cleanup, the crew performed one last safety check on the flying apparatus, the steel bicycle cage, the wires and ropes and the rest of the equipment, and one by one the banks of stage lights were extinguished, and it was time to go home.

A new face stared at her, cocking its head sideways to better see her. Pear-shaped, the wooden head rose to a peak upon which was perched a toque in blue and white. He had jug ears, a perfectly round red nose, and two cobalt glass eyes. A seam divided the face in two and served as a rudimentary mouth. He was about her height, perhaps an inch or two taller, and much wider in the belly. Dressed in baggy pajamas in the same colors as his cap, he wore shoes three sizes too large. A clown of some sort, a puppet who could move on his own. He poked her in the ribs. "Are you real?" he asked.

Kay tried to answer him, but she had no mouth. She was surprised to discover that she could move her arm independently and point to the smear of paint standing in for her lips.

"Zut alors!" said the clown. "Don't move a muscle." He passed in front of her and retrieved an object and then hid it behind his back, crossing around to her side. "You must trust me. This won't hurt a bit."

With one hand, he quickly pinned her head to the table. In the other hand, he held a small keyhole saw, its jagged teeth sharp as a tiger's. She wanted to scream, but she could not make a sound. Thrashing around to escape only made him tighten his grip. "I assure you, *mademoiselle,* this won't take a minute."

68

The cut itself did not hurt, but merely vibrated against her wooden head, and almost instantly she felt a strong urge to breathe, as if she had been suffocating and gasping for the first swallows of air. After a few strokes, he stopped sawing and gently removed his hand and then stood to admire his handiwork. She clacked her rough lips together, opening and shutting her new mouth.

"*Voilà!* Later a little sandpaper to smooth down the edges, but for now, *bienvenue!*"

"Where am I?" The sound of her own voice surprised her, having been locked in her throat for so long.

"You're in the Back Room," the clown said and waved his arm with a flourish, showing her the scope of the surroundings. She sat up to take a better look and immediately regretted her decision. Colors and shapes mixing and spinning before slowly settling into view. It was a surprisingly small space. In the middle was a rectangular worktable, littered with tools — hammers and saws — and a miniature lathe with what appeared to be a wooden leg pinned in place at the top of the thigh and bottom of the foot. A sack of overflowing cotton batting stood next to a glass jar half full with fine sawdust. Beaded curtains ran from the floor to ceiling to her left, covering what she remembered as the entrance to the toy shop proper. Opposite the curtain was a bare cinderblock wall broken in the corner by a wooden door to the outside, its single window covered by a sheet of brown butcher's paper and locked on the inside by both a deadbolt and a strong chain. Along the other two walls rose industrial metal shelves upon which sat an assortment of other puppets who were lined up along the edges. Still as a statue, the clown had been holding his arm up in the air as Kay gathered her wits.

"What is the Back Room?"

"It's where they make the puppets."

"You are a puppet?"

"My name is Nix. At your service." He dropped his arm and bowed deeply.

"Am I a puppet?"

A mischievous leer was pasted on his face as he rose. "That you are."

On the shelves, all the other puppets twitched and moved, burst into applause. They clapped and hooted, waving their arms and legs, jumping for joy. Their voices were strange, out of key for adults but not childlike either, some register in between. She was frightened by their enthusiasm but not by Nix's revelation. Long ago, she had grasped her situation. She understood that somehow she had been transformed into a puppet and was relieved to hear his confirmation.

A fat marionette, twice the size of Nix, with a barrel stomach and a giant walrus mustache launched himself from the shelf, leaving behind his wires and bars, and waddled over to her, leaping up and landing beside her. He was astonishingly spry in the way that fat men sometimes are. Offering his hand, he helped her to her feet. Nix grabbed her other hand, and they both steadied her as she wobbled on spindly legs, knees buckling once or twice. Her gaze darted back and forth between the two walls as those weird creatures came to life. Some sat in groups of two or three, feet dangling over the edges of the shelves, watching intently. Others stood leaning against the metal sides, affecting a more casual air. She counted twelve altogether, plus the two men at her sides. She wiggled her fingers, and they let go.

"Careful," Nix said. "The first step is a doozy."

She teetered like a toddler and nearly fell to her face. For the next steps, she shuffled forward before daring to lift her foot again.

"Bravo, good show," the walrus man said. "They call me Mr. Firkin."

"Pleased to meet you, Mr. Firkin. How is this all happening?"

"We come into life of our own accord. We lucky few can move about as long as the people are not watching. Midnight to first light, we are free. Well, freedom is all relative, of course. Free within the confines of the Back Room. Free to move about, talk with one another, reconnect with old friends and meet new ones. Like you."

She remembered that there were people who would be wondering where she was. "And we cannot leave the Back Room?"

"Why would anyone ever want to leave?" Nix laughed.

"Not on our own accord," said Mr. Firkin. "What would people think if suddenly puppets could move like ordinary folk?"

One by one, like raindrops trailing down a windowpane, the others slid off their places on the shelves and moved toward the table. The marionettes and rod puppets marched her way. The hand puppets appeared to be gliding on the hems of their cloth bodies, silent as ghosts. Some of them leapt to the floor as Mr. Firkin had done. Others climbed the legs of the table to join the rest as they surrounded her, curious, tempted but tentative. Three of the creatures, large marionettes in nineteenth-century dresses in dark formal colors, stayed behind, whispering to one another like sisters. She counted a devil, a fairy, a hag. A black man with white hair in a white judge's robe, and a white man with black hair in a black judge's robe. A rod puppet dared to touch Kay's hair and then quickly drew back her finger. A glove puppet with long ears, wide black eyes, and a sharp muzzle sniffed at her feet with his black rubber nose.

"He looks like Pluto." She laughed.

"Well, he's not," said Nix. "He's just an old dog who does nothing but bark and get into trouble." On cue, the hound woofed twice and then sat back on its skirt, wagging a thin leather tail that curled at the tip.

"These are the players," Mr. Firkin said with a flourish. "Our company."

"And who are the giants? Where have they gone?"

None of them wanted to be the first to speak, as though they were operating on a covenant of silence. Nix shrugged his shoulders, and Mr. Firkin looked away when Kay confronted him. From their place at the back of the crowd, the Three Sisters cracked. "They are the puppeteers," they said in unison.

"The makers and unmakers," the wooden

fairy said. "In service to the man in the glass jar."

"Tut-tut," said Mr. Firkin. He put a finger to his lips to silence her. "Enough of your philosophy. The man is called the Quatre Mains, the woman is the Deux Mains. They decide when you are to stay in the Back Room and when you get to be part of a show. They choose who performs, who must wait."

"And what if I don't want to wait?" Kay said. "What if I want to go home?"

The tallest of the Three Sisters sauntered to her side and draped a thin arm over Kay's shoulders. On her sharp angular face, she wore a melancholic expression, a look of long suffering and heartbreak over the absurdity of life. She stroked Kay's face with a delicate finger. "You don't go home, dahlink. Not by your own doing, in any case. You are here for duration."

5

In the alley behind the Back Room, a mockingbird was singing, trying out a few bars from a dozen different melodies, looking to impress any potential females in the area. How strange, Kay thought, to wander so far north. He might be repeating those same songs for a long, long time. The bird reminded her of her husband and how long and ardently he had wooed her, how long she had resisted. For the first time since her transformation, Kay was missing him. Not in the way she used to long for him after a few days apart, but in a deeper way, a feeling she had not had before, a realization that their destinies had changed, perhaps inexorably. The thought that he, too, might be lonesome troubled her, yet she knew that little could be done.

The bird sang on in the last of the night. Mr. Firkin stood by the door, but guarding against trespass, though he seemed more anxious about a visitor from outside than an escapee from within. Perhaps it was all for show. After they had examined her, most of the puppets returned to their tasks. Nix practiced juggling with three small heads taken from a bin of spare parts. He must have just begun to learn this new trick, for he would often miss and clumsily drop one of the wooden balls, the head bouncing across the wooden floor, with the clown in pursuit. The Russian Sisters — they had made their introductions and proved her hunch — lounged indolently nearby on makeshift furniture, sighing when the mood struck them and holding their hands dramatically against their foreheads as though stemming a migraine or an existential woe.

Beautifully carved, the Sisters were tall and willowy, adorned in long elegant gowns of crushed velvet in dark shades of mauve, aubergine, and navy blue, with high lace collars, and on their feet they wore button boots. Their long hair was pinned and coiffed in a modest style that threatened to unwind, and their beautiful faces were adorned with matching aquiline noses. Irina toyed with a strand of pearls at her neck, and Masha twirled a parasol to a rhythm only she could hear. They adored being watched, and after a time under scrutiny,

Olya motioned to Kay with a languid wave of her hand to come join them.

"Sit, *lapochka,* and tell us of the outside world. What news from the mortals?" Her voice dripped, low and rich, into the air.

"How long have you been here in the Back Room?"

"Forever and a day," Masha said.

"I do not know," Irina said. "How long is eternity?"

Olya shot them a glance that indicated they had said too much. "Pay no attention to these mopes. They have short memories. Things were not always thus."

"It is June," Kay said. "Or at least it was when I arrived. The passage of time is hard to judge inside a box. We were just married, my husband and I, this past April, and we came here for work."

"Does this marvel have a name?" Olya asked.

Unsure of the answer, Kay hesitated. "I have forgotten it for the moment, but he teaches French literature and is a translator, and I am an acrobat. A gymnast, really, but I thought it might be fun to spend the summer in Québec with the cirque."

Irina stifled a laugh. "I'm sorry. Expectations are often thwarted by the smallest accidents."

"An acrobat?" Masha smiled. "That will serve you well, pet, when it comes to the next puppet show. The Deux Mains adores a nimble doll. But your husband, tut. How careless of him to misplace you, to let you wander this way. Never enter a toy shop after midnight."

Kay thought of how she had entered this space, remembering being outside the toy shop looking in. The sensation of being followed. The lights on for the first time ever and at such a late hour. A twinge in her hand reminded her of turning the doorknob and stepping into the store in her bare feet. Where were her shoes? She must have taken them off to fool her pursuer, to erase her tracks. At last, she had come so close to the man beneath the glass. Darkness arrived completely as she'd lifted the bell jar. She'd shut her eyes and then awoke to find her life in pieces. Memory, what a strange thing, not bound to any time but to a place. This box of a room, alone with these weird creatures. The Russians were smiling at her. She wondered if the Quatre Mains and the Deux Mains were nearby, in another room in the building, perhaps asleep in a bedroom in the upper story. Or tinkering below in the cellar. Or not there at all.

"Tell me about the others," Kay said at

last, shaking off the dust of her own spell.

"The old-timers," Masha said. "Some have been here so long that they no longer have a name. Take the judges." She gestured toward two large puppets arguing together over a chessboard. From the few pieces left on the board, it was impossible to tell who was playing black and who was playing white. "They are simply the Black Judge and the White Judge, but I can no longer tell who is whom. Do you know, Irina?"

"They were in some farce together, ages ago, and I am not sure if either knows his proper title. What does it matter? They are made for disputations." Catching her fingers in her strand of pearls, she pointed at another pair. On the bottom shelf, an elaborately decorated rod puppet with ram's horns and a horrid black goatee, his crimson body filigreed with swirls of gold leaf inlaid in the finest teak, played at hide-and-seek with what looked like a bunch of sticks in a gossamer shirt to which had been affixed a pair of wire and lace wings. "The Devil seeks his due," she said. "He is a foreigner, an Indonesian wayang, a minor deity of some lascivious intent, but we just call him the Devil."

Masha called out to the girl hiding behind a spool of twine. "Hey, girl, what do we call you these days? Is it Peaseblossom? Or Cobweb? Asphodel? Or perhaps we should just call you Twiggy."

"Get on out of that," the girl said, angry that they had given her away. Her voice emerged from a bundle of sticks woven together in the shape of a face, and her eyes flashed like lit embers. "I am the Good Fairy, as you well know." The Devil laughed and sprang to her at once, and she giggled in mock terror, sticks scraping on the wooden floor.

When the Devil passed by, the Dog barked, the sudden motion startling an old woman rocking on the edge of the counter, her short legs dangling in the air. At her side was the girl who had been so curious about Kay's hair, a mere waif in a rag dress, a thatch of brittle yellow straw standing up on her head, staring back at them. "The gramma is the Old Hag," said Olya. "Don't worry about hurting her feelings by calling her so. Deaf as a block of wood." She dropped her voice to a whisper and hunkered in close to Kay. "And the little one is Noë. Be careful, dahlink, for she is med as a hetter. I will tell you a secret. Noë has tried to make her escape many, many times, and that is why old Firkin posts himself at the door. We cannot have such madness let

80

loose into the world."

"And why does she want to leave?" Kay asked.

The Sisters tensed and lifted themselves from their recumbent positions, sitting up like respectable ladies. Each gave the others a knowing look, signaling a tacit agreement to let the truth alone. Masha spoke: "Who knows why anyone goes crazy? The mind invents its own miseries. I myself prefer to be the very model of happiness. And I advise you to do the same."

Kay could not stop watching the straw-haired girl. At first she seemed merely still and self-possessed, but in time her inner enchantments began to leak out. Noë twisted her fingers together and pulled them apart. Through her thin shirt her clockwork heart beat like a dove's. In a lull in the symphony of conversation in the room, she could be heard humming to herself, not un-like the mockingbird singing in the predawn world outside.

"Come, *zaichik,*" Olya said. "And meet the Queen before the night is through."

Taking her hand, she stepped off the edge, floating to a soft landing. Still unused to walking after such a long spell, Kay had to lean on the Russian woman's arm. Seated by the curtains dividing the Back Room

81

from the toy store, on a throne made out of oatmeal boxes, the Queen was the most life-like, the most beautiful of them all. Carved from tiger maple, the grain running length-wise from brow to chin, her face and classical features were set off elegantly by a corona of jet-black hair cascading to her shoulders. Her robes were dyed pomegranate, and in one hand she held a scepter cunningly painted in shades of gold. At her feet sat a horrid creature, a green foam puppet, his misshapen head dominated by a large pair of plastic googly eyes, a primitive mishmash inspired by Picasso, the saddest face Kay had ever seen. He mewled like a kitten as she approached, covering himself under his mistress's hems.

"Pay no attention to that Worm," Olya said. "His name is simply that, and he is more to be pitied than feared." Five paces away, she kicked out her foot and the puppet slid farther beneath the Queen's skirts, quivering and muttering complaints. They stopped in front of her and curtsied.

"Majesty, may I present . . . ah, my little angel, I have forgotten your name, if I ever learned it."

"Kay," she said and rose to face her. "Kay Harper."

The Queen tipped her chin in greeting.

Olya bowed as well before continuing her tale. "She is the latest sent over to us by the Original in the Front Room. Stitched and sewn by the Quatre Mains and the Deux Mains themselves in the last moon. Kay Harper comes from beyond. She is an acrobat, Majesty. A tumbler."

"You have been on the stage?"

"I have," she said. "Just recently in the cirque, but for some years before in both competitions and performance."

"That will serve you well, when the time comes."

"So I have been told."

"If you are chosen." The Queen corrected herself with a beatific smile. "Remember your training, and you will have many a happy time with the puppeteers. I am afraid that some of us forget how to behave." With her toe, she nudged the squirming Worm below the throne. "You will want some opportunity now and then to play a new part. Change is everything in this place."

"Yes, Your Majesty."

The Queen bent closer, looking Kay in the eyes. "If you follow a few simple rules, all will be as it should. We are free to move about after midnight and before the first light of day, as long as we are ourselves alone. And we do not leave the Back Room

83

and certainly never venture into the Front Room. You must not bother the toys on the other side. Live simply and know your place."

A bell rang. From the vicinity of the beaded curtain, Firkin shook an old-fashioned school bell with great vigor and announced in a booming voice: "Time, ladies and gents. Places please. Rosy dawn is sticking her fingers in our eyes. Places. Time."

The Queen sighed and descended her cardboard throne, and Worm slithered away quick as a grass snake. All of the puppets were moving now, putting away their games and trinkets, scurrying about to return things to how they were. Noë shouted at the Old Hag with the news, and the Dog bounded across the shelf, burning away the last excess energy. Attending the Queen, the Judges fixed her wires to her wrists and ankles, and with a great heave ho they positioned her on a coatrack, where she was to hang, the life draining from her features after one wan smile in Kay's direction. The others retreated to their places, their expressions, too, changing into frozen smiles or frowns. Olya pulled at her hand. "Dahlink, we must find and put you back where they last left you. Do you remember? Day is coming. Hurry, hurry."

After three days, his feet fell off. Theo had walked the length and breadth of the Old City, from the first light at dawn till well into the night, looking for her. Mornings he would start on Dalhousie and work his way through the narrow streets, poking his head into all the small cafés and shops they used to frequent, and then ride the funicular to the city above and join the mobs of tourists crowding the squares, popping into the old churches and galleries, lining up for the changing of the guard at the Citadelle, or descending underground to the museum of buried streets near the Frontenac towering over it all. American accents filled the air, a woman's voice turning his head once an hour. He saw her all the time in bits and pieces, the sweep of her hair, the figure of a girl in the back of a horse-drawn carriage, a pair of shoes peeking out from a sidewalk table. There, not there. The shopkeepers and the reenactors in the square — the merchants in their tricorne hats, the maids in their bonnets — came to recognize his constant presence, sadly shaking their heads to the question in his eyes. He would show them her picture on his phone again and again, "Have you seen this woman?" Following the police department's advice, he visited the American Consulate on the Terrasse Dufferin, bringing with him her passport and his story, and the young bureaucrat behind the desk assured him of their concern and support. They offered him a cup of tea and promised to do everything they could. But all such promises failed to convince him that anyone was looking for her.

She was gone. He could not eat, he barely slept, he talked to himself all the time.

Worn to the bone, he retreated to the apartment in the late afternoon to steal a few hours' rest. A half-dozen messages blinked on the answering machine, all from his mother-in-law, Dolores: "Is there any progress? Are you out looking for her? Where have you looked?" And more ominously: "Did you two have a fight? What have you done?" Just listening to her voice made him tremble, and he wished there was something he could do to reassure her, some way to bring her up, wheelchair and all, to the steep cobblestoned streets, to let her know that he, too, was going mad over Kay's disappearance. *What have you done?* What did Dolores imagine he had done?

His papers and books lay on the table, the French-English dictionary open at *M* for *meurtre.* Muybridge could wait. Next to the manuscript sat a stack of bills and letters Kay had asked him to mail, including a card for her mother's birthday and a picture postcard to a friend from school. Her plate and coffee cup lay in the sink. One of his old shirts she liked to wear to bed peeked out from beneath her pillows. A paperback on her nightstand, placed facedown to mark her place. He flipped it over to save the spine. A closet of clothes and shoes, a dresser drawer crammed with underwear and socks, though most of their things were back home in New York. In the bathroom, her hairbrush lingered on the windowsill, her makeup and lipstick, and her toothbrush just where she left them in the medicine cabinet. Such paltry evidence that she had ever been there. He stripped off his wrinkled clothes and stood in the shower under a hot stream of water for a long time, trying not to think. Stepping out into the steamy bathroom, he draped a thick towel over his head like a hood and sat on the edge of the tub, holding in the heat. Wrapped in a cocoon, he very nearly missed the knocking at the front door.

"Just a sec," he yelled and threw on a robe as he flew to the front door, crying, "Don't go, don't go."

When he saw the two men standing on the threshold, his first thought was that they had come with the worst possible news. Dressed in dark suits and ties, they had the unmistakable aura of the police, and why else would they come to the apartment unless to break it to him in person? The older of the two had silver hair atop a world-weary face. The younger man remained yet to be wizened. He was as fresh and crisp as a soldier, one of the few black men he had encountered in Québec. Water dripped down Theo's forehead, and he wiped his skin with the end of the towel.

"Theo Harper? Sorry to disturb you, we're with Sûreté du Québec. Permit me to introduce myself. I am Inspector Thompson and this is my partner Sergeant Foucault. May we come in?"

"Is this about my wife? Have you found her?"

As he stepped into the apartment, Thompson said, "No, no. We've come to ask you a few questions, if you don't mind."

"That's a relief, I suppose, if you haven't found her body, there is still hope." Theo ushered them in and closed the door behind them. "Can I throw on some clothes? You could make yourself a cup of tea, if you like, the kettle's in the kitchen."

"Please, take your time, get dressed. Foucault, will you do the honors? A cup for you, Mr. Harper?"

He was halfway to the bedroom and nodded over his shoulder. Behind the door, as he dressed, he eavesdropped as the two policeman talked to each other in French.

"First impressions?"

"He seems nervous," Foucault said from the kitchen. *"Avoir l'air coupable."*

"Il a tué sa femme?"

"It's often the husband. Or the boyfriend." Foucault was pouring the third cup when Theo emerged, and they sat at the dining table cluttered with his papers.

"Excuse the mess," Theo said.

"Are you a writer, Mr. Harper?" Thompson asked.

"A translator." He watched their faces for any sign of embarrassment, but they might as well have been stones. "I am working on a translation from French to English of the life of Eadweard Muybridge. Do you know him?"

"No," Thompson said. "But you are here to translate a book? I thought you were American."

"Oui, je sais parler français. My publisher is here in the city, but I can work anywhere. We live in New York, where I teach college,

89

but my wife was fortunate enough to land a role with the cirque for the summer. She is an acrobat, a performer."

Foucault was scrutinizing him while Thompson asked the questions. He began to feel like a man under the lamp. Thompson added a cube of sugar to his tea and stirred it casually. "And how do you find Québec?"

"We love it here. Until she went missing."

"You were having no problems? Between the two of you? It must be a challenge to have a spouse in the theater, always being watched, admired."

"Inspector," Theo said, "I know this is the routine, but I assure you, we are fine. I told all this to the desk officer when I filed my report."

"And her family? Why have they not come to join in the search?"

"She only has her mother left, back in Vermont," Theo said. "And Dolores is in a wheelchair these past five years. Doesn't get about very well. But we are on the phone every day."

"Too hot." Thompson blew across the surface of his tea. He set down the cup and held up both hands to put a stop to Theo's objections. "No offense, Mr. Harper. Just some details, minor things to clear up to help us with the investigation." He nodded to his partner.

Foucault took out a small memo pad and flipped to the page he desired. "Tell me what you remember about the last time you saw your wife. Anything you may have forgotten to mention to the desk officer that you can remember now?"

"It was the afternoon, right? One day like any other. We had slept in, and she had to go to the warehouse where they prepare for the show. But they perform outside, a few blocks away. She left, and I sat down to do a little work."

"You weren't fighting? Arguing?"

"Of course not. What makes you think so?"

"Can you tell me what she was wearing when she left the flat?"

He screwed his politeness back into place. "Blue jeans. Gray canvas shoes? A simple blouse, white I think. I don't remember exactly. What she always wore on her way to the show."

"The show." Foucault frowned. "And you said in your report she went to dinner with others from the cast? Did she come back to the flat to change her clothes?"

"No, I would have seen her."

"You were here the whole time?"

"No, I went out to eat. At the Brigands on the rue Saint-Paul, I'm sure they will remember me. Give me an alibi."

With a clatter, Thompson set down his cup into the saucer. "Alibi? There is no need to talk of alibis. You went to eat, you came home. Okay. Does she keep any clothes down at this theater? Perhaps a change of something nicer to wear. A sundress, perhaps?"

"I suppose —"

"You suppose," Foucault said. "We went down there and checked, monsieur, and that's exactly what we supposed. Her jeans and shoes and blouse were still in her locker, so if she went out, it was either in costume from the cirque or she had a change of clothes."

"Okay, so she changed her outfit before going to dinner. What difference does that make?"

Foucault pressed forward. "So you have no idea what she was wearing the night of her disappearance?"

His face reddened. "How could I?"

Thompson pushed back his chair and stood, defusing the tension for the moment. "I apologize, Mr. Harper. As I say, we have to ask these questions first, and thing is, I'm sorry to say, but we may have some bad news. There is a body, a woman drowned, washed up on the shore of the Saint Lawrence, and we have no way of identifying her at the moment. She is young, fits the general description of your wife —"

"Kay?" Theo covered his mouth and tried not to cry out.

"But" — Thompson held up his hand — "she was wearing a dress, no shoes, and we thought it couldn't be her. Until we went down to the warehouse and met the caretaker."

"Egon Picard," said Foucault.

"Monsieur Picard told us that the actors often leave clothes in their locker, so we thought to come talk with you to see if you remember. It was a simple yellow sundress. Perhaps you could come with us to the medical examiner, if you please, and we can take a look."

"To see if it is her?"

The two policeman looked at each other and then back at Theo. *"Oui,"* Foucault said, and laying a hand on Theo's shoulder, he helped him to his feet.

They rode in silence to the morgue, Foucault at the wheel, Thompson keeping company with Theo in the backseat. A seagull lolled in the blue summer sky, as though it was following them. As they pulled into the parking lot, Theo could no longer bear the suspense.

"Am I a suspect? Do you think I could possibly harm my wife?"

"You're not under arrest, Mr. Harper. There's no crime, as such, that's been committed. We don't even know if this is your wife. But you should steel yourself, just in case. A body taken from the water after so long is not a pretty sight."

When the attendant pulled back the sheet, the corpse was as sad and gruesome as Thompson had warned. Theo cried out involuntarily and looked away quickly from the body on the slab. For the first time since Kay's disappearance, he broke into tears, a ragged sobbing that would not stop. The ruined creature was not his wife but some other poor soul quit of this world. Asked if he was certain, could he look again, Theo shook his head, saying, "No, no, that is not her."

6

The drowned girl accompanied him to the circus. After the emotional tumult of the interrogation by Thompson and Foucault and his afternoon at the morgue, Theo did not want to be alone, but he had nowhere to go, so he headed instead to the plaza where the free theater played. The dead girl who walked beside him was the spit and image of his wife; he could see how they had mistaken the corpse for Kay. Water dripped from her body and her footsteps squelched on the pavement. Blue at her extremities, the skin on her face slack, she no longer looked like a woman in her twenties but a horror beyond all hope.

"Where have you been?" she asked. Now the voice, that was identical to his wife's, and he was surprised to hear it. "Why didn't you come save me?"

He did not know how to answer her, so he said nothing, and he did not want the passersby on the street to think him crazy for talking to a ghost, but no one seemed to notice her along the way, despite the fact that she wore nothing but the white sheet from the morgue and that she smelled of fish and the brackish water of the Saint Lawrence. He wished she would go away and leave him alone.

At the lot leading up to the stage, the crew and actors bustling about did not see her either, though those people who recognized him had a kind word or gesture of sympathy for his troubles. He saw Sarant limbering and unkinking her spine. She seemed embarrassed that he had approached her. "Any word?"

Theo shook his head. "But the police came by to question me, if you can imagine, about her clothes. Two detectives, Thompson and Foucault."

"Yes, they were here as well," Sarant said. "Loose ends, more questions. What was she wearing, that sort of thing. I really didn't have anything more to say." She was unnerved by Theo's sideways glances and kept trying to determine what he was looking for or what he might be trying to convey. At last she touched him lightly on the shoulder and hurried off to the dressing rooms. The drowned woman watched forlornly as Sarant departed. Theo wandered through the crowd, looking for a familiar face, watching Reance pace the length of the stage, but he could not catch his attention. Dusk was sneaking up on them, and as the first patrons began to arrive, Theo found Egon in a spot near the front entrance.

"Two, please," he joked.

Egon smiled at him. "You're here for the show?"

"I thought we could watch together, if you are free."

Egon found two milk crates for them in the wings. He offered him a swig from his flask, and Theo took a discreet tug. The dead girl stood between them, absentmindedly watching the last of the crowd make its way onto the grounds, and then she suddenly took off, picking her way through the clots of people milling about, although not a soul responded to her sepulchral presence. Theo lost sight of her at last and was greatly relieved. Out in the audience, Reance was working his preshow shtick, giving the folks a close-up before it all began.

"Police came by today," Egon said. "Asking a lot of questions. You would like these two blokes, Thompson and Foucault, salt and pepper."

"We've met. They came by the apartment.

97

It seems I'm under suspicion."

A gong was struck. The overture blasted away any chance for further conversation. House lights down, stage lights up, and descending from a platform the slumberland bed with the sleeping boy, the phantasmagoria of dreams commenced once more. Theo nearly broke down in tears when Sarant and the flowers came around, imagining Kay instead of her understudy in the role. As they watched Sarant balance atop the silver ball and contort her body into an arch, he poked Egon in the ribs and asked in a hoarse whisper, "Why would they think I had anything to do with her disappearance?"

"It's always the husband." The little man shrugged. "They wondered if I had seen you that night. But how would I know to look for you? We hadn't even met."

"But I wasn't here. I was working that night and only stepped out for dinner."

Illuminated by the footlights, Sarant wobbled, threatening to fall, and a gasp raced through the crowd. Theo wondered if the contortionist had been distracted by the presence of a corpse peering out of the darkness, but she recovered and slowly unwound herself back to the stage to welcome applause. As the show went on, he kept trying to find the ghost, but she proved elusive, blending in with the spectators ringing the stage. Theo and Egon sat in silence through the *entr'actes* and the grand tumbling finale. He could not resist the temptation to watch for Kay, though he knew that she would not appear.

After the show, they walked back through the quiet streets to Egon's cell at the warehouse. The tourists were steps ahead of them, peeling off to their cars parked along the side streets, or making the hike back into the Old City through a light fog that obscured the way.

"Come inside for a moment," Egon said at the door. "You look like shit, and perhaps you could benefit from another drink."

He followed Egon to his room and accepted a tumbler of Scotch. The women on the walls looked down upon them, and the empty warehouse was as quiet as a cathedral.

"Perhaps I should not say this, but I trust you and think you tell the truth. One of the detectives let slip a small clue to their thinking. He said that when you first reported her missing, you said something about a murder to the attendant who took your statement."

"Murder? I said nothing of the sort. The

99

sergeant was the one who talked about what happens to people who go missing. Do they think Kay was murdered?"

"As I said, a *faux pas*. Madness."

"A body washed up," Theo said. "A Jane Doe who drowned in the Saint Lawrence last week. They had no idea who she was. Naturally, when they couldn't identify her, they thought it might be Kay. They took me to the morgue."

Egon choked on his Scotch, sputtering to catch his breath.

"I am still in shock. It was horrible. Not Kay, of course, but close enough. She was black and blue and swollen from the water."

"And you are sure?"

"No, not Kay. There was a resemblance, and I can see why they dragged me over there." He was trying not to cry. "But it was just too much for me."

"Let me freshen your drink. What an ordeal."

The liquor wormed its way through his body. He sat awhile with his thoughts, debating whether to confess his fears. "I'm going crazy with worry. Can't sleep, can't eat. Every day I get out in the morning, first thing, and go out searching. I see her everywhere, but when I get close, she morphs into another woman."

Egon handed him the bottle. "Tomorrow I will help you look. Now, go home, get some rest. Take the Scotch with you and drink it till you fall asleep. Keep up your spirits, *mon ami.* She is out there somewhere."

The fog had thickened during the interval, a summer storm rolling in. Thunder boomed over the Saint Lawrence, and lightning illuminated the Frontenac. The rain started to pelt down before he was halfway home. The smell of cold water against the hot cobblestones. Heavy drops, rills tumbling along the curbs, puddles in the intersections. His wet clothes clung to his body and his shoes bubbled with water at each step. Drenched and weary, doused with drink, he slogged into the apartment, leaving a trail of wet footprints on the rugs. He laid down the bottle of Scotch, took off his clothes, and toweled off. Kay would have relished getting caught in the storm, she would have spread her arms and thrown open her face to the falling rain. She would have loved it, and he would have worried about catching a cold. Theo tumbled into bed, certain that if he could sleep, just sleep, he would be better in the morning. In the middle of the night, he was awakened by the sensation of rainfall. Drops of water on his bare chest and face, and in his stupor he wondered if he had been crying in his sleep. Through the shadows of the room, he realized that it was the drowned woman on top of him, straddling his body, and as his sight adjusted to the half-light, he could see the beseeching look in her eyes and hear her whisper again, "How have you forgotten me?"

The others taught Kay the motion of puppets.

Noë fetched a set of rods from a bin and affixed a pair to her wrists and a pair at her ankles. The wooden sticks clacked against the floor as she walked into the middle of the Back Room, once nearly tripping over a tangle at her feet. The puppets gathered round in a semicircle, and Kay imagined herself back onstage, under a spotlight of attention. Mr. Firkin stepped forward as the master of ceremonies.

"The trick is to remember not to move until you feel the pressure from the puppeteer's hands. Ordinarily when the humans manipulate you, there are two people required for a doll like you, one to move your arms, and another to control your legs. They will flank you on each side and push or pull on the other end of the rods. Perhaps it's best if four of us act the parts, one at each extremity, so to speak. Let's put the Devil on your left and the Good Fairy on your right. Judges, perhaps you can make her walk."

The four puppets hurried to their appointed spots. She felt a soft tug as each took the sticks in hand and the overwhelming sense that she was no longer in control of her own body.

"If you were a real girl," the Good Fairy whispered in her ear, "you would have an opening where they could use one hand to make you talk and move your mouth. Not like that crude thing you use now."

Kay clamped shut her makeshift lips, recalling how Nix had taken a saw to her face. Putting a finger to his mouth, Mr. Firkin motioned for them to be quiet. A curious look came over him as he drew deep into his own thoughts. When at last he found the information he had been seeking, he chuckled like a professor.

"Are you familiar with your center of gravity? The fulcrum of your balance? For most people, it is situated between the navel — or should I say belly button — and the, ahem, groin. You might feel it as a small acorn in the pit of your insides. Of course, for others the center of balance might be virtually anywhere. A divot at the base of the skull. The midpoint between the flanges of the lungs. I knew one misfortunate soul whose center was in his left knee —"

"I am a gymnast," Kay said, "and quite familiar with balance and gravity."

"Yes, of course," he said, flustered. "How quickly I forget, and, of course, that's why you are here. Well, you must relax outward from that point, let yourself go limp around it."

She exhaled a long deep draft, and in her next breath slackened her muscles, trusting the foursome to keep her upright. Her knees buckled slightly, and she teetered as they held fast. Giving herself over to the others demanded all her concentration. Old yoga practices kicked in. She emptied her mind and let herself go. Her right arm shot forward when the Good Fairy lifted the rod, and then the Devil brought up her left and caused her to clap her hands. A puff of dust rose from her canvas fingers. The crowd cheered for her, and then she felt the push of her left foot as she took her first step. Working together, the puppets moved her arms and legs, and she was walking. She squealed like a toddler with delight over a sudden and newfound power. They moved slowly at first, allowing her to get used to the sensation, but soon they quickened the pace, forcing her to new directions, even made her walk backward. She enjoyed the ride with a different driver, finding that she was made to move this way. And just when she thought it over, they made her leap into the air and held her suspended eighteen inches off the floor, and in a careful and delicate movement, they unfroze her from space and let her glide back to the earth, landing softly as a dove.

"Again," she cried. "Again, again."

"Excellent, wonderful." Tall Olya spoke above everyone's head. "Don't wear yourself out, dahlink. There's time enough to walk and fly and perform their magic."

The Judges were already untying the rods from her ankles. The Devil in front of her removed the strap from her left hand. "You'll be tempted to play the part. Give in, give in."

On her right side, the Good Fairy said, "Pay him no heed. He's nothing but a big ham. All that talk about performance. Feh, just wait till they come for you."

"Who is coming for me?"

"Why, the Quatre Mains and the Deux Mains, of course. You don't think you'll be allowed to stay in the Back Room forever."

"When will they come?"

"We never know. But they will get you."

"Suppose I leave before they come for me."

"Oh, you can never leave," said the Good Fairy. "You are not allowed to leave on your own accord."

Worn out by her perambulations, Kay sat on a box of foam noses and ears and considered her surroundings. She had not given much thought to the extent of the Back Room, how its yellow walls circumscribed a world with gunmetal shelves, bins of odds and ends, bolts of fabric, the vaguely menacing hammers and saws and awls. The novelty of the place inured her to its limits. All around her, the puppets returned to their business, arranging themselves in familiar cliques. The Queen sat on her oatmeal-box throne. Nix took up his juggling, tossing three ping-pong ball eyes with nonchalance. The Three Sisters lounged by a toy samovar, sipping tea in tiny glasses.

"Do you mind if I join you?" Kay asked. "I have no idea what to do or where to go."

"You are trapped," Irina said. "In the same bourgeois drama we all are. The melancholy parade of day and night marches by, and not a one of us knows where it leads."

Masha chimed in. "Tomorrow and tomorrow and tomorrow. We are forever waiting for tomorrow and looking for a better day."

Making room for her on the box that served as a settee, Olya bid Kay come sit by her side, and with great show she pantomimed another glass of tea, wincing slightly as she handed it to her. The tea was hot, to Kay's surprise, and when she pretended to take a sip, she was astonished by how strong and sweet the taste was. Almost immediately she realized that in the whole time she had been in the Back Room, hunger and thirst had deserted her. She hadn't had so much as a bite in what . . . weeks? Months?

"Spasibo." She remembered her Russian manners.

"Is nothing," Olya said. "You are surprised to find the tea to your liking? Usually we drink a bitter brew. For you, a pinch of sugar."

"It's good," Kay said. "But how is it possible?"

"My dear girl," Masha said. "All things are possible with imagination. You might as well ask the same about all of life. How does the thrush know when is spring and time to return? How is cherry tree both flower and fruit and then a scrag of bones in October? Tea knows how to be tea."

"But how do you make the real tea out of imaginary nothing?"

Like three magpies, the Sisters cocked their heads and stared at her, puzzled by the abstract nature of her question. She wondered if she had unwittingly crossed a line, and the long pause disconcerted her. They looked lifeless again, reverted to their puppet state. Snapping her finger in front of their glass eyes, Kay tried to wake them from their stupor.

Olya blinked first. "Dahlink, we are practicing."

"Practicing for what?"

"In case we are called to play our roles."

Masha leaned in and whispered confidentially. "True freedom, *golubushka,* comes in knowing your limitations. We are all waiting here for whatever happens next."

Looking over the lip of her teacup, Irina smiled at her. "When the puppeteer calls, the puppets must be ready."

From the doorway came the ringing of the school bell and Mr. Firkin shouting that the night was nearly over. The Dog began to bark excitedly as the puppets whirled into motion, restoring the Back Room to its previous state. Before the Sisters could get away, Kay grabbed Olya by the brocade sleeve of her dress. "What roles are you talking about? Who is calling?"

"Everyone must prepare for the puppet

show," she said and pulled away.

"Places, please," Mr. Firkin cried. "Is everything as it should be? Quickly, quickly, now. We must not let them notice anything amiss, or there will be hell to pay."

The lights went out. Thin strips of sunlight filtered through the edges of the back door and the cardboard window covering. The room was warming, the glass ticking as it expanded, the air rising from the floor. If only she could ride the wave and escape. Normally she faced a blank wall, but this morning she dared to change position and did not look away. The rest of the puppets assumed their inert countenances, dead eyes, blank expressions, as still as corpses. Quiet descended, heavy and expansive. She was alone again.

The days were all the same in the Back Room. For the first few hours, she remembered her life before this life. Fleeting images crossed her mind. Her mother cutting out a silhouette from black cardboard, asking the five-year-old Kay to please sit still. At a high school gymnastics meet, the auditorium hushed while she prepared a dismount from the balance beam, her foot slipping, her hips wiggling, her shoulders throwing off her equilibrium, and then her father's soft voice reaching her from the bleachers: *be still.* Her husband — not yet her husband — peering intently at her across a table of Indian food, the tail end of an argument over some silly ex-boyfriend, and she asks do you love me and he says: *Still.*

Inside her head, she laughs at herself, as if she had any choice in the matter, since she could not will herself to be anything but still during the daytime. She wanted to move. She wanted to be more than a doll on a shelf. She wanted to see the man in the glass jar and wondered if he was waiting for her, out in the Front Room. Her thoughts disturbed her rest: when would the Quatre Mains and the Deux Mains come for her? What role would she play? She could no longer move on her own in the daytime. Nothing to be done but to wait in stillness.

7

She left a hole his mind tried to fill. Theo dreamt of finding Kay all the time, but every morning, she was still missing. He woke up tired and disoriented, and all he could remember was the hellish sensation of having been watched on his journey. Spied upon by tiny eyes of creatures hiding among the trees and hedges in the parks or from the old stone buildings that lined the twisting streets of the Basse-Ville, gremlins squirreled away in second-story windows shrouded by lace curtains.

He shared the tale of the watchful eyes with Egon as they stopped for coffee at a sidewalk bistro near the Terrasse Dufferin. From their table, they could see the length of the grand esplanade that runs above the Saint Lawrence, crowded with tourists taking in the sights, the weather warm enough for shorts or skirts and sandals. The little man nodded demurely, and Theo wondered if he had somehow offended him, drawn a subconscious comparison between the gremlins and the diminutive size of his only friend in Québec. A breeze rippled the flags that flew above the square. A light sky above the river was purled with clouds. A perfect day in July. Kay had been gone for three weeks.

"I used to feel that I was being watched, too," said Egon. "Or rather, it was a case of being scrutinized all the time. Even now you can see it in their eyes, how quickly some people turn away when they first notice me."

A pair of tourists shambled up in matching *Québec je t'aime* T-shirts.

"Then they look away. Guilty buggers. There but for the grace. And then they look back. Curious as the killed cat. And then away again to show you how liberal and unprejudiced they are: that's okay, you are a little person, I do not mind."

The couple, who must have heard him, frowned as they passed.

"I prefer the children, *les enfants horrible,* no more than two or three years old. They will look to their hearts' content, unabashed, and point their fingers right at you as if to say, *Maman,* explain that to me. How can it be? A man just my size, what a glorious conundrum. But I get what you are feeling,

112

Harper. Maybe you are a little bit paranoid, understandably."

"Paranoid?"

He drained the cold dregs from his cappuccino and scraped the last cloud of brown foam with his index finger. "Perhaps you feel you are being watched because of that incident with the police. And all those who are pointing a finger at you. Unjustly, I might add. But don't worry. I defend you like a wolverine."

"Who is pointing a finger? What are they saying?"

He licked the back of his spoon. "I don't like to repeat gossip, but there are stories going around. These are actors, don't forget, and worse, circus people. I overheard Reance tell a chorus girl that you lied to the police about the body of the drowned girl, who was in fact your wife, and you are hiding the truth because you killed her. The police have no way of identifying her. She is perfectly anonymous, no dental records, no fingerprints on file. Reance is being profoundly ridiculous. A slanderer. I'm not sure I should mention the other one, it might upset you."

"Upset me? What could possibly be worse than that?"

Waving away the question, Egon fished in

his pocket and laid a loonie coin next to his saucer. On the boardwalk in front of the Château Frontenac, a small crowd had gathered to watch a juggler in a striped shirt atop a unicycle. He was working with three bowler hats, catching each by the brim, and then sending them spinning like plates into the air. After a few moments, without a single hesitation, he flipped one atop his head, and the next, and finally the third, so that he looked like a triple-decker ice cream cone. The tourists applauded, and Theo and Egon were on their way before the empty donation hat could be passed to them.

They walked to the overlook and stood along the cast-iron railing and watched the boats go by on the Saint Lawrence. "Kay's mother has been in touch with the cirque. She says you haven't been returning her calls."

Theo closed his eyes against the sunlight reflecting off the water. "I don't know what to say to her anymore. She asks questions with no answers."

"She's distraught about her daughter."

"Naturally. I know. I just cannot face her."

"I've been getting this secondhand, realize. She spoke with the stage manager, who told someone who told me, so it is not from the horse's mouth, so to speak. Her mother thinks you two had a row, a blowup, and Kay has run away from you and is hiding. Afraid of you."

"Her mother barely knows me. Lost my temper? Why would Kay be hiding from me? We were happy." Just as he said the words, he heard himself speaking of her in the past tense, and his voice caught in his throat. He pictured his mother-in-law back on her farm, fretting the days away over Kay, going about what chores she could manage in that stoic New England manner. While his first thoughts were sympathetic, he quickly grew angry about her suspicions. She had never liked him, not from the start. Perhaps the ten-year age difference with her daughter bothered her more than anything, though he could not be sure if a more fundamental distrust existed. She was unfailingly cordial to him, hospitable on the few occasions when they'd spent the night under her roof, but she focused almost all of her attentions on her daughter, as though he was not there. The last time they saw Mrs. Bird, at the wedding earlier in the year, she had seemed so fragile in her wheelchair. But there was a fierceness to her as well, a mother bear protecting her cub.

"Could be she has a point, the mother-in-law," Egon said. "I don't mean that Kay is afraid of you, of course not. And I don't see her deliberately hiding from you. But perhaps she isn't here at all. Perhaps she left the city. She took a wrong turn, bumped her head, ended up somewhere other than Old Town. We have been up and down these same streets a thousand times. Perhaps we have been looking in the wrong place."

Blown by a sudden gust of wind, a derby rolled down the boardwalk, spinning on its brim until bumping into Theo's feet. From a distance, the juggler came running toward them in an odd and curious manner. He moved like a mime pretending to run, a slow-motion gait in exaggerated steps. Theo thought of Muybridge's photographs of the racehorse, how they needed to be viewed at the right speed to convey the illusion of galloping. Played too slowly, the sequence of images produced a herky-jerky notion of a horse, like this juggler who seemed to have slipped off the sprockets. Panting despite his awkward chase, the young man stopped in front of them and bowed deeply at the waist, like a puppet loosed from its strings. With a quick thank-you, he retrieved his derby and then trotted away.

"Nice catch." A voice came from the other direction. It was Inspector Thompson with his partner Foucault. Theo wondered if they had been tailing him the whole day.

"We noticed you across the street," Foucault said, "and thought we should say hello."

"Any leads, detectives?" Egon asked.

Thompson joined them at the fence and grasped the iron bars. "I wish we had some news for you, Mr. Harper, but there's nothing. We're looking. We've recanvassed the neighborhoods and businesses between your place and the theater, but nobody saw a thing that night. Nobody watching the street at that hour."

Except the gremlins, Theo thought. Except the little eyes peering through the little holes.

Egon lit a smoke and flung the match over the edge. "Is there any chance that she went somewhere else?"

Foucault mimicked his senior partner and joined the line at the fence. "We notified the provincial police straight away, and even the Mounties in case she's gone off the farm entirely, so there are police officers all across Canada keeping their eyes out."

"Of course anything is possible," Thompson said. "Is there any reason to think she might have left the city, Mr. Harper?"

"None that I know of."

"Did you two ever argue, Mr. Harper? I

mean, above and beyond the usual why do you leave your socks about the place?"

He denied it with a frown.

"Did she ever talk about going home to the States? Any reason to believe?"

"What have you heard? Have you been talking to that bastard Reance from the cirque? Has my mother-in-law been calling you?"

"As a matter of fact," Foucault said, "she told us that Kay worried about how possessive you can be, prone to jealousy. You didn't lose your —"

"Her mother has no right to make such accusations. She thinks I stole her daughter away. I assure you everything was fine between me and Kay. We are happy."

Thompson drummed on the iron bar with his fingers. "I apologize for my partner, Mr. Harper. Just considering the possibilities, so that we may dismiss the unlikely."

Stepping away from the fence, Theo faced them all. "Listen, Kay wouldn't leave me. She wouldn't go off on her own. Don't listen to all these false stories about a temper. I have no temper. I didn't do anything to her, and never would. She's here, I can feel it in my bones."

The changeover always happened slowly. A

118

spark flickered deep within, perhaps only in her mind or, as she now thought, at her soul's center of gravity. The inside flame would go on and then off and on again until it caught hold, and suddenly she would be conscious, not quite aware of where and who she was, but able to think. In those moments of limbo, Kay remembered vestiges of all she had left behind: the circus, the balancing act, a man following her through darkened streets, Father, Mother, husband. He would be worried about her, why she had not yet come home. So late, she should send a text to explain how they got carried away, one drink becomes many, and how she tried to shake that persistent old lecher. She should be home with her man, his books and papers messing up the kitchen table. The Muybridge Obsession. Her husband whispering French to himself as he worked. His old-fashioned fountain pen marching across the blank page. In his own world, he could still be working and not have noticed how late it had gotten and the fact that she had not yet come home. Or when she did, he would be at her side in bed, his hand resting on her hip, but he was not here. And no hips, no breasts, her figure gone back to a child's, the dawning awareness of the state she was in, a wire frame, cloth body, arms, and legs, stuffed, a head full of dust. Her puppetness came gradually upon her. The flatness of the shelf was now hard against her back, and she was very nearly overcome by how stiff she felt.

The overhead lights beat down like so many suns. She sat up, surprised once more that she could sit. Only the Dog had awakened before her. He sat by the door staring at the knob, forever hopeful that he might be let out. Hanging from the coatrack, the Queen opened one eye and yawned. After a long slow stretch, she began worrying the knots holding her in place. Nix, who slept curled into a ball, unfurled to full length and sprang to his feet, toddling over to wake Mr. Firkin. In the bustle of the midnight morning, she did not notice anything out of the ordinary until all the puppets had risen. The two Judges and the Hag were missing. The mismatched chessmen sat atop the worn and folded board, and in the old woman's rocking chair sat Noë, her knees drawn up and her straw head resting on her crossed arms. Leaping down from the shelf, Kay scurried across the floor and pointed to the empty spaces. "They're not here. They've gone!"

The Three Sisters untangled their wires and strolled over to the place where the vanished puppets should have been. Olya laid a hand on Kay's shoulders, and Masha and Irina inspected the spot like two children wondering where their lost toys had gone. The others came over as well. Even the Worm inched his way to bear witness. Some bowed their heads, and others looked wistfully at the curtain to the toy shop.

"Where are the Judges?" Kay asked. "What happened to the Old Hag?"

"They've been selected," said Mr. Firkin. Beneath his walrus mustache, he was smiling. Murmurs of delight filled the air. The Devil waltzed the Good Fairy across the floor. Nix turned three cartwheels and ended with a heels-over-head backflip. Even Noë overcame her immediate regret and clapped and whistled.

Seeing the confusion on Kay's face, the Queen took her aside from the boisterous celebration. "You should be happy for them. They've gone to a better place. The Quatre Mains is putting on a new show, and he must have selected those three to be in it. They have the chance to do what they have been created to do, you see. Who knows, they may be out in the great world, perhaps a children's show in the city square, if they are lucky. And if you are good, and the puppeteers find a part for you in this show or the next, then you will have your chance, too. There is nothing like a performance to lift the spirits."

"So they are just in a puppet show for now? They will be coming back?"

The Queen stared at her shoes. "You can never tell. The ways of the artist are mysterious. Sometimes the puppets return, sometimes they never come back. Sometimes they last forever. Do you remember the wooden man in the bell jar?"

"What do you mean never come back?"

"Don't worry yourself, child. Just be happy for them. They have a chance to be under the spotlight." She patted Kay atop her head and then went off with the Dog, playing fetch with a ball with a nose attached to it.

The night went on as other nights had, though with a lingering bitter-sweetness. There aren't too many occasions when a new role comes your way, but on the other hand, she expected to see everything in its proper place — the Judges exchanging pawns and bottle caps, the Old Hag cupping her ear to catch the latest mischief. But they had vanished.

With no companion of her own, Noë seemed particularly forlorn. Kay found her in a far corner, whittling with a nail file at the stub of a pencil, intent on her task. Dark circles ringed her button eyes, and here and there, pieces of straw had fallen — or had been pulled — from her head. She jangled her right foot rapidly over the edge of the box on which she sat, and she hummed a song to herself under her breath.

"What are you making?" Kay asked.

"A point." Her voice had an odd rasping sound, like a duck with a cold. Noë glared at her, but Kay did not take the hint.

"A pencil point, I get it. What do you want a pencil for?"

"In case I ever find a paper, so I can write a note. You don't happen to have a paper?" She whittled more furiously, the shavings popping from the wood.

Kay shook her head, and then suddenly remembered where she had seen paper of a sort. On tiptoe, she stole over to the abandoned chess set that the Judges had contrived from a few real chessmen and the odd flotsam and jetsam of the Back Room — a few bottle caps, an eraser, the lid to a tube of glue. Among these treasures was a spent matchbook, the outside printed with a picture of a dancing woman and the advertisement for a club called Les Déesses and an address in Montreal. But the inside was gloriously blank. She tucked the matchbook under her jumper and wound her way back to the corner. Making sure nobody was watching her, she sat next to Noë, her bottom resting on the cold bare floor, and handed over the piece of cardboard.

"There," she said triumphantly. "Write to your heart's content."

"Are you sure nobody saw you? There are spies everywhere."

Using her body as a shield, Kay made the corner secluded from the rest of the room. The straw-haired girl printed in block letters: *HELP. Get me out of here.* When she finished, Noë folded the cover to hide the note and concealed it under her blouse. "We need to get a message to the outside world to come rescue me."

"But you can never leave. Besides, why would you want to leave the Back Room? Is it because the Old Hag was chosen to be in the show? Don't worry, the Queen said that she will return."

"Maybe she will, maybe she won't. I've seen them come, and I've seen them go, and I've rarely seen them back in here, no matter what she might say." Her eyes danced in her skull. "Depends on what the puppeteers decide, or what the man in the bell jar tells them to do. Listen, kid, you haven't been here so long, but it is a hell of a way to live.

I don't want to end up on a shelf. Or worse. We gotta figure out how to get this note under the locked door. We gotta find some way to let the people outside know that we are trapped in here."

Kay studied her friend's sad face. "I will help you," she said.

They hatched a plan in the corner. When Mr. Firkin rang the bell for the end of the day, Noë would run across the room as though to part the curtain and escape into the toy shop. She would never make it, of course, but in the diversion as the others ran to trap her, Kay could slide the flattened matchbook under the back door, for no one would suspect her of such a thing. Heads together, they conspired in whispers, and she felt an almost human intimacy in how their voices mingled, how the secret bound them together in the moment.

Had it not been for the Worm, they might have carried off the plot. The moment Mr. Firkin called for time, Noë let out a banshee cry and raced for the exit, her wooden feet clattering against the floor. The Devil chased her, wailing and gnashing his jaws. Nix dropped his juggling, sending the balls bouncing wildly, and stepped in her path, and the rest of the puppets moved forward in the rush, the Dog barking at the sport, the Queen aflutter, even old Firkin gasping to intercept her mad dash for freedom. Seeing her chance, Kay slipped away to the back door, the matchbook clutched in her hands, looking for a blank space to slide it through, when the Worm threw its body across the bottom draft, its crazed eyes spinning, and hissed at her to stop.

8

The trial had to go forward without the Judges. In their absence, the Queen presided from her oatmeal box, and Mr. Firkin agreed to play the prosecutor, with the Devil on defense. The puppets spent most of the night constructing a courtroom out of wooden boxes, old tools, and spare parts. Ordinarily they would have preferred a few rehearsals, but given the gravity of the charges, they decided there was no time and ultimately improvised as they went. The Worm acted as bailiff and led the prisoners past the jury of the Three Sisters, the Good Fairy, and Nix. To have included the Dog in passing judgment would have made a farce of justice, so he was left to wander, sniffing at the two women in the dock.

Kay was penitent, head bowed, hands folded as if in prayer. Next to her, Noë stared straight ahead, her straw hair sticking out like a dandelion puff, a hint of anger shining in her button eyes. The Queen brought down her gavel and Mr. Firkin rose for the prosecution, a scrap of lamb's wool serving as a wig.

"Mum." He bowed first to the Queen and then to the jury box. "Ladies and gentleman, the province intends to show, beyond the doubt of a shadow, that the defendants on the night before tonight, that is to say last night, did willfully and knowingly conspire, plot, scheme, and connive to make good their escape from this place. Using a forbidden pencil and paper — Exhibits A and B, my friends — they did write a note and then tried to slip said note under the door." He turned on his heels to face the accused and pointed his finger at their faces. "This is well known to be in direct violation of the rules, what you are allowed to do. Furthermore it is, on a personal level, disappointing. And upsetting. Especially from those of you who have been here a long time and should know better." He dabbed his eyes with the tail of his shirt.

"Thank you, counselor," the Queen said. "Does the defense wish to make opening remarks?"

The Devil stood on cloven feet and paced in front of the jury box. He was trying to make eye contact with the jurors, but they would have none of it, averting their gazes at the last possible moment. "Who among us is not guilty of having a dream? My friend the prosecutor would like you to think that a crime has been committed. He'll show you a pencil stub, a matchbook, a note. Mere props in this sordid drama. And he'll say that my clients were attempting to contact people outside the Back Room in some wild cock-and-bull fairytale notion that said matchbook, said note would convince a human bean —"

The Good Fairy burst out laughing and had to cover her mouth. The chuckle infected the whole courtroom. Two swift bangs from the Queen's gavel silenced her.

Raising a black eyebrow, the Devil continued. "As I was saying, as though this pitiful scrap of paper, this so-called Exhibit B, would a) be found by a real person and b) mean what it was supposed to mean. To wit, that there was a puppet inside the toy shop asking to be saved. Imagine such a thing, ladies and gentleman of the jury, and you will have an imagination that outstrips my own. The absurdity of such an SOS, why, it beggars credulity. As if a body would happen to pass by, discover said note among the debris of the alleyway, and break down the door. No, my clients were not attempt-

129

ing their escape. They, my friends, were only pulling your collective leg."

The Three Sisters put their foreheads together in a private consultation, with Olya keeping watch at the Devil's retreat. From the bench, the Queen motioned for Mr. Firkin to begin.

"Call Nix the clown," he said.

"Objection!" the Devil roared. "Nix is a member of the jury, Your Honor, and you cannot expect him to be a witness for the prosecution as well."

After a second's thought, the Queen ruled. "As we are so few in number, I will allow it. But, Mr. Nix, your own testimony must not prejudice your deliberations. Bailiff, if you please."

Carrying a miniature book in its mouth, the Worm sidled up to Nix, who placed his hand on it and swore to tell the truth. Mr. Firkin hitched his thumbs into a pair of suspenders he had fashioned for the occasion. "Now, then, if you will kindly tell the jury — including yourself — where you were on the night in question."

"Last night? Here, same as always, m'lord."

Firkin paced before the witness box, contemplating the phrasing of his next line of attack. "Tell us in your own words what you saw those two hoodlums getting themselves up to on the night in question."

"They were conferring in the corner, Mr. Firkin. I could not hear what they were saying, but I had my eye out. Not literally, of course. And that one —"

"Let the record show," Mr. Firkin intoned, "that Nix the clown is pointing to the codefendant, Miss Harper."

The Queen gaveled on the makeshift desk. "There is no record, Mr. Firkin, just so you know. We have no stenographer. We have no paper on which to write, and our pencil is currently Exhibit A, so I see no need for a record."

Hiding her voice behind her hand, Noë whispered in Kay's ear, "Do you see a pouch on the Queen? For this is fast becoming a kangaroo court."

"I heard that," snapped the Queen. "May I remind the defendant that my feelings are very easily hurt?"

Nix jumped in to fill the awkward silence brought about by the embarrassing remark. "I saw Kay Harper fetch the matchbook, Your Grace, and next thing, Mr. Firkin here is saying it's time for us to go to bed. Quick as a wink, Noë makes a break for the curtain. Chaos ensues, I don't mind telling you, but you were there. You saw it. Every-

131

one here is a witness. I had to stop her from trying to run through between the strands of beads. She would have been injured. Or worse. She may have awakened the Original."

The Three Sisters crossed themselves. "Without a cat in the room," Olya said, "the mice feel free."

Mr. Firkin scowled at her to keep quiet and then clapped Nix on the shoulder to show how well he had done. "Your witness, Devil."

"I have no questions for this clown. The province concedes the point that he stopped her in what he believed to be an attempted escape. His bravery is not germane to our case." He winked and gestured for Nix to step down.

On his way back to the jury box, Nix waved to the defendants and honked a toy bicycle horn concealed in his trousers pocket. When the laughter died down, Mr. Firkin announced in a loud voice, "The prosecution calls the Devil."

"Your Honor, please, this is preposterous. I cannot be expected to testify against my own clients."

"Overruled," she said and beckoned him to sit. There was no show of swearing him in.

"May I remind you," Mr. Firkin said, "that as an officer of the court, you are bound to tell the truth, even if that is against your nature. Did you not last night pursue Noë as she tried to escape through the curtains?"

The Devil nodded. A fat white spider slipped from one of his horns and hung from a silken thread.

Picking up the matchbook, Mr. Firkin said, "Please the court, Your Majesty, Your Honor, I place into evidence Exhibit B, and now ask the witness if he did not retrieve said matchbook from one Worm. And then, Old Devil, did you not read the note for yourself and give it to me as guardian of the entrance to the Back Room?"

"Firkin, Firkin. You know that I did."

Having no rebuttal questions for himself, the Devil was dismissed.

With his thumbs again hooked around his suspenders, Mr. Firkin took a dramatic pause. "Call the two defendants to the stand."

"I really must object, Your Honor. My clients are not required to incriminate themselves, and it is most unusual to put two into one box."

"Mr. Devil," said the Queen, "we are not amused. The hour of our long sleep is at hand, and much remains to be done. We

133

must finish the trial, decide the punishment, and then make ready."

"String them up." Someone in the room was throwing his voice.

The gavel crashed down. "Order, order. If that voice was not a marionette's, well, that is just in extremely poor taste. There will be no stringing, there will be no up. Now, Kay and Noë, please step forward and be quick about it."

The two puppets held hands and walked gingerly to the witness box. The Worm slithered in to give the oath, but one joint sneer scared him away. Mr. Firkin marched forward like a Dutch uncle and handed the matchbook to Noë. "Did you write this note? Would you please read it out so everyone can hear?"

Noë nodded. "I don't see why I've got to say the words. Everyone already knows what I wrote: 'Help! Get me out of here.' "

"And you, young lady." He trained a stern eye on Kay. "What were you thinking by trying to slip it under the door?"

Kay sighed and did not know what to say. He left her quaking in her chair and returned to his own, a faraway look in his eyes, as if he were contemplating the eternal verities, or perhaps he was merely daydreaming or thinking of nothing at all.

The Devil rose to cross-examine the witnesses. In the hollow of his left clavicle, the spider had found space to knit a web. The Devil snatched the matchbook from Noë's fingers and read the message again to himself. "Surely, you were only joking. You were having your way with us."

She shrugged her shoulders.

"And you, Kay Harper, you were in on the gag?"

"I was just trying to help."

"Heh-heh. Help with her little practical joke?"

"No. Help her go home."

With one voice, the Sisters in the jury box gasped. The Good Fairy snapped a twig. Nix gave his horn a desultory toot. The Dog, who had been resting under the witness chair, began to whine. Kay searched the room for a sympathetic friend, but they had all turned their faces from her. The Devil was behind her, leaning against the back of her chair, his long fingernails clacking against the balsa wood.

"You cannot go home," he said. "You cannot ever leave the Back Room. The Quatre Mains might come for you, but even then, he may bring you back, just as he has done with each one of us at one time or another."

"But she wrote a note." Kay looked at

Noë, who was sobbing quietly, her face buried in her hands. "She said that someone could come and save her. Rescue us."

"A thin hope," the Devil said, "to base your dreams upon. Yes, if someone knows you are here. And, yes, if they come for you after midnight when we can move about. And, yes, if they know it is you — who you used to be — and not how you are now: a mere puppet. And, yes, if in escaping, they trust you will follow and not look back."

"Oh, dahlink," Olya cried out. "If they get past the puppet in the Front Room. If they love you, if they know where to find you. If, if, if. Too many ifs."

"Better," the Devil said, "to put away such dreams."

"I am sorry that I ever had them." She thought of her husband and wondered if he had forgotten her by now. The Back Room was as quiet as she had ever heard.

At last the Queen cleared her throat and broke the silence. "Since you have confessed and apologized for what you have done, and I know that in your hearts you promise never to try to run away again, this court finds that you have been punished enough."

And with that, the trial was over, the verdict rendered, yet they all sat still and in place, like dolls in the window, until the time came to put away their playthings.

The beauty was in the conception of the problem, and the elegance was in the solution. It all started with a horse. Muybridge had been commissioned to photograph the horse in motion, ostensibly to determine just how it moved, whether or not all four feet left the ground at once. Hard as it is for the modern mind to conceive, in centuries past, no one really knew. The eye was not quick enough. Artists guessed. Scientists speculated. Until Muybridge figured out a scheme to use a series of wired cameras tripped by the animal as it galloped. The mare's name was Sallie Gardner, and the twenty-four pictures were made on June 15, 1878. Theo sat at the kitchen table surrounded by his abandoned work, the translation of the life of Muybridge. He studied the famous images, in which he could clearly see that as the horse moved forward all four feet left the ground at the apex of its stride. The legs folded together under its belly, the horse appeared to be flying in midair. Flipping on his smartphone, Theo watched a short video that ran the photos in sequence. At regular speed, it lasts for three seconds, but the anonymous poster had looped and slowed the images, capturing the motion of the filly's fluid stride. He could not stop watching Sallie Gardner and her jockey, hitting replay again and again. Eventually the light behind the tiny image began to bother his eyes, and he wiped clear the screen and set down the phone.

The pages had fallen out of order, the translation broken from where he had left off his work. In fact, the whole apartment was a shambles, the bed a wreck of sheets and blankets, Kay's pillow hugged to death, the sink awash with dishes, dirty towels and stacks of laundry in the bathroom. He had let the place go. Kay would be horrified by the clutter when she walked through the front door, though he had given up listening for her key in the lock. All the usual reminders of their daily routines were falling away. He had stopped believing she was just in the other room.

Kay used to jump slightly when he entered or at the knock on the door or the ring of the phone, just a reflex, no more than her muscles flexing, but he had always noticed how easily she startled in such moments. Yet for all her expressive energy, she was most compelling in the stillness of their time together. She had a way of curling herself into the smallest possible space when alone, reading a book or watching TV, and it often surprised him to find her wedged into the corner of a sofa or hiding behind the wings of an armchair. He would watch her surreptitiously and study the emptiness in her expression or the concentration behind her eyes. More than the sound of her voice, the music of her laughter, her body next to his in bed or walking hand in hand on a warm summer night, more than action, he missed the stillness of her and felt that slipping away. He could be alone with her, but it was difficult learning to be alone without her.

In the midst of all his desperate searching for her, he had to fight the thought that Kay might never be found. He had to push away the fear that she was gone forever, that he would never see her again. On the surface, he allowed the possibility, and in long conversations with Egon or the police, they had broached the subject now and again, and he thought how kind they were, trying to prepare him for the eventuality, or should we say possibility, probability, likelihood, chance. But underneath all their palaver, he refused to accept any other reality than that she would return, alive, whole, the same as she had been. She would have been shocked to see how he had let himself go.

He stabbed at the disorder, piling his

books and papers into neat stacks. Washing the dishes, gathering the sheets, linens, and piles of clothes for a drop-off at the laundry. He cleaned out the fridge, discarded every open carton, and he made a hash from what remained edible. For the first time in weeks, he sat down to a normal homemade meal alone in the apartment.

Between bites, he took out his phone and leaned it against his glass and searched for more Muybridge. In his fascination with animals in motion, Muybridge had made scores of other studies — a running bison, a charging lion, an ostrich, an elephant, a parrot in flight. And then he photographed people, how they moved in the simplest of tasks. All very clinical, the bodies in question either barely draped or without any clothes. Theo was entranced by the sequence of a nude woman descending a short staircase over and over, and he suddenly remembered what happened the night Kay disappeared. The light in the toy shop. He had been eating at Brigands bistro on rue Saint-Paul, just down the street from her favorite store, when the lights went on in the abandoned building.

In all of his interviews with the police, when Thompson and Foucault had asked him to re-create the events of that night, he had neglected to mention the incident, perhaps because in comparison to Kay's disappearance, it seemed inconsequential in his confused mind, but now he remembered clearly his surprise that evening. He had told them all the rest, leaving the apartment and walking to the restaurant, what he ate, how long he stayed, at what time he arrived back home, and the long wait to hear from her, the message in the middle of the night. Perhaps the lights in the toy shop meant nothing at all. The juggler in the bowler hat had reminded him of the puppets, and a string of synapses fired in his tired brain, but despite the late hour, he needed to go check that shop, if only to fill in the puzzle.

"Wait just a minute," she had said, tugging on his crooked arm. "Stop, let me see." Kay acted like a child when they passed the Quatre Mains. She could not resist staring at the dolls and puppets on display, sometimes putting her hands on the glass to peer inside and stare at the wonders. And nearly every time, Theo indulged her whim, for in those moments, the little girl emerged, the one he had never known, the essential child inside, like the core of a matryoshka, the Russian nesting doll. Some bright spirit responsible for the grown woman he loved.

The chilly night air foretold the end of

summer and the autumn soon to come. He stuck his hands in his jeans pockets and ambled along the sidewalk, vaguely excited about remembering the missing detail. A few stragglers lingered at the outdoor café tables, and a fiddler's reel from an Irish pub spilled out onto the cobblestoned street. At the corner nearest Quatre Mains, a ghost appeared, and at first, he mistook her for the drowned woman and shook with a spasm of fear, but it was a scullery maid in white cap and apron, her face ashen and nicked by makeup scars, with an iron necklace and a length of chain ringed around her neck. She nearly ran him over, and then looked as though she recognized him for a brief moment. *"Pardonnez,"* she said, smiling. Both hands were clenched to hold a hurricane lantern which glowed with the flicker of faux whale oil that gave a deathly pallor to her makeup. He laughed, realizing she was one of the actors from *les Visites Fantômes de Québec,* the nightly summer ghost tour through the Old City streets. Looking back once, the phantom sped away to join her hidden comrades.

The puppet shop stood just as always, dark and quiet. The dolls had not moved. The bear with the red fez had not bicycled away. The aboriginal doll underneath the bell jar, the one Kay so adored, stood like a guardian to another world, his black eyes staring into the distance. Theo tried the door, but it was locked as always. Perhaps his memory was just playing tricks, and no light had ever flashed in the abandoned store. He pressed his nose against the window as she had always done, but he could see nothing but darkness behind the puppets.

9

The giants returned. Kay had no idea how long she had been in the dormant state but was startled to be aware of them in the middle of the day. Judging by the slant of light coming through the edges of the covered windows, it was perhaps four in the afternoon. Something had happened to the order of things, and though she could not move, Kay was attuned to the changing nature of the world. Beyond the curtain, the giants were moving about. She could tell by their heavy footfalls and agitated voices reaching her ears. The bells on the front door ringing like mad with people going in and out of the shop. They spent hours in the Front Room, and not just the Quatre Mains and the Deux Mains as expected, but others as well, new and different voices, swearing in French and English, the smell of cigarettes, bottles banging on the counters, the tromp of boots and the packing of boxes. Kay hoped for night to come, then midnight, so that the puppets might be awake and someone could peek around the edge, but they must have started early in the day to have been working for so many hours. Frustrated that she could not see what was happening, she let out a deep and loud sigh. Behind her came a whisper: "Shush!"

"Who is that?" Kay asked.

"It's the Good Fairy. You shouldn't be talking."

"What's going on out there?"

From the four corners of the Back Room came warnings to be quiet. She resisted the urge to speak again and instead listened carefully, trying to calm her fears by falling into the hum of conversation and the random bangs and bumps. In a while, the noises slowed down. Men at the front door were saying *adieu.*

"No," the Deux Mains said. "We can do the back room ourselves. Nothing but odds and ends. *Merci.*"

The lintel bells chimed one last time. A key went into the lock, and then silence once more. Kay waited a long time before daring to speak.

"Does anybody know what is happening?"

The Queen issued an edict. "You are not

to speak until you are spoken to. Everyone keep still. A move is afoot."

Kay did not like to be chided by the Queen, but she respected her wishes. In the privacy of her own contemplation, she conjured a number of scenarios. The men were cleaning out the front of the shop to make room for the puppets languishing in the back. She pictured herself and her comrades taking the place of those old toys in the display window next to her favorite. Or, possibly, the men were with the police who had been looking all this time and finally found her and would be returning in the night and bring her back to her husband, who had not forgotten her after all. The thought quickened inside like a pulse that made her feel nearly human again.

Without warning, the beads rattled and the curtains parted. Backlit, the giants stood in the opening, two shadows great as mountains. The puppets stirred with excitement, barely contained exhalations rising softly from where each one lay.

"Good evening, my beauties," the Deux Mains said. "We are off on our next adventure."

Mad with curiosity, Kay turned her head to face them, breaking a cardinal rule. She gasped when she saw the Quatre Mains hand over the primitive wooden puppet to the Deux Mains, who laid it carefully in a bespoke leather case which she sealed and locked with a clasp. Together, they put the bell jar in a separate container lined with cedar shavings. From there they began loading tools into milk crates, gathering the spare parts, and throwing them into bins. One or the other crossed her line of vision frequently, but they were little more than a blur in their haste. The puppets held their tongues and stiffened, and the giants only spoke out of necessity.

"Shall we take them all?" the Quatre Mains asked.

She wondered what was meant by his question, whether some would go and some would stay, whether it was a temporary measure as when the Judges and the Old Hag had departed or more permanent, for it surely seemed as though they were packing to leave for good.

"Who would leave a soul behind?" the Deux Mains replied. "They are the spirit of our shows. Take each and every one."

A wave of relief doused the fuse of panic. A giant approached, two legs and a forest-green cabled sweater, and with his fingers rolled Kay over on her back. Wrapping his grip around her, he lifted her high into the air, her limbs gone limp, and raised her to his face. His eyes were like two china plates, blue and gray with black saucers in the middle, and his nose was pocked with old scars like a hill on the moon. Deep wrinkles lined his face, fissures in the parchment of his skin, and wiry hairs looked like strands of twine sprouting from his eyebrows and the caterpillar of his mustache. He brought his other hand to her head and with the nail of his index finger inspected the jagged cut of her mouth, his touch gentle and curious. When he cracked a smile, his teeth looked like old stones weathered by scores of winters. He smoothed her hair with his free palm, his gesture reminding her of her husband's affection. "A little mischief," he said. He laid her in a partitioned wooden box, her space no wider than a coffin and lined with newspaper shreds. She watched as he brought the others. To her left, he laid Noë, after a quick brush of her straw hair, and to her right, he placed Nix. The Deux Mains had three dolls in hand when she arrived, and Kay had only the briefest glimpse of her. She was a dark-haired woman, with olive skin and green eyes, younger than the Quatre Mains, perhaps by a dozen years. Setting down the Three Sisters, she then covered Kay and her companions with a flat divider, darkening the space. Olya, Masha, and Irina were stored atop them, and then a lid was fixed to the box that now contained six. Strips of packing tape sealed them in. Judging by the muffled sounds, a second box was prepared, which Kay could only assume held the Queen and Mr. Firkin, the Good Fairy and the Devil, and the Worm and the Dog. And then the giants went away again.

Midnight arrived in the catacombs, but the puppets were buried in confetti. Kay could hear them awaken into the half life, but for all her squirming and wriggling, she could not move. They were all stuck in space like the dead and buried. To shake the claustrophobia, she blew out a string of quick puffs and tried to calm down. From the left came a gentle sobbing, and she imagined poor Noë full of sorrow. On her right, Nix began to whistle the "Entry of the Gladiators," which she recognized from her circus days, the old chromatic tune to send in the clowns.

"Pipe down." A voice overhead, Olya's, cut through the noise. "For God's sake, if we are to share the same grave, we can't have that whistlink and that sobbink night and day."

"Olya," Kay said, "is that you? What is

happening to us? Why did they pack away the man in the bell jar?"

"Do not despair, Kay Harper. We are just on a holiday. Taking a little trip."

"We are leaving the Back Room?"

"Dahlink, the Back Room is not a place, it is a state of mind. We go where the wind blows. We might travel for a bit, we might find a new home."

Her sister Masha cleared her throat. "Is not the first time, kitten. Live for a century, learn for a century. I remember the time we were just in the middle of a performance of *Macbeth,* when they had to skedaddle."

"The three witches," said Irina.

" 'Bubble, bubble, toil and trouble,' " Masha answered. " 'Fire burn, and cauldron bubble.' "

"How did it go, sister?" Irina asked. " 'Fillet of a fenny snake.' You remember the Worm, eh? How he hated the part. 'In the cauldron boil and bake; Eye of newt —' "

"All right," Olya said. "That will do for the Memory Lane. These poor gills are worried sick."

Irina could not resist. " 'By the pricking of my thumb, Something wicked this way comes.' "

"Enough," Olya shouted. From the box next door came soft titters. "Calm down, everyone. Now and then, it is time to go. The Quatre Mains knows best. Perhaps he has heard whispers in the dark, rumors in the audience that this puppet or that is too lifelike, too real, and they start poking around in his business."

Masha offered another theory. "Or perhaps the two puppeteers have simply grown tired of this place. The road is in their blood. Gypsies."

"Living out of a suitcase," Irina said. "Better than living in one, eh?"

Nix laughed. "You saw they packed away the Original, too. I am sure we will not come back to this place. Our happy home."

"But what about my people?" Kay asked. "How will they know where to find us?"

"We are your people," Olya said. "You are one of us, and you go where we go."

Kay stared at the partition above her head, wondering how long she was doomed to be in this cubicle. How long till she could be free, to see the outside world again, to hold her husband in her arms. She searched her memories for his image, his name, but found it had slipped her mind. She did not know how she would bear such a prison.

Early in the morning before the moon had set, a knock came at the back door. As if in answer, the shop bells rang once from the

151

front door. The giants had come for them. A wave of August filled the Back Room. Footsteps, the sound of an engine in the alley behind the toy shop, and then the box was being lifted in the air, let loose from gravity's bounds. They were leaving, they were in motion. Kay wondered if he would stop looking now that she was truly gone. She whispered her good-byes.

In the end, Theo packed Kay's things to take home with him to New York. Her suitcases sat next to his in the foyer. All that was left to do was box up his books and papers, the unfinished Muybridge. Fortunately, his publisher had granted him an extension, under the circumstances, and he promised it by December. The sublet on the apartment expired as well, and Theo's few acquaintances had come to say *au revoir*. Thompson leafed through *Animals in Motion* while Foucault was engrossed in a newspaper account of the photographer's trial and acquittal. Sipping a beer in an easy chair, Egon appeared more relaxed now that the cirque's run was over and summer near its end.

"Just so you know, Mr. Harper," said Thompson. "Theo. We questioned Reance a number of times, questioned all the women who went out with him that night as well. I know you have your doubts, but believe me, if he was involved, we would know."

"The criminal mind always has a hiccup," Foucault said. "A giveaway. Working a suspect is like playing poker. Do you play, Monsieur Harper? Any fool can win with your winners. The trick is to lay down your obvious losers but bluff when the time is right. Too often and they con on to your game. Too rarely and you're depending on luck again. Most players make a psychological mistake. There's a tell, a subconscious move or gesture that gives away whether they have the nuts, are limping in, or completely bullshitting. Play with a fella long enough and you discover the tell. If you pay attention. If you are good at that sort of thing. We must have had that guy in a half-dozen times. Not our man. No tell."

Theo wondered if they had been playing him all this time, too, trying to guess what his tell might be, what his gestures might be saying. He knew that they thought, at first, that he was responsible for his wife's disappearance. Hell, they even had Kay's mother believing he was guilty. But over time, Thompson at least had come to regard him above reproach, though perhaps for Foucault it was all a ploy, an elaborate double bluff.

"Do I have a giveaway?" Theo asked.

Rising from his easy chair, Egon lit up a cheroot and went to the window to blow smoke out to the street.

Thompson closed the book with a bang. "Theo, you surprise me. Once and for all, you are free and clear. We'll keep working on the case. We have all your contact information —"

"I can be here in two hours, if I fly."

"Good." Thompson patted him on the knee and motioned for his partner to get up. "I can't tell you how sorry I am that this happened here in Québec. And that we have so little from where we first began. We'll keep looking. *Tiens bon.*"

They departed via the stairway in the hall. From his perch, Egon watched, and seeing them pass on the street below, he flicked the butt of his cigar through the open window. "Useless," he muttered.

"Not a clue," Theo said. "Almost three months and not one damn lead. Not even a theory as to how she vanished."

Into the box, he piled the Muybridge texts and then laid a neat stack of manuscript pages atop the books. Awaiting trial, Muybridge wondered in his misery if he would ever take another photograph. After he was acquitted that was all he ever did. Freed from the burdens of his marriage and the trial that changed his life, Muybridge pursued his art with a fanatic's obsession. Seeing his work all together made Theo uneasy, for so much remained to be done, but he could not imagine how he could ever find the will. School would start in a few weeks, and he had no idea how to prepare for the semester or simply face the students in the classroom. Not with Kay missing a world away.

"I'm running out of money," he confessed. "If I could stay in Québec, I would. And I feel like I'm abandoning her somehow, to be leaving like this."

The apartment looked so impersonal with all their things removed. He should leave a note behind, in case she returned to find him gone. Or if she was dead, so her ghost would not wander the rooms searching for him. Egon sat by without a word of comfort.

"Where will you go?" Theo asked.

"Maybe I'll try to latch on with another show. There's a group of puppeteers doing some interesting things in Calgary, and I've always wanted to spend some time in the wild West. Or I know a showman down in Burlington."

"Well, if you decide on Vermont, you'll have to say hello to my mother-in-law. Though you might not want to mention our connection. She still thinks I am guilty as hell."

They did not want to say good-bye, but neither knew what to say instead.

"When is your plane, *mon ami*? Tell me you have time for dinner or at least a drink."

He smiled and put the lid on his translation. "Tomorrow morning, first thing."

"One more for the road, then. If we can't paint the old town red, at least we can pour some beer in our bellies."

The summer crowds had thinned in the faded end of August. They walked alone through the city streets, heading for the Brigands. "Did I tell you about the ghost I saw last time I ventured here? One of the girls in the *Fantômes* show came running down the street, nearly bumped right into me. Scared the life out of me."

"What would we do without the tourists, my friend, who come to see our ghosts and follies? And the lovely young things dressed up for a show?"

A sidewalk table was free, so they decided to dine al fresco, to watch the people stroll by. Their orders were quickly taken, and when the pints came, they fell into respectful silence and anticipation, savoring the cold smooth taste of ale. He had loved it here when they first arrived, the look and feel of the Old City reminding him of some wayward part of Europe broken off and drifted west across the Atlantic. Kay had adored the whole experience, foreign yet familiar. She would have been sorry to leave.

"There's a shop up ahead that was her favorite. An old toy store filled with antiques, but it was never open. We couldn't figure out what happened there, whether the owners just up and deserted it or if the banks had foreclosed. A shame, really, such lovely things in the window. She adored the dolls, and one puppet in particular, an old Inuit carving that stood under a bell jar."

"The Quatre Mains? I know it well," Egon said. "Let's go have a look after we eat. We'll break in, and I will steal it for you."

After the fish and chips had filled them, after the drinks had whetted their daring, they staggered into the street, bound for thievery. He would do it for her, he thought, why not? With each step, the puppet transformed into a talisman. If he could rescue it, why not his wife? But the window display was empty. The dolls were gone. The bear had ridden away with the little dog. The tin soldiers off to another tin war. Every last trace. All that remained were cobwebs in the corners and two dead bees on the bottom shelf.

"Looks like the sheriff has beaten us to it. Or some five-year-old bandits," Egon said.

Theo bent his head and pressed it against the window. A fat wet tear dropped to the ground.

"Come now, you mustn't. We will get Inspector Thompson and his sidekick to investigate where all the toys went."

The front door was still locked when Theo tried the knob, and he waved for Egon to follow him around the corner. An alley ran in the shadows of an old and decaying section of the ramparts to the Vieux-Québec. It seemed to lead to a dead end, a place no one had visited for centuries. In the gathering gloom, they skulked behind a row of old stone houses, uncertain as to which was the back of the Quatre Mains. A heap of litter by the back door gave it away — papers and cardboard boxes, castaway wheels and springs and sprockets, a single wooden leg, a bisque head caved in at the right eye, and the tangled wires and handle of a marionette.

The door to the back was open. Egon stepped inside, and gingerly Theo followed. He found the switch to the overhead light which threw into relief the bare metal shelves and the yellow walls and the well-worn floor. Tiny footprints in the dust made him wonder about mice. A chair crafted from empty oatmeal boxes lay on its side. Small piles of sawdust dotted the surface of the center table. A wisp of cotton tumbled into a corner. Separating the back room from the store proper was a dark beaded curtain, filmed with dust that rose like pollen when he brushed past. All of the toys were gone. Even the man under glass that Kay so adored. Nothing but a stray ribbon, scraps of paper, price tags, a spent matchbook.

"Looks like someone left in a hurry," Egon said.

Theo cast his gaze upon the bare walls, filled with regret that he and Kay had never been allowed inside when it was bright and full of life. He could picture her delight in being lost among the puppets, and he was seized by the enormity of his departure. The toy shop refused to give up its secrets. They left as they had arrived, no closer to understanding.

BOOK TWO

10

The girl in the second row, three seats back in French 201, unless that Poindexter would take her usual spot. A woman in a yellow poncho crossing Amsterdam Avenue in the rain, who looked so surprised to find him chasing after her. Three times on the subway: once a pair of legs, once a woman in Kay's favorite red Donegal sweater, and once a face on the D train heading in the opposite direction. Her voice calling out for a wandering child — where would their children come from now? — on the steps outside the Cathedral of Saint John the Divine. He considered going inside, saying a prayer if such magical thinking would bring her back. Right now, on the spot, Kay marching down the center aisle to the pew where he knelt. The buzz of his cell phone in the middle of the night and fumbling under the pillow for it only to miss a telemarketer from Kissimmee, Florida, or

Waterloo, Iowa, and then he was awake half the night imagining those lonely salespeople consigned to such a purgatory. Every time he checked the mailbox, he turned the key with the hopes of a child on Christmas morning — nothing but coal, bills, and junk. When the leaves began to change colors. When he was drinking her favorite chai, or passing by the corner where she had first touched his arm, first kiss, last kiss, the spot in Central Park where he first knew she would say yes if he asked, when he asked.

Theo missed her most on Tuesdays and Thursdays. During the fall semester at the small college upstate, he had only two days of classes teaching both French language and literature, more than enough to keep him busy, what with the unfinished Muybridge translation loitering in the background. In years gone by, the long train ride up the Hudson Valley had offered him a chance to read or write, but now he spent most of the trip looking at the passing landscape, his thoughts filled with Kay. Rocking, in constant motion, he dozed and dreamt of her in his arms, the warmth of her skin, the scent of her body, her hair, the taste, the sound, the touch — until he roused himself from slumber, embarrassed if someone happened to be sitting next to him. Then he would turn away, press his forehead against the window, and try to forget for the rest of the trip. "Not her, not her," he whispered along with the rhythm of the train rolling on the track. And a bump would jolt him, bang his skull against the glass, and he would dig in his briefcase, find a book, grade a paper, set a lesson plan in his lap.

The first week back at college was marked by sheer awkwardness. His colleagues offered perfunctory greetings, a few words of consolation from the more kindhearted who had heard the news, but mostly the staff and faculty avoided him as though grief were contagious or they, too, suspected him of foul play. Even his comrades in the Modern Languages wing were cold to him. Frau Morgenschweis would not look him in the eye. Señora Martinez said how sorry she was on his first day back and then went silent. Only Dr. Mitchell, who knew seven languages and taught Greek and Latin, was the same as ever, blithely unaware of gossip and office politics.

"Dr. Harper." He nodded when their paths crossed at the communal coffeepot. "You were away this summer, eh? How is that new bride of yours?"

The question stunned him. "Ah, Dr. Mitchell, you haven't heard? My wife has gone missing."

"Missing?" Behind his wire-rimmed glasses, Mitchell blinked his eyes in confusion and empathy.

Theo shook his head and tried to keep his composure. "Literally, actually missing. She disappeared in the middle of a night in June, and we haven't seen her since. Not a trace."

"Jesus, I'm so sorry." His voice cracked. "The police are looking for her?"

"Yes, since she vanished. Up in Québec, where she was performing for the summer. I was there to keep her company and work on my translation."

"My dear." Mitchell gripped Theo's arm and hung on tightly. "Have you asked the chair for a leave of absence?"

The touch of another human, even such a small gesture, filled him with a profound lonesomeness. He knew that he had to free himself or risk a breakdown in the faculty lounge. "I looked for her all the time, called the detectives every day, but she just seems to be completely gone. I thought that work might help me deal with it better. I'm surprised you hadn't heard. I understand there was a memo —"

"I never read the memos." Mitchell leaned

his head close enough so that the pink of his scalp shone through the thatch of his thinning hair. "If you need anything, even just a sympathetic ear . . ."

Loosening his grip, Mitchell patted him on the shoulder and went away, talking quietly to himself.

The classroom offered Theo refuge from his sorrows. If they knew, the students had the sense or apprehension not to bring up the matter. For the first few weeks of the semester, Theo busied himself with the new freshmen, sorting those who had decent instruction in high school from those who had only the rudiments of French. Another class of six students commencing their second year worked on enriching their understanding of grammar, the study of sentences, irregularities, idioms, and style. Most of all he loved his seminar on Flaubert, where he could almost lose himself in the discussions, but even in the middle of a conversation with his bright and curious students, his thoughts drifted to Kay.

One young woman interrupted one such reverie by snapping her fingers to gain his attention and wake him from a trance. "Dr. Harper, professor, excuse me. But I was just wondering why this novel is called *Madame Bovary* if we have to wait so long for Emma to arrive? I mean, initially you think it is a book about Charles, and then his mother. And then there's Heloise. I mean, isn't it all way too convenient that his first wife just ups and dies?"

He blinked. His voice seized up, the words went dry in his mouth. Of course, Kay could be dead. He had been open to such a possibility, as early as the day they showed him the body of the drowned woman, but until that moment in the classroom, he had not considered it as a twist in their story. The student's question hovered in the air, but she herself evaporated from view, as did the others around the table. Everything was going away and leaving him resolutely alone in the room, and the only sound that reached his ears was the ticking of the cheap clock on the wall above the door. The student cleared her throat.

"Mademoiselle Parker, is it?" he asked. "Convenient? That's one way of looking at the death of Heloise, but I would say inevitable. From the moment Charles first sees Emma and is smitten, the whole story is set in motion. And it becomes her story. Emma's." He looked at the clock again, finally noticing the time. "And I'm afraid I've kept you all late." He dismissed them and sat at the table while they filed away.

Later that afternoon in the student union, he was puttering around with his Muybridge in a corner when a clutch of students came in and sat in a group of easy chairs overlooking the quad. They were loud and disruptive, and he recognized two or three from his Flaubert class, including the skeptic Parker. Hidden from their view, Theo could eavesdrop on their conversation with a modicum of effort.

". . . so he just went blank," Mlle. Parker said. "And I was all rise and shine, but he just sat there and spaced."

"You know his story, right? Word is his wife just vanished into thin air this summer."

"What do you mean she vanished?" Parker asked. "Like ran away on him, 'cause that I could see."

A third voice chimed in. "No. That's just it — they don't know what happened to her. Went all missing person on him. They say she might be dead."

"Get out. You don't suppose he killed her and dumped the body?"

They shared a nervous laugh.

"C'mon, guys," one of them said. "Not nice. But no wonder he's that way. Seriously lost."

Parker leaned across the table. "Hey, you

169

never know about the secret life."

Kay's joints rumbled, her stitches pulled at the seams. The vibrations meant that they were moving once again. On the main roads at constant speed, the hum of the engine and the rolling wheels lulled them to sleep, but a bump or a pothole and everybody was awake and complaining. If the jolt was harsh enough to cause the shocks to spring, her neighbors in the cardboard mausoleum swore and cursed the driver. They had been packed into some sort of van or truck, the puppet box wedged into place by other crates and cartons, shifting only slightly on the steepest of hills or the sharpest of curves. The back of the vehicle was dark, dank, and dismal. Inside her compartment, Kay suffered with the heat. The straw laid down as a cushion made her itch and twist to find comfort and relief. But most oppressive was the dullness of the routine. They would mosey for a few hours and then rest. She imagined that the drivers had stopped for lunch or to use a bathroom or to stretch their legs. And then back in the van and move some more until night fell. One or the other, for both the Deux Mains and the Quatre Mains took a turn at the wheel, would come to the back and open the door,

170

and the stale air would belch out in a rush as fresh air billowed in. After they checked their cargo, the giants departed. Above her, the Sisters yawned like three little kittens. Only when they were all shut in for the night, Kay dared to speak.

"Olya? Masha? Irina?" she called to them.

"Dahlink," they sang together.

"I've been awake all day between naps. How can that be, without the moon or without the stars?"

Directly above her, Olya spun slowly in her chamber, her wooden shoulders scraping the edges. "We are no longer in the Back Room, and we are free of its rules."

Irina laughed bitterly. "Free as one can be, shut in a coffin."

"Until we get to the next place," Olya said. "We will be in a kind of limbo, between one world and the next. The Original must be traveling with us."

"Purgatory in a box," Masha said. "Shut up and sealed is worse, if you ask me, than knowing where you are and what is to be expected. At least in the Back Room, you could see your friends every once in a while. Here the scenery never changes, the company never varies."

On her left, Noë quietly sobbed. "What I wouldn't give for a little light, a gulp of fresh

171

air. I'm going crazy in here, I tell you, cooped up night and day, never knowing if it is night or day except for the constant driving, driving, driving, then stopping probably at some cheap hotel out in the sticks. This is no way to live. Without your friends, your family. A chance to move and play, a chat across the table."

"Ah well," Olya said. "No use complaining, nobody is listening, nobody cares. Least of all the Quatre Mains, who could do something about it. You must make the best of your lot in life. Think of Kay, this is her first trip. Give some consideration to her feelings."

"Hers? What about my feelings? What about some consideration for the rest of us, bundled like packages? Like bottles in a case —"

From the right side, Nix trumpeted. "Oh would you please shut up? It's like this every time. Whine and moan and carry on. You know it's not forever. You know we had to leave the toy shop, they have come looking for Kay. Most likely we're bound for a better place, a happier tomorrow. Songs to be sung. Capers, jests, a chance to perform again. So you have a little inconvenience —"

"Feh," Irina spat out. "An inconvenience?

Better they would just dump us in the back of the van in a great big heap and then lock the door. At least then we could move about, see how the others are."

Masha hollered from her chamber. "Are you there? Can you hear us? Good Fairy? Devil? Are you all right, my Queen? Mr. Firkin, are you with us?"

The six puppets went quiet and waited for a reply. The other tombs were quiet. A cricket had crawled into the back of the van and began to chirp. The song echoed and filled the space.

"I wish I had a shoe to throw," Noë said. "And silence that bug."

"Where are they?" Irina whispered. "Do you think they are here? Maybe the Quatre Mains forgot them at the Back Room."

"Don't be ridiculous," Nix said. "Perhaps we have stopped at some little burg and the masters decided to put on an impromptu roadside show. No doubt the Queen and Mr. Firkin are behind the proscenium awaiting their cues."

The cricket picked up the tempo.

"Or maybe they can't hear us over this godforsaken cricket," said Noë. "I would give my left arm for a shoe. Hell, I would throw my left arm at it if it would *just shut up.*"

173

Olya restored reason. "Let us take a measured approach. The other box could be tucked away behind who knows what matter of junk. On three, I want us to all shout 'Hello! Can you hear us?' Loud as you can. One, two, three . . .'"

They shouted, and within a few seconds came the shouted reply: "Hello! We are here! Are you there?" Even the Dog howled a high lonesome greeting.

"Are we there?" Masha laughed.

"What dopes in the other box," Irina said. "What a ludicrous question —"

Nix interrupted. "I'll not have you insulting the Queen. Or Mr. Firkin. Or whoever it was." He spoke as loudly as he could. "We're here! Wherever this may be . . ."

"We have stopped for the night," Mr. Firkin yelled. "We are searching for a new Promised Land."

Irina hollered, "Let's hope it doesn't take forty years!"

"Keep your spirits up," the Queen bellowed regally. "It shan't be long."

On her word, they each fell silent. Kay was reassured by the presence of the other box of bodies. She had grown accustomed to them all. Indeed, she had a fondness that surprised her in its intermittent tenderness, for they were only puppets, after all. Above

174

her, the Sisters shifted in their compart-
ments, trying to get comfortable. Nix was
softly whistling a circus tune, and the
scratchy sound from the left could only
mean that Noë was tossing her straw head
from side to side. Outside and far away, a
car occasionally passed by, a melancholy
sound, and Kay guessed that they were
indeed parked at a hideaway motel. Just as
all had gone still and quiet, the long night
stretching ahead, the cricket song started
up again.

"Stupid fucking cricket," Noë said. "I'd
like to hammer it. I'd like to squash that . . .
pest."

From the upper berth, Olya whispered,
"Hush."

"You're restless, Noë," said Kay softly.
"Would you like me to tell you a story?"

A low murmur of assent drifted from next
door.

"Once there was a bendy girl. When she
was just a baby, she could stick her toes in
her mouth, and before she learned to walk,
she could tumble the whole way across the
floor. When she was quite small, she used to
watch the other bendy girls, and soon she
copied what they could do — balance on a
beam, vault over a horse, swing like a
monkey between two bars up in the sky. All

she ever wanted to do was jump and fly like a bird, and in time, she grew up and became so good at it that now all the little girls would watch her instead. And she had a string of admirers, young men entranced by her body and how supple it was and what fantastic things she could do with it. They had been drawn in by the motion, and at first their flattery was gratifying, but in time, she realized how empty were their looks and praise, for she was much more than a bendy girl. One after another the boys proved their intent, how little they knew or understood her, until at last she felt that one more admirer might just make her explode, so she went into a castle tower high above the clouds, locked the door behind her, and climbed to the topmost window where she could be alone. One day she heard a sound coming from beneath the ocean of white, a sound she had not heard before: a man speaking words she did not comprehend, yet so curious and beautiful that she ran down the steps, unlocked the door, and stepped outside to follow the sound. She ran across a meadow of asphodels in bloom and entered a birch forest, the white trees shimmering in the sunshine, till she came to a clearing. By a pond stood the stranger, the words he spoke appearing in circles above his head, like a man in the funny pages, and she came closer to try to read what he had written in the air."

The van had grown still again. Even the cricket was listening.

"He said, 'How do you do?' when he saw her, for he did not know the bendy girl, and she asked him what the words meant, and he said that he could teach her. They spent the day with the words and they were so enchanted with each other that they fell in love. She bent herself around him, and he fell apart, collapsing like a dying star, nothing more than strands of sentences, a man made out of words."

In the darkness, Kay could sense Noë was facing her, her breathing close, her fingers pressed against the partition. "That was you," Noë whispered.

"Was it? I am trying to remember. There seem to be two worlds — one of words and one of motion — and we are tied to one or the other, never quite able to be in both."

Long afterward, when everyone else was asleep, Kay heard the two sets of footsteps approach and the languorous voices of the giants. The aroma of coffee hit her like a dose of speed. The doors opened and closed, bang, bang. The key clicked in the ignition, and the wheels crunched onto a gravel

177

berm, the van lurching from reverse into drive. The Deux Mains rolled down her window to let in the first sweet smell of autumn.

11

Muybridge wept like a child after the verdict was read. Collapsed in his chair, he sobbed so effusively that the prosecutor and several men of the jury fled the courtroom to avoid the spectacle. Not guilty.

Just five months after the trial, his wife, Flora, died suddenly of the 'flu or fever. Their son — if indeed the infant was Muybridge's and not her lover's, as she had boasted — was sent to an orphanage, and though he paid for the child's care, Muybridge had little to do with him for the rest of the boy's life. Word of Flora's death reached him in Panama, where he was traveling under the name Eduardo Santiago Muybridge. He had departed almost immediately after the trial, on a commissioned expedition to photograph the people and the scenery of the Central America Pacific coast. Big painting-like landscapes, with clouds added to the skies in the darkroom.

First in Panama and then steaming north, stopping in Costa Rica, Honduras, and El Salvador before his final stop in Guatemala. He spent nine months on the trip, forgetting her, and on his return to San Francisco, he made a gift of a portfolio of his best images to Mrs. Stanford, seeking her patronage. She, in turn, recommended the photographer to her husband, Leland, who was looking to find a way to stop time. Together they hatched the experiment that led to the "moving images" of the famous *Sallie Gardner at a Gallop,* the horse in motion.

Theo set down his pen and wondered about that year away. Did Muybridge grieve for his dead wife on the wide blue Pacific? Or did he throw himself headlong into the work, setting up the huge negative plates, the portable processing tent? He liked to imagine old Muybridge among the natives, the strange Englishman with the wild white beard, so thoroughly eccentric to the men and women of the coffee plantations, the half-naked children clambering over the ruined Spanish colonial churches abandoned to the relentless fecund vines. And though the plates were in black-and-white, Theo could feel the greenness of the landscape, hear the birdcall, see the lizards and insects wither beneath the heat bearing down.

Through his office window, he could see the approach of autumn in the reds and golds of the trees lining the rolling lawns on campus. It would be getting cold soon. How Kay hated these first frosty nights, the time it took for her body to acclimate to the new season. Perhaps I should take a leave of absence, he thought, and go somewhere tropical for the winter. He could picture himself with Muybridge in the jungle, and then returning home next April and there she would be, waiting for him, wondering why his skin was so dark, his hair so light. Wondering where he had been all this time.

And where are you now, Kay? What fills your day? Who do you talk with now that we are apart? He held a running conversation with her, as though she were across the room instead of inside his head, and he knew that what she said in these imaginary dialogues was just the sound of his own voice talking to himself, but it was the best he could do, it was all he had. A kinder, more sympathetic version of the woman he loved.

"Why did you leave me?" he asked.

"But I haven't left you. It wasn't a matter of choice."

"Where are you now?"

"Just beyond reach."

Just beyond actually being there, an illusion shattered by harsh reality a hundred times each day, like a forest of memories chopped down to stumps.

The knock at the door was so soft that he could not be sure if anyone was behind it. The hinges creaked slowly, and from the edge Dr. Mitchell's face appeared, already contrite for the interruption. Theo waved him in.

"Dr. Harper? Theo? I thought you might be here today. I'm not disturbing your meditations?"

"Have a seat." Theo smiled. "To what do I owe this rare pleasure?"

Taking a chair across from him, Mitchell considered his opening gambit. He ran his fingers through his hair and drummed his fingers on the desk. Theo studied him, suddenly aware of how little he knew of the man's private life after working together these past five years, whether Mitchell was married or single, straight or gay, as some had speculated. Despite their long acquaintance, they had spent no more than a few moments alone together. Aside from the faculty meetings when he spoke only to defend the classics, Mitchell kept to his office and classes. He was an enigma, a scholar so deeply serious that he seemed to exist in a world apart. Behind his glasses, his eyes shone clear and strikingly blue. As usual, he paused before speaking, gathering his thoughts from the confluence of memories and languages, faces and stories milling about his brain.

"I've come to talk with you about your wife."

Shifting in his chair, Theo willed the man to go away, but Mitchell stared at him like an owl. "I can understand your reluctance." Mitchell smiled and continued. "And I certainly respect your privacy and don't mean to pry, but you've no doubt heard? Or then again, maybe you haven't. Fact is, there's been some gossip, I'm afraid, and while I don't believe a word of it, I must speak with you like this. How does Virgil have it? 'The monster Rumor flourishes by speed, and gains strength as she goes.' Best to snuff it out quickly, before Rumor gains wings."

"What is it you want to know exactly?"

Mitchell cleared his throat and searched for a suitable way to broach the subject, but, finding none, he simply began. "There's a vicious story going about that you and your wife had . . . been floundering on a rough patch of ice."

Theo smiled at the delicacy of his metaphor. "Nothing of the kind. We were having an extended honeymoon of sorts, at work but happy as could be."

"Students get all caught up in what they are reading and impute the lives of fictional characters to real people."

"Well, we are reading *Bovary,*" Theo joked.

The allusion escaped Mitchell, who read little that had been written after the birth of Christ. "You said she simply vanished one night. The police have no clues, no theory of the case?"

"I thought —" Theo began, but cut himself off and considered where the story might lead. "The night she disappeared, she was out with a group of performers from the show. There was a man, an older man, who was seen attempting to follow her home after the party."

"A snake in the grass."

"Of course, I confronted him, but he denied everything. Said she took off in the wrong direction and he never saw her again. The police questioned him as well, but there wasn't any evidence. No . . . body. Not a trace."

"I am sorry for your troubles, Theo. Gossip can be difficult to strangle. Perhaps you

184

remember when you first joined the faculty, all the stories about that student, that boy who made such astonishing accusations. A more benighted time, it's true, but still I understand how quickly rumors spread and what a strain you are under."

Grateful for an ally, Theo confessed. "I feel bombarded by suspicious looks, whispers behind my back. All the more hurtful, given the truth. I miss her horribly."

Slipping a finger behind his eyeglass lens, Mitchell wiped a tear. "I'll spread the word, if you like, to have the professors and the staff put a stop to this mindless speculation among the students. They can be reasoned with."

"I'm grateful. I can't tell you how much I appreciate your looking out for me."

Mitchell nodded but appeared to be reluctant to take his leave.

Theo stole a glance at the framed wedding picture next to his computer, vaguely concerned that he might betray Kay by speaking directly of her. "Excuse me for not knowing, but are you married, Dr. Mitchell?"

"Heavens, no, never," he said. "But I have been in love, and I can only imagine what hell you've been going through."

They regarded each other for a moment

before Mitchell hoisted himself by the arms of the chair, and clutching the back of the rail, he hesitated. "But your work is proving adequate distraction? I understand you are commissioned to make a translation."

Theo stood to be on an equal plane with his colleague. He thought of his morning's jaunt to Central America and the difficulties of translation. "Do you know the photographer Eadweard Muybridge?"

The name did not immediately register, and Mitchell shook his head. With some excitement, Theo rummaged through the books stacked at the elbow of his desk, procuring at last his treasured copy of *Animals in Motion,* the dust jacket tattered at the edges. He gave it to Mitchell with the delicacy of handing over a roll of papyrus. With a childlike curiosity, Mitchell leafed through the book, raising an eyebrow at the pacing lion and the kicking mule.

"I see your man Muybridge is an Aristotelian. Come with me."

They walked down the quiet corridor of the old stables that had been converted to offices and small classrooms. As he passed each open door, Theo could not resist the urge to peek inside, catching a few teachers busy at their lectures, Frau Morgenschweis's famous seminar on *Faust,* and in the empty spaces the blaze of October leaves framed by windows. Mitchell's office was crammed with books and papers, cheap posters on the walls, and reproduction busts of the great minds of antiquity staring down from the shelves like gods. Despite the clutter, Mitchell knew precisely where to find the book he had in mind.

"*De Motu Animalium,*" he said. "Among his many interests, Aristotle was a zoologist of sorts. *On the Motion of Animals.* Feel free to borrow it. A bit peculiar in spots. Science has not been kind to some of his ideas, but he is to be praised for the vigor of his speculation. Your Muybridge animals illustrate one of Aristotle's points. He says that the motion of animals can be compared to automata, puppets, wound up and released. Your pictures catch them in midair, at a precise instant. What is a photograph other than the quest to stop time? To hold that one moment before the eye and plant it in memory? So that we do not forget."

For a moment, Kay could fly. Lifted from the ground, like Dorothy's house in *The Wizard of Oz,* the carton of puppets spun in the air, rocking them in their cardboard tombs. Noë cried out softly, and Nix chuckled. As suddenly as it had launched, the box

187

descended, landing with a soft thud. The pent-up air let out a gasp when a knife punctured the packing tape seal, and when the flaps popped open, the temperature inside dropped a few degrees in an instant and took Kay's breath.

"We'll need the Sisters," one of the giants said. "And the new girl beneath them."

Olya, Masha, and Irina were freed. The ceiling no longer sagged under their weight, and soon the cardboard fell away, and Kay felt the sun warm her and saw the light of day bright in her unblinking eyes. Every instinct screamed to close her eyes lest she be blinded, but she could not and soon found that she could stare into the blue without fear. A pair of hands lifted her from the box and laid her in a patch of grass next to Irina as the giants unloaded other gear from the back of the van.

The world was a beautiful place. Soft as a bed, the ground yielded to her feathery weight. A breeze caressed her in intermittent waves. Birds sang in nearby trees, the leaves rustling, the branches gently creaking. A stray memory toyed with such sensations, a man warm and pleasant lying next to her in the tall grass declaring in the shapes of the clouds they watched a camel, a duck, a white rose. At the edge of her thoughts, she detected the giants moving, carrying boxes from the lawn into the back of a small building. Faraway music floated by, the song of a carousel, and children's laughter in the wind. How she had missed the sound of children, their unabashed joy in the face of newness and wonder. A shadow appeared and blotted out the sun.

Squatting on his haunches, the Quatre Mains reached for her and Irina, taking one in each hand. His grip was firm but gentle, and Kay nestled in his hand as he walked across the lawn, swinging in the rhythm of his gait. He pushed with his hip and opened a door into the dark. When her eyes had adjusted, she could see they were traveling along a narrow hallway, past faded posters on the walls, dodging bits of scenery, foam rocks, a stack of leaning stage flats, a fake chandelier, tattered sofas, rickety chairs, obstacles in a warren of corridors.

A rack of costumes — gowns and robes and a pair of angel wings — rolled toward them, and Quatre Mains stopped to let it pass. At the back end was another giant, a red-haired man in a dingy black sweater, and he paused to say hello. Kay had not seen anyone other than the two puppeteers in ages, and the fact of the man amazed her. The two giants talked to each other in

189

French, so she could not understand half of what he said; but he was real, not a myth at all, and she wanted to join the conversation, be heard, or attract his attention in some way. Wave her arms and legs, shout, just to see if he recognized her for who she really was — a woman trapped inside a puppet's body. But the red-haired man took scant notice of her or Irina. He simply nodded when the Quatre Mains lifted each puppet to give him a closer look.

"Just the week?" the man switched to English.

"Eight shows through Sunday," the Quatre Mains said.

"Well . . . *bienvenue à Montreal.* Much success to you."

Backstage a makeshift rehearsal space had been arranged. A single mahogany banquet table dominated the room, and lying there were some of her old familiars along with a few puppets she did not recognize. With casual disregard for their comfort, the Quatre Mains dumped Kay and Irina on the table and hurried away, muttering about how much remained to be done. Kay had landed awkwardly, her left elbow resting on the sharp shin of a marionette she could not see. Though she was hyperaware of her circumstances, she could not move, and dared not say a word, for the giants might reappear with more of their colleagues and other materials fetched from the van.

Late in the afternoon, the Deux Mains arrived and rearranged the puppets in two straight lines. Working quickly, she picked up a puppet and did something to it that Kay could not see, but she could hear the clip of scissors and the pull of thread through cloth. One by one, she worked on the others, adding a touch of paint to a worn face, a scrap of cloth transformed into a new dress. Midway through the repairs, the Quatre Mains joined her. They worked in silence for the most part, concentrating on their tasks, but occasionally, they shared a few thoughts.

"This one," said the Deux Mains, holding up Olya. "She'll need three changes of costume."

"Let's start her as Jo in *Little Women,*" the Quatre Mains answered. "You think she would be the best Jo? Even though she usually plays the oldest, yes, I can see her as the lead. And the other two can be Amy and Meg. And, of course, the new one will play the narrator."

"Can she double up as one of the Little Women as well?"

"She can be Beth." He laughed. "Perfect,

191

our late, lamented mistress of ceremonies."

The Deux Mains held up Kay for inspection. In the corner of the puppeteer's mouth hung a needle, a loop of red thread dangling like a strand of blood. She took a long look at Kay, allowing her a long look in return. Kay had not yet had such an opportunity to get a thorough sense of the woman, and she drank her in like an infant studying its mother's face. And as she watched her, she saw her jade eyes darting, searching for imperfections. Steadying her fingers against Kay's wooden face, the Deux Mains dipped a paintbrush and wicked in the puppet's eyebrows, laid a fine edge, and quickly stroked in long eyelashes. As she worked, she pursed her lips and the curled tip of her tongued darted. Caught in the flow of her craft, the Deux Mains worked with a satisfied smile, laying Kay on the table. She brushed the lint from her blue gingham frock and then reached into a box and found two sets of dowel rods and fixed them at the wrists and ankles. In one swift motion, the Deux Mains had the puppet on her feet and walked her a few paces forward and tested how fluidly her arms could be raised and lowered.

"You'll do, little one. You'll do just fine." She held her up to show the Quatre Mains.

"Is she ready for her debut?"

"This mouth isn't right. What sort of hack butchered her so crudely?" He laid her facedown on the table and sifted through a toolbox for a hammer and a chisel. The first blow skited into the wood at the back of her skull, and then he yanked out the blade and repositioned it for another strike. Kay felt no pain but was in shock over the sudden rough treatment as he chipped away at her mouth. With trial and error, he rasped out an opening and found a lever to fit into place, and then he sawed away her lower jaw and planed and sanded the edges for a good fit. He screwed the whole apparatus into place and fiddled with the lever. Her wooden jaws clacked together and opened wide, just as she had been able to do as a person. The Quatre Mains bent round to see her face as he spoke and made her mouth the words "I am nobody's puppet." With a satisfied grin, he set her down with the others.

As they were tinkering with the last of the puppets, a cell phone blurted out a melody, startling in its novelty after all this time. The Quatre Mains answered, and when he was through with the call, he rejoined the Deux Mains at the worktable. "That was Finch. They'll be here in fifteen minutes and are bringing the new man. Name of Delacroix. Finch and Stern have given him his parts. Not too many lines. Mostly the slapstick. If he can get down the blocking, we should be okay for the show."

They arrived in peals of laughter, announcing their presence in the theater long before they reached the rehearsal space. Delacroix was a pencil-thin Frenchman, mouth at rest in a sneer, fingers stained by Gitanes, but deeply attentive to the rapid instructions fired at him in both languages. Stern came from the other pole, a refuge from a commune, a bushy white beard covering his chin and reaching down to the collar of his red plaid shirt. But the biggest surprise was Finch. She was a giant among giants, a head taller than the Quatre Mains. She had a pleasant long face, big mitts for hands, long legs and feet, broad hips, and a bust like the prow of a ship. How would she ever fit in the tiny space below the puppet stage? How would she ever get those fingers into the opening of a glove puppet? Like many large people, she moved with a panther's grace, the delicacy of her care a well-earned compensation for her size. The three new puppeteers handled the cast of characters, hefting each puppet to judge its weight and the intricacies of the mechanisms. They tried out Kay's newly hinged jaws, walked her a few steps forward and back.

"This one is the narrator for the whole show," said the Quatre Mains. "She'll do the *entr'acte*'s jokes and stories as well as play the part of Beth."

"Seems reasonable," Delacroix said. "Nothing I haven't seen or worked with before."

"That's good," said the Quatre Mains, as he clapped him on the back, raising a cloud of dust and dander. "We have thirteen blackout scenes along with the prologue and epilogue and a few in-between monologues, which needn't concern you much. And one of the scenes involves only two characters that Finch and Stern have created out of their stormy imaginations. So, an even dozen for you to learn. I propose we take on the six most difficult before our supper, and when you return, you can pick up the rest, *toot sweet* as they say. Not too many lines, and you can be on book since nobody in the audience will be able to see you most of the time. As a matter of fact, in one skit, 'Lassie, Go Home,' all you need do is bark like a dog. You can bark, can't you?"

"Arf, arf," said Delacroix.

"Oh no," said Finch. "Bark like a collie."

"Woof, woof."

195

"C'est bon," the Deux Mains said. "Shall we get to it?"

The rehearsal lasted well into the night, a swirl of talk and motion that left Kay baffled. The Deux Mains handled her most of the time, carrying her to a small ledge built into an opening of a tall flat where Kay sat, legs dangling over the edge, facing a sea of empty chairs. When the Deux Mains addressed the stage, she moved the lever behind the puppet's head so that her words, *sotto voce,* appeared to be coming out of Kay's mouth. And then Kay would be ducked away and laid to rest on the floor as the other puppets started another sketch. She enjoyed playing both the narrator and Beth in the *Little Women* skit with the Three Sisters and a matronly figure who was vaguely familiar. It all happened so quickly and furiously that she could not be sure of any part, much less the whole, of the show. The giants moved like dancers, their hands in constant motion, backs bent, heads hidden, slipping on the glove puppets, twisting the sticks and wires to make the marionettes flit across the stage, talking, laughing, swearing when they made a mistake. The Quatre Mains lorded over the chaos, calling out the titles for each new blackout sketch, hollering up to the invisible person manning the lights over a missed cue. In the end, all the puppeteers collapsed to the floor, congratulating one another on their performances, and after putting away all the puppets in the backstage room, they shut off the lights for the night.

Exhausted, Kay could hear them retreating and was grateful for the peace and quiet. Far from the inner sanctum, a door closed and was locked. She heard a giggle in the darkness. A small lamp burst into brightness. She sat up, surprised that she could move on her own, and saw Mr. Firkin with his fingers on the switch.

"Mes amis, mesdames et messieurs, welcome!"

Around her the puppets awakened and rose.

12

"I'm dead," Kay said. "But you already knew that, having read the book."

Out in the dark, a single person gasped. The audience was settling into place, waiting, saying entertain us, make us laugh or cry, willing themselves to be carried away in the promised dream. They listened for what she had to say, words conjured by the unseen voice, and watched the puppet manipulated by invisible hands, until at last they believed. The Deux Mains lifted Kay's hand to her forehead to shield her eyes from the stage lights. In that simple gesture, she became real, and they were hers.

"I am your host, Beth March," she said. "And this is 'A Little *Little Women* and Other Puppet Tales.' You know the story of the four March sisters: Meg, Jo, Amy, and me. Well, I'm the sister who bites the dust. No need to feel sorry for me, though. I kind of like it here, up in the wings, watching it

all from above. Gives a girl a certain freedom. And, besides, let me tell you a secret:
all art needs a little sadness in it, a small
tragedy to balance the human comedy."

She stood on the ledge like a jumper at
the window. The Deux Mains made her tot-
ter before settling into a comfortable position. "Don't worry, dear friends. May I call
you friends? Perhaps not right away, but I
hope we are friends in the end. We are not
here to talk of life's tragedies but to entertain you with a number of sketches, some
happy, some sad, in our little revue. Like
life, our show has plenty of laughs along the
way. Sit back, relax. Pay no attention to the
man behind the curtain or the hands that
fiddle with our strings. Let us be friends."

The spotlight went off and Kay was swept
into hiding. The Deux Mains hurried to
another opening for the first scene. From
her resting place, Kay could hear the crowd
roar with laughter during the ribald bits
from "The Regina Monologues" and "Adam
and Eve and Bob and Carol and Ted and
Alice." Some sniffled during the rocking
chair denouement of "The Olden Girls,"
and Kay eagerly waited for the key moment
in "Lassie, Go Home," where young Timmy,
played by Nix, fell down the well, and
Lassie, played by the Dog, barked inces-

santly instead of rushing off to find help. The first woof, woof from Delacroix brought a few chuckles, the second, a ripple of titters, but by the fifth plea for Lassie to just go home already, the audience was in shock, and when Lassie lifted a leg, they were fully in on the desperate joke.

The Russian sisters played a series of roles in many of the scenes, but Kay's favorite was "Cinderella Goes Shoe Shopping," with Irina in the title role and the other two as the stepsisters complaining about their feet. Mr. Firkin played the hapless clerk trying to serve all three at once. But it was the ending that fascinated and terrified Kay. By some magical trick, the shoes — also wired — began to dance by themselves in a frenzy, clattering on the stage as the puppeteers stomped on the floor behind them. All five puppeteers worked the actors, but the Quatre Mains handled pairs and pairs of shoes, furious with the sticks, so many flying wires that he indeed seemed to have four hands.

Most of the time, Kay's role as MC was to fill in the intervals between the skits, but for "Punch and Judy's Final Grudge Match," she played the part of the ringside announcer as Stern's Punch was relieved of his slapstick and pummeled senseless by Finch's Judy. Unlike most of the puppets in the show, the Punch and Judy were strangers to her. They had not come from the Back Room, and it took her a while to figure out where she had seen them before. They had been in the front display window of the old store in Québec. They were stock characters, mere toys compared to her friends. Kay caught herself longing for someone she used to love. The man in the bell jar.

Every performance sped by, barely time backstage for the troupe, soaked with sweat, to change the puppets' costumes, shift props, wheel backdrops into place. The giants possessed a manic energy, their faces lit with joy as they pulled strings, worked the rods and levers, donned the glove puppets. Bending to her, the Deux Mains smoothed the wrinkles from Kay's dress and checked the straps to ensure the rods would stay in place.

"The grand finale," she whispered to Kay. "Keep it real."

In the darkness, the giants took their places. Finch, Stern, and Delacroix handled the Three Sisters and the puppet playing Marmee. The Quatre Mains took control of the rods at Kay's feet, and the Deux Mains operated her hands and mouth. A spotlight shone, and they walked Kay to the edge of the doorway.

"The death of Beth," she intoned. "Or, the last of a little woman."

With an assist from Finch and Stern, she maneuvered into bed. A pneumatic device arranged under the quilts of the sickbed made it appear that a doll was breathing her final death rattle. The March sisters and Marmee had gathered around her, watching, their simulated breathing in sync with Beth's. The only motion came from the trembling of the strings. Their stillness added an air of dignity. The expressive limits of their wooden faces matched perfectly the emotions of the moment. They were born to grief and in their grieving expressed most clearly the defining sorrow of their faces.

A puppet seagull flew by the window. The tape recording of its call sounded like a laughing maniac.

"She's much too young," Meg cried.

"How can she do this to us?" Amy asked. "How can she leave us? Oh, Beth."

"I cannot bear it," Marmee said. "My angel."

Jo faced the audience. "She was the only decent one among us. Beth, I will write about you. You won't be forgotten, and your sacrifice will make me a better writer."

"She goes," Marmee said. "She flies from us."

By the alchemy of light and a puppet ghost made of the sheerest silk, Beth floated from the bed and disappeared into the rafters. The surviving Marches bent their heads to the empty bed. The lights were lowered on the tableau and lifted to Kay's spot by the door. The theater was hushed.

"Of course," she said, "that's not how her death plays out in the novel. No deathbed contrition, no gathering of the sisters. Beth slips away quietly one night, just like that." She snapped her fingers in sync with the puppeteer. "The book goes on, and there are even a few sequels, as if there are sequels. For Beth, the story ended. As it does for us all. There's only one ending."

With the Quatre Mains moving her feet and the Deux Mains her arms, Kay walked to the middle of the stage, the spotlight following her. Dressed in black, the puppeteers revealed themselves, but the audience continued to focus on the doll.

"A sister, a sister . . . a sister lives on as long as there are those to remember her. A mother, a child, a brother, a father, and her sisters and friends. You won't forget your old aunties, will you? We can try to forgive Louisa May Alcott for the bum ride Beth got, for that rude treatment ill deserved just to make a better, more dramatic book.

Because, well, in the end the writer pulled it off. Beth is still alive in us all these years later. All the Little Women made eternal through . . . what? A book? Art? Love? Or is it all the same?"

The light circled just her face. "No strings attached." The audience groaned, and laughed at their reaction to the pun. For a brief second she seemed to stand there on her own, without the assistance of the puppeteers. "Are we still friends? Of course we are. Good-bye, my dears, *adieu.*" And then a quick blackout.

When the applause began, the lights went full. Deux Mains had Kay take a bow, but then she dropped the puppet, allowing her to hang limp as the other puppeteers emerged from behind the scrim. The reaction of the first night surprised her, and the acclaim continued through the whole week. Only the matinees proved more subdued, perhaps because of all the children brought by parents who thought puppets were for children or who failed altogether to read the warnings. No matter how enthusiastic, the clapping and cheers enthralled her. The puppets made their exit, spent but exhilarated, an atmosphere of fatigue and euphoria in equal measure.

After Quatre Mains and the others battened down their sets and props, the puppets rested until midnight. Replaying the performance in her mind, Kay was always surprised by the return to autonomous life, which was made even stranger by the presence of the inanimate ones, the lifeless Punch and Judy, the seven glove puppets who played the dwarfs to Noë's "Snow White and the Codependents," and the seagull, nothing more than a children's toy. Scattered among the dead were some of her old cronies from the Back Room. The Sisters whispered together in a corner. Mr. Firkin regaled Nix with a particular moment in the show when he "had them eating out of the palm of my hand." Kay longed for the others who had been stowed away — the Devil and the Good Fairy, the Queen and even the Worm. And then there was the curious case of Marmee, who was always hounded by the Dog backstage. Usually she kept to herself, knitting one night and unraveling her work the next, like Penelope waiting for Odysseus to return. Nearly the entire week had passed before Kay had the courage to approach her and inquire directly.

"How is it that you are alive like us?"

Marmee lifted one eyebrow and leered at her.

Kay continued, "Do I know you? You look familiar. . . ."

"You mean to say you don't recognize your old friend? Oh, the Quatre Mains would be so happy to know how readily and easily you've been fooled." She laughed and hunched her shoulders and rocked on her heels. "Are you sure you can't guess?"

"Something about you reminds me of the one we called the Hag."

"That's it!" Marmee touched the tip of a knitting needle to the side of her wooden nose. "First try, good for you. Isn't it wonderful? Aren't I marvelous? They took off my old head and gave me a new one. Freshened up the stuffing and patched me right well. I feel forty years younger."

Kay wanted to reach out to touch her, see if she was real, but a tremor ran along her arm from fingers to shoulder. A bubble grew inside where her stomach used to be, and she felt dizzy enough to sit. "How could it be? You are still you? Not someone else, for you sure look different."

"Looks aren't everything, chick. There's such a thing as essence. What's inside you. I've been all kinds of puppets over the years. Once I played a bawdy in a honky-tonk show, and once I was a rod puppet on a well-known TV show for children. But

206

things change. As long as you hold on to your essence, you have everything."

"But you were taken away with the Judges. What about the Judges? What about their essence?"

Drawn in by their conversation, the other puppets eavesdropped, curious but quiet. Marmee looked about the circle and confronted the question.

"They were unmade. You'll find what's left of them in a box of spare parts. The stuffing back in Québec. Maybe it was the Original's idea, or maybe it was a whim of the Quatre Mains. He saw no need for them any longer, so . . ." She clapped the dust from her hands and wiped them clean.

"You mean they are gone? For good?"

"For good, for ill, for what you will. But, yes, they are kaput. No more."

The others seemed unfazed, accepting the finality of her pronouncement quite readily. Drifting away in twos and threes, they talked quietly among themselves. Nix cracked a joke that made Mr. Firkin laugh and then chide him with a warning of "too soon." Puppets changing shape, disappearing altogether. Kay's notions of order were disturbed, so she found a dark corner in which to hide and contemplate and take exception to just who ruled the world.

■ ■ ■ ■

Theo spent a rainy Saturday archiving all the photographs of Kay he could find. From a fat album, he scanned in their wedding photographs and then dragged a few dozen images from the social media sites she haunted. He reached into the cloud and ran off prints until the color ink faded to sketches. He plucked another hundred off an old digital camera he had forgotten about, and from his phone, he downloaded a batch from Québec, the latest, the last. Some that she had taken he had never seen, and he searched for some clues, but there was nothing. Any image from that night was locked in her phone, wherever that might be, wherever she might be. He saved what could be found to the hard drive and then made two separate backups on his portables to leave nothing to chance.

A thousand faces. A thousand memories.

They had met through friends of a mutual friend at a rooftop party in Manhattan. Kay was with a man who worked in marketing. Theo had shown up alone and was having a miserable time until he met Kay on a corner of the roof overlooking the Flatiron Building. The summer humidity dampened everyone, and she had taken off her light jacket and stood in a sleeveless blouse and skirt, her bare legs and arms alluring. With a swizzle stick, she stabbed at the lemon in her melting drink. She smote him with a smile. They were the last to leave the party.

Reaching for another tissue, he wiped his wet face and blew his nose. He was surprised at how quickly he could be torn apart. The photographs were safely preserved, at least, but they only recorded a part of her story. Kay's mother had the other pieces to the mosaic. On their trips to Vermont, she had shown him all the scrapbooks — baby's first steps, school days, the gymnastic meets all duly memorialized by newspaper clippings and faded ribbons pressed between the leaves.

"I'm sure Theo doesn't want to look through all that stuff," Kay had said. "Don't subject him to that torture, Mother."

"But I do, I really do," he said. "I want to know what you were like before we met."

Dolores flashed a triumphant smile. "Now you see, Kay. I know him better than you do. Come sit by me. . . ."

How long had it been since he had spoken with his mother-in-law? Two months? Their conversations had been a chore and a heartache, her questions filled with recriminations over Kay's disappearance. At first, her tone had been accusatory, looking for signs of his culpability, but in time he thought he had convinced her of his baffled grief. When he returned to the city to begin the school year, Theo tried to reassure her, despite the lack of any news. "How could you give up?" she had asked. "Why aren't you staying in Québec to keep looking for her?" He explained that he could not quit his job. Their savings had been slowly draining away, and while the college might have considered a leave of absence, the truth was he needed the distraction of the classroom. And his translation. Thank God for Muybridge.

Her latest phone call had been one long wail of grief and frustration. "Why did she ever marry you?" Anger had bubbled between Theo and Dolores from the beginning. She resented how he had taken her daughter away from her in a time of need and had intimated on many occasions that he was too old for Kay. He bristled at her interference and how quickly she could make Kay feel guilty for having, at last, a life of her own. The accident that had put Dolores in a wheelchair had changed her, or so Kay claimed. She used to be such a sweetheart, Kay would say, but Theo was not so sure. Over the months of his court-ship and marriage to Kay, he tried his damnedest to be liked by her mother, since love seemed a too-distant horizon. Why did she marry him if her mother trusted him so little?

He was so lonesome that he nearly picked up the telephone to call Dolores, just to have the chance to talk about Kay with someone who knew and loved her as well, but he could not bring himself to dial her number. And there was no one else. Kay's few friends in the city had been solicitous at first, but they, too, had gone on with their lives, and there wasn't a soul in New York to commiserate.

Night fell earlier than usual. Perhaps the rain hastened the darkness. Framed in the window directly across the street from his apartment, a couple sat down to dinner, an ordinary evening. Theo watched them eat, chatting over the salads, losing steam when it was time for ice cream. She took away the dishes, and he sat at the table slumped forward, holding his head in his hands, thinking deeply about a serious matter. He did not move until she returned and laid her palm on the back of his neck, and he threw an arm around her hips, pulling her close, and rested his head against the softness of her belly. They remained in this silent embrace for a long time. When they left the dining room together, shutting off the lights, Theo rose wearily and lay on the couch in front of the television.

At two in the morning, he awoke suddenly, mildly surprised to find that he had fallen asleep during the movie. A light glowed from his desk, and seated in his chair Muybridge leafed through Theo's translation. He was shabbily dressed, his jacket threadbare at the elbows, his shirt unbuttoned at the neck, the collar frayed. A corona of white hair framed his great head, and he seemed oblivious to everything but the book in hand. Theo rolled off the couch and approached him, but the ghost did not look up. Taking a fountain pen from his breast pocket, Muybridge crossed through an entire page and then recapped the top with a click that echoed in the silence.

"Not at all how it was," he said to himself. "The bastard Leland Stanford took all the acclaim for the pictures of that horse Sallie Gardner. As if it was his idea in the first place. Treated me like a hired hand. Me. An artist."

"Treachery," Theo said.

Muybridge looked at him, an aching sadness in his eyes. "Do you know Stanford published *The Horse in Motion* under his own auspices? Didn't give me the slightest credit. I had been to Paris and London and was about to present my own paper to the Royal Society. I called it *Attitudes of Animals in Motion,* and do you know what they called me? A fraud. All because of Stanford's claims. They'll believe a rich man over a poor one every time. One day you are a sensation, the next a failure. It was embarrassing, humiliating. My reputation was ruined. I should have sailed back that day and shot that son of a bitch."

"Wouldn't be the first time," Theo said, and then clamped his fingers over his mouth.

Muybridge scowled. "That's not a very nice thing to say."

"My apologies."

"Harry Larkyns was keeping private with my missus. He had it coming."

"My remark was uncalled for. I'm sorry."

Pulling at his prodigious white beard with his dark-stained fingers, Muybridge considered whether to forgive him. "Have you ever been married, señor? Maybe you would not be so quick to judge."

Theo rubbed the sleep from his eyes. "I was married. Am married. But my wife is missing. One day she was here, and the next

213

she was gone. Some people think she might be dead. Maybe you have seen her on the other side."

"The other side?"

"Heaven . . . or wherever people go after they die." He tried not to sound too optimistic. "I thought since you were dead —"

"Dead? Who said? What gave you the idea I was dead?"

"I didn't mean anything by it, but you died in 1904 while you were creating a scale model of the Great Lakes in your garden on Liverpool Road. You were seventy-four. A nice long life. I wrote the book on you. Translated it, anyhow."

Muybridge sat back in the chair and folded his hands across his belly. "Of all the eccentric theories. You think I'm some sort of spirit, a ghost? My good man, have you considered that I might be a figment of your overwrought imagination? A hallucination brought about by a spot of indigestion. You haven't exactly been eating well since Kay disappeared, and that ham sandwich you had for your dinner — really, sir, you should always check the expiration dates."

Theo was deeply distressed by Muybridge's reasoning. He sat back on the couch and stared at his own feet, ghostly white in the darkness, but every time he looked up, the apparition was still there.

"You need to find someone to talk to," he said at last. "Do you have anyone with whom you are especially close?"

The question drilled into him and punched a hole in his stomach. "Just Kay."

"Obviously she's out of the question. What about your old pal Egon up in Québec? What about this Dr. Mitchell who seems to have taken an unusual interest?"

"You and I could talk. . . ."

Muybridge shook his mane. "That would be like talking to yourself."

"That's all I ever do, really. It feels like I'm talking with her, most of the time. Constructing the monologue as though it is a dialogue, but part of me knows that the whole internal conversation is one-sided. She really can't hear what's going on inside my head, but I talk to her just the same, as if she somehow can hear what's on my mind. In my heart. I would be crazy to be talking to myself."

As Theo spoke he watched Muybridge fade away, a photograph reversing the process of development. Dark areas became shades of gray, then mere shapes, outlines, and finally nothing. He was alone again. If she was out there, waiting for him to come find her, Kay would be different from the digital images in the archive, in the picture he carried around in his head, the face he saw when he talked to her. She would have changed. He went into the bathroom to get ready for bed. Many of her things were just as she had left them. Bottles and jars and creams and brushes. The yellow towels she had chosen. A red silk robe hanging from a hook on the back of the door. Looking into the mirror, he thought he would start again in the morning. Reach out and find someone with whom he might talk. Surely there was another person left in the world.

13

They would be going back into the boxes come morning, so the party after the final show lasted till the wee hours. Nix held court, juggling the seven dwarfs with great skill. Mr. Firkin provided the voice-over, a running patter of each name called out at the high point of the toss. Gathered around a toy piano, the Three Sisters belted out a set of show tunes, enticing the whole cast into a stirring rendition of "Do You Hear the People Sing?" from *Les Miz*. As the evening wore on, the tunes grew more maudlin, and by two in the morning, the Sisters were entwined in obscure weepy Russian songs only they knew. In her guise as Marmee, the Old Hag reunited with her dear pal, the Dog, who had recognized her at once. They spent a happy hour playing fetch with a red foam nose.

"Look at her," Noë said. "Twenty years taken off with a new head."

Kay considered her friend in the dim light of a corner nook. "Have you ever been changed? Got new parts?"

"Not me, sister. I've always been thus. As least since I first joined the company. Before that I was a punk in real life. Spiked hair, nose ring. A tattoo of a black rose on my hip. Me and him snuck into the Quatre Mains toy shop one night, looking for a little privacy, if you know what I mean."

"Your boyfriend?"

Noë snorted. "You could call him that. I don't even remember his real name, he was just a boy I met at a jazz festival on the Terrasse Dufferin, and we hit it off, I guess. We snuck into the toy shop after midnight to fool around. He shouldn't have messed with that old puppet. After the change, he didn't want anything to do with me, and I felt the same. He loves it here. Guess it beats Mum and Pop back in Ottawa. Guess crawling on his belly is a better gig than busking on the boardwalk."

At their feet a low chuckle rolled across the floor. The Worm had slithered over to eavesdrop on their conversation, and when she saw him there, Noë stomped her foot right by his head. "Go away. Shoo."

It made such a piteous whimper that Kay nearly felt sorry for the poor thing. Inch by inch the Worm wriggled away to safety.

"So that thing has forgotten about that night with you?"

"I don't give a fig about him. He was nothing to me. I do think about my family. My parents, every day. Isn't there someone outside who misses you? Your man?"

Kay tried to recall his face, and when she could not picture him, she was filled with shame and sadness. "I was married once upon a time. A white gown with a veiled white hat, and in my arms were damask roses and calla lilies. We were outdoors by a lake and a honeybee kept swarming around my bouquet, and the groom kept swatting at it with these pathetic waves of his hand. He was trying to not call attention to the bee, trying not to embarrass me. And I can remember thinking: he should not hold himself back. Who cares what people think? Do something big. A grand gesture. Throw himself on the bee like it was a hand grenade. The guests wouldn't have minded, everybody was watching. Even the minister might have had a good laugh. And then the bee started buzzing around my veil, there was a spray of baby's breath, and still he's with the polite swats. So I just handed him the flowers and unpinned the hat and tossed it to the side. A breeze picked it up and carried it to the water. He gave me such a look. The surprise in his eyes, but I just smiled and nodded to the preacher to keep going. What else could I do?"

"You certainly didn't want to get bit by that bee."

"One of my cousins rolled up his pants and waded out for the hat after it was all over, but I didn't care. The moment had passed for Theo." Her eyes widened as she finally remembered. "My husband's name was Theo, and I don't think he ever got over the shock of me taking that hat off right then and there and just saying the hell with it. But it was the bees, you see, and who cares about the hat? He just didn't know me well enough; I guess you never do."

"I'll bet he misses you," she said. "I don't doubt that he thinks of you all the time. If I were him, I'd be looking for you still."

Overcome, Kay wrapped her arms around Noë and embraced her. The puppet's straw hair brushed against her cheek. They sat side by side, Noë resting against Kay's shoulder, and watched the diminuendo of the cast party. The Sisters had run through their Russian repertoire and were reduced to ballads of murder and wrongdoing and Irish folk songs filled with homesickness. The rest of the troupe gathered around the piano and joined in at the longing refrains.

It felt good to be touched by another be-ing. Theo had loved her surely, and she had loved him in return, but it all seemed so long ago, a world away. She remembered he liked to sing in the car, whiling away the long hours of a road trip, searching the radio stations for recognizable tunes. His voice was sweet and lovely, cracking in the reeds of the upper register, and plaintive and silly when he attempted falsetto. Once in a while, she would join in, and he tried to harmonize while she carried the melody. In the dying of the night, she had briefly remembered his name, could hear his voice in her head, but why could she not picture his face?

A small octagonal window near the apex of the ceiling let in the first hint of day. Mr. Firkin called for places, and the party groaned to a halt. The puppets shuffled to the positions in which they had been left the night before. Noë uncurled from be-neath Kay's arm and told her, "You must promise me to never forget who you are. And if you ever have the chance to run away, just go and don't look back."

In the darkened room an octagon of morning fell across the table, and from her spot, Kay followed the shaft of sunlight progress as the sun moved higher in the sky. It was not quite noon when the giants finally arrived. Four of them, in any case. Delacroix was gone, a temporary addition to their merry band. Finch and Stern busied themselves immediately, striking the set and lugging away the scenery and props. Back in the boxes went the puppets, segregated as before between the animate and the inanimate. Kay had been loaded into the bottom compartment as before and waited for the Three Sisters to be interred on top of her. She drank in the last of the light before the coming darkness.

"Thank God we finished when we did," said the Deux Mains. "Delacroix was beginning to suspect."

The Quatre Mains boomed out his answer immediately. "No, he was a clueless sprat."

"I overheard him say something to Finch. He definitely noticed the difference among them, how easily the Sisters moved, how naturally the Dog behaved versus, say, the seagull."

"That seagull is nearly impossible to get right. I really need to work on the wings. Perhaps another joint would make it fly more naturalistically."

"I'm telling you, he was this close to understanding the secret of the puppets."

She held her index finger and thumb an inch apart. "You could read it on his face, see it in his hands. You can feel it in the motions of the sticks. Life of their own. Finch had to —"

"What?" Finch had reentered the room. She towered over the open box and smiled down upon the puppets. "My ears were burning, were you talking about me again?"

"Tell him," the Deux Mains said. "Tell him your theory about Delacroix."

Finch laid a finger against her pressed lips. "Mum's the word. He had his suspicions, but what could he say without coming across as a complete loon? That some of these dolls are alive? Or were alive once upon a time? No, that would be plain crazy. The closest he came was expressing surprise at how they moved and talked and acted. Uncanny was the word. I said it was a case of superior craftsmanship."

The Quatre Mains stepped beside her and laid a chummy hand against her back. "Craftsmanship. I like that. Good quality construction."

"A touch of the artist." The Deux Mains linked arms with Finch. The trinity lovingly gazed upon the puppets as if they were looking at little children asleep in their beds. And then they sorted the rest of them into

223

the box and closed them for the next stage of their journey. For Kay, it was like dying and being buried all over again.

She blushed when Muybridge asked if she would be willing to take off her clothes and be photographed in the nude. Because he was kindly, because he reminded her of a grandfather, because he was distracted and earnest, she said yes. The readiness of her answer surprised her, but she needed the money from the modeling, and she was not ashamed of her body, not averse to shaking convention. "It is for science," he said and bowed his head slightly and fumbled with his unkempt white beard. He reminded her of Walt Whitman and Nast's illustrations of Santa Claus. "I am undertaking the greatest study ever made of the human form in motion."

That afternoon he explained to her how the cameras worked, how they were timed to capture images in sequence that revealed subtle patterns when viewed as a whole. "You will be in good company," he said, and then he showed her his invention to project the moving images. In a darkened studio, he played his favorites: a smiling boy crabwalking on his hands and feet, two boxers demonstrating a jab and feint, and a nattily dressed man with a straw hat taking a turn across the stage, swinging a cane, and pivoting on the point before jaunting off in the other direction.

"Such a dandy." She laughed. "I'm afraid I have no special talents. . . ."

"No need to worry," the photographer said as he turned on the lights. "We will have you do simple things, ordinary actions of the everyday. Nothing is outside the scope of my study, my desire to record. I am interested in all things human." He spoke with such detachment that she was completely at ease before the cameras.

Theo noticed her, this young woman whose story he invented, time and again in Muybridge's *Human Figure in Motion*. Sometimes she appeared shy, hand across her eyes, her posture betraying her embarrassment. In other sequences, she could not be more natural. Seated on the floor, a white shift draped across her lap, she awaits the approach of a young girl of four or five who presents her with a small bouquet, and in the final frames, she rises to accept the flowers and kiss the child on her cheek. He and Kay had talked about children in their whirlwind courtship, but it had been no more than a passing dream, a promise for the future that now felt shattered. He stared at the woman embracing the child, the look on the model's face genuine and unabashed. It seemed to him a tenderness in a dozen images, a moment of unintended beauty in Muybridge's obsession.

"Your door was open." The voice behind his back startled him, and he swiveled in his chair to find Dr. Mitchell, pensive and curious. "You have a visitor. Should I show him in?"

"Harper!"

Theo recognized the voice at once and was surprised to see Egon in the threshold. "I can't believe it. What brings you here?"

"You are a hard man to find. I looked for your address through all the phone books of New York."

"You had my number. You could have called," Theo said.

"No cell phone for me," Egon said. "Gives you cancer of the brain. Besides, this is too important. I remembered all our talks in the evenings this summer and, of course, you are a college man, a professor, and then it becomes a matter of deduction to find you. I had to see you, so I scraped up the cash. It's about Kay."

"Is there some news?"

Egon waved away the question and launched breathlessly into his story. "Remember telling me how your wife loved the puppet shop? After the circus closed, I had no place to stay. You and I had seen that the Quatre Mains was vacant, so I made a little home for myself in an empty room upstairs."

"You just snuck in there?" Mitchell said. "Like a squatter?"

Laying a finger against his nose, Egon nodded. "Not so bad. Downstairs was the remnants of the toy shop, but upstairs there's an old bed, a kitchen, a kettle, running water. And I said, Egon, you are so lucky. Whoever was there skipped out in a hurry. Left half their shit behind. This will be easy as a wink. So, I settle in, keep quiet, have a place to call home. Better than the streets, eh?"

"Wouldn't you worry about being found out?" Mitchell asked.

"As long as nobody sees me go in and out, and I keep the lights out in the storefront, I am invisible."

Theo cleared his throat. "I wish you had let me know, I could have helped."

With a small bow of thanks, Egon continued, "Anyhow, one night the wind rattles at the windows like to blow the house down, and it sounds like there is something alive after midnight in the toy shop. I crept down the stairs. Holy cows, there was a storm inside like a tornado blowing across the floor in tight circles sending all the dust and papers and old bits and pieces of broken toys flying. I was tempted to run out, but the wind stopped after a bit, and everything went quiet."

"You were drunk," Theo said.

"Maybe I had one drink too many? Maybe I see the truth. I lay in bed, not able to shake the feeling that some sort of enchantment was at play. A spell, a haunting. I don't know how to say it, but that the room was looking for something alive."

"The room itself?" Mitchell said. "I've often felt that same sensation. The house with a soul."

"So, next morning, I wake up early as usual, because I like to be about before anyone else, and I creep downstairs to the back room, and there are all these neat little heaps of debris arranged on the floor like a miniature landscape. Like that wind blew in and arranged them just so. I poke around in some of these mountains and there are doll parts, a wooden finger, a curl of hair, and cotton stuffing and sawdust and such. And that's when I find this." He reached into the inside pocket of his vest and produced an ordinary matchbook, holding it up like a talisman. "Tell me what you think after you have read it."

Theo examined the matchbook. On the printed side was a silhouette of an exotic dancer at a Montreal club called Les Déesses. He turned it over and read the inscription on the blank side: "HELP. Get me out of here." The letters penciled in a faint, unsettled hand, as though the message had been written in a hurry. He handed it to Mitchell, who seemed equally puzzled.

"Don't you see?" Egon asked. "The message was from someone inside the toy shop, trying to get out."

Shaking his head in disbelief, Theo took the matchbook from Mitchell and examined the note more carefully.

Egon looked him in the eye. "Some might say this message is a mere coincidence. I say the place is haunted. Or something terrible happened here. And I cannot help but feel that I was led there by the memory of a puppet in the window. The puppet you said your wife adored. I am not a superstitious man, did you ever think so? But I can't help but feel that I was led there to find the note. I hope I have not upset you, Harper, with all this speculation, but it was a powerful feeling. Down to my bones."

Like a magician, Theo twirled the matchbook between his fingers.

14

The van stopped and started, rolled forward a car length, and idled again in park. While they were in line, the giants switched off the air conditioning and cracked open the windows, but it was hotter than hell in back. Kay squirmed in the straw. They had been playing the theatrical vagabonds, setting up their shows and staying for a day or two at provincial hamlets, performing cleaned-up variety skits in high school auditoriums and Grange halls for clutches of country people desperate for entertainment, or afternoons with restless children, the worst of all, a crowd of tots expecting *Sesame Street* and getting an old slapstick Punch and Judy instead. Now they were waiting in the heat and the dark to get to the next place. Soon after the engine had been stopped, the giants began talking English with another person. Muffled by the boxes, their voices were indistinct, but Kay could tell by the rise and fall that a strange man was asking a series of questions to which the giants replied softly and politely. The doors opened and the people moved toward the back. All at once, the cargo space was flooded with light.

"Puppets," the man said. "Now I've heard everything."

"We are going down to perform a few shows here in Vermont," the Quatre Mains said, "with our American friends."

"So you said. Would you mind opening up a box, so's I can have a look?"

"Any which one?" the Quatre Mains asked.

"As long as it has these puppets you were talking about. Let's try this one here." He tapped the edge where Kay lay. The giants removed the box and placed it on the pavement. Opening the lid, the Deux Mains took out the Three Sisters and lifted the separator above Kay and Noë and Nix. It was like looking up from an open grave. Dressed in a green uniform and a wide-brimmed hat, he towered over them and bent for a closer examination. His grip felt strange on her body as he held Kay in the air and poked around in the straw with his free hand.

"So you made all these puppets?" the green man asked.

"Every last one of them," said the Quatre Mains. "Wood and foam and stuffing and sticks."

"They seem so lifelike. Ever get scared that they'll wake up in the middle of the night and come to get you?"

The Deux Mains laughed. "We keep them under lock and key when we're asleep. No use taking any chances."

The green man looked over her. "My partner's giving me the thumbs-up, so your paperwork must be in order." He handed Kay to the Deux Mains, and she could have sighed with relief over the familiar touch. "Welcome to the United States of America. Enjoy your visit to Vermont."

The giants repacked the puppets and were about to close up the van when the green man interrupted. "And good luck with your puppet show. No, that's not right — what are you supposed to say? Break a leg. Or break a string, I guess, since they're puppets."

Once they started rolling again, Kay whispered to Noë. "Did he say we're in Vermont? Back in America?"

"Land of the free," Noë answered. "The Green Mountains."

"My mother lives here," Kay said. "This was home once upon a time."

Mornings before school, her mother used to fix Kay's hair, separating and plaiting the strands as she sat behind her. Kay could still feel the gentle tug of her mother's hands as she worked, the pressure to keep still, and the final gesture when she finished, her palm stroking the braid to make sure it stayed in place. Her mother's hands. She and Kay would fold the washing together on a summer's day, taking the sheets from the line stiff from the air, a crisp snap, Kay on one set of corners, her mother on the others, and stepping forward hand to hand to bring the ends together to her mother's grasp. Her mother's dusty hands patting a ball of dough, rolling it out with a wooden pin the color of honey, and scooping the thin circle to lay it into a pie pan, and pouring the mountain of Granny Smiths or peaches that glistened like golden crescent moons. Her hands holding knitting needles like two pens converting, through clicking manipulation, a fall of yarn into a scarf, a blanket, a cardigan. Her mother's hand inside a sock monkey moving along with the funny voice to tell her a bedtime story. Her mother's hand against Kay's face on her wedding day, holding there for the first time in years before letting go as if to say goodbye forever.

That she could not remember her mother's face bothered Kay. Her forgetfulness was more than a character flaw, rather a sign of a deeper disturbance that had beset her ever since she had joined the troupe. Her past had shattered like a mirror and could be apprehended only in shards and slivers. Her mother's face had been the first she had fixed upon and was the most familiar of her entire life, and Kay knew that something had gone terribly wrong in its utter blankness. She could not recall her husband's face either, despite their intense intimacy over the past few years. A face she had stared at for hours, days, weeks. Eyes that darted and followed her own when they had been kiss close. A smile that had lingered across a table as they earnestly discussed their future together. And now the picture of his face slipped in and out of memory with disturbing frequency.

The giants stopped for the night but left them in the back of the van. Cold air seeped into the space; a crisp autumnal chill bore right through the boxes so that even the straw lining was no protection. Not that Kay minded the cold, no more than the close air and claustrophobia of her miniature casket, but still she could feel the changes of the season. And they must have parked in some remote and deserted place, for the night was eerily quiet, punctuated only by the quick hooting of an owl. Her mother used to say that's the song of a speed owl, the hoots strung together like the ringing of a telephone. She missed her mother till dawn.

Frost had formed overnight, and the stiff grass crunched under the weight of the boxes as the humans unloaded the vans. A woodpecker trilled and hammered at a tall tree. The early sunshine warmed the crates till they ticked and creaked, and happy voices filled the air. She could hear Finch and Stern and new people talking and laughing as they moved about, and the aroma of coffee and fresh bread reminded her of hunger and the welcome of breakfast.

A shadow fell across the boxes. "Let's have a look at them." The man's voice was touched by a slight Irish accent.

"Right here and now?" Finch answered.

"Give them a splash of sunshine. Let them see what they've been got up to."

Finch and Stern opened the boxes and laid out the puppets on the dew-damp lawn. A few fat white clouds gathered over a chain of plump mountains in the west. Pines and firs mixed with birch and maple, nearly leafless in the late autumn, and ringed the perimeter of the landscape to the horizon. A yellow farmhouse stood across the road, smoke doodling from a brick chimney. The Quatre Mains and the Deux Mains were approaching with mugs of coffee in their hands. The vans had been parked next to an old red barn, and Kay could just make out the words on a small hand-painted sign: Northeast Kingdom Puppet Museum.

The Irishman walked among the puppets, picking up those who caught his fancy, trying his hands at the sticks and strings to make Irina dance. Smitten by the Good Fairy, he cradled her in his arms, turning her over and peeking beneath her bodice to see how she had been assembled. Nix made him laugh. Noë brought a sadness to his eyes. When he drew close to Kay, he showed a kind smile on his ruddy face as if he already knew her.

"They're grand," he said. "Excellent carving and handiwork, but they'll never do. Too small for our shows."

"But we've come all this way," Finch said, "on a promise."

Clapping her on the back in solidarity, the Irishman laughed. "A man's words is his only honor. We have a few weeks yet to Halloween. Time enough to make, what, ten or twelve out of this lot if the fair weather holds."

Finch turned to the Quatre Mains, a look of panic in her eyes. "What does he mean? Make them new?"

With a raised eyebrow, the Quatre Mains stopped her. "As long as we keep their essence, that shouldn't be a problem."

"Come inside," said the Irishman. "You'll love how we've converted the barn into a museum. I subdivided the ground floor into a warren of rooms, and upstairs there's a great big loft that runs the length and breadth of the building. Down below along the backside of the building there's an old sheepcote that leads out to the pastures. No animals now, of course, only room for all our little friends. We used to get barn swallows in the summers here, but the puppets scared them off."

The Deux Mains grabbed his arm. "What will we do with our puppets?"

"Ah, bring in them dolls," the Irishman said. "No use getting soaked in the morning dew."

The five of them gathered the puppets, and Kay and the Good Fairy ended up in the Irishman's arms. Through the stippled sunlight they marched off to the faded red barn. At the door into the darkness, a placard read: "Enter at your own risk. Donations welcome."

All around him at Grand Central, people made their reunions. Couples met in a kiss. A serviceman in his dark green uniform found his scruffy younger brother. An old man in a porkpie hat and carrying a tattered gym bag searched for a prodigal son. Theo began to wonder if he had made some mistake bringing Egon home with him from the college. Egon had scurried off to the bathroom as soon as they had pulled into the station, and Theo was left alone in the middle of the crowd. Perhaps the whole cockamamie idea was backfiring. Haunted toy shops. Messages on matchbooks.

"When duty calls, Egon answers." He was suddenly at Theo's side.

They joined the queue for taxis as the daylight began to fade, neither one broaching the subject at hand, their small talk instead falling to the long trip from Québec and friends from the cirque and the latest chapter of the life of Muybridge. Only after he had been fed at an Indian restaurant uptown and they walked back to Theo's apartment and poured a dram of bourbon was Egon prepared to share his news. Ensconced upon the living room sofa in his

238

robe and slippers, the clock scrolling toward midnight, when all else had been said and the matter was no longer avoidable, Egon spun out his tale.

"You've seen the SOS on the matchbook. Well, that's only part of the story. I need to tell you about the other strange things that have happened in that little shop of horrors. After the first week or so of my residence, it became clear that I wasn't going to be found out inside the shop, so I relaxed a bit, kept a light on in the back bedroom facing the alley."

"You shouldn't wait so long if things get desperate," Theo said. "You could always contact me —"

Egon held up a hand to stop him. "Thanks all the same. Look, I've been hand to mouth before and I will be again. That's not what scares me."

Ice rattling in his drink, Theo leaned forward in the easy chair. "Something worse than a storm inside the house?"

"During the day I am at the library trying to do my research to find you, and at night, I poke around the place. After I found the matchbook, it's like a treasure hunt, and that's when I notice a hatch to the attic. In the ceiling right above my bed. Curiosity killed the cat, but not me. I rig up a stack of boxes and books on top of a chair and climb right up there. Wobbled the whole way. The attic was dark as a tomb, and then I feel a spiderweb brushing against my face, which freaks me out. Turns out to be a long string hanging down, and when I pulled it, a light-bulb came on and made a halo. I nearly fell through the hole when I saw what was up there. Dolls staring at me with their glassy eyes and old stuffed bears and rabbits and a giraffe with a broken neck. Worst of all were the puppets."

"Good grief —"

"Broken marionettes with twisted wires and slumped together like a pile of dead bodies. An old ventriloquist dummy who looked like he would spring to life and murder me if I moved. Puppets missing an arm or a leg. Even one with no head. And imagine all this time, I had been sleeping just below them in an empty and abandoned flat."

"Gives me the shivers."

"Nearly gave me the shits in my pants. I tell you it took forever just to move from the spot, but I screwed my courage to the post and began to investigate."

A siren on the street below punctuated the mood. They both laughed and sipped their drinks.

"You get used to the noise, *n'est pas*? New York, feh. Like I was saying, it was a morgue for these old toys, the spillover maybe of what could not be fixed in the workshop? And just in the shadows were piles of old newspapers and magazines, the kind of junk in a million attics, but I was curious and poked around some more and found a book."

He hopped from the sofa and reached into the front pouch of his bag, pulling out a black notebook with a tassel bookmark and a strap to keep the cover closed. With the solemnity of a courier, he handed the journal to Theo. Most of the pages were covered with words in an elegant cursive, and he could see they were scripts, lines of dialogue and sparse instructions for the motions of puppets. It was a performance log, a new title every fifteen or twenty pages.

"Plays," Theo said. "For puppet shows."

"Exactly," Egon said. "So I'm up in the attic, three in the morning and not another soul, I hear a sigh. My heart nearly stopped. Over in the corner are these two heads lying in the dust, one black and one white staring at each other like they've just been interrupted having a *tête-à-tête*. Like they can't understand what happened to the rest of them, where did their bodies go? Comes

241

another sigh from one of these broken-down puppets, and you don't have to ask me twice. I scramble, bat outta hell, and get to the hatch just as one of them heads moans, so I jump and the whole tower of boxes and books comes tumbling down, and I land on my tailbone nearly dead on the floor."

"You could have killed yourself."

"I'm near paralyzed, but I can't spend another minute there, so I crawl down the steps one by one to the bottom floor and I lock myself in, half convinced I'll wake up dead in the morning."

"It's a wonder you didn't end up with a broken neck. What do you think made the sound that scared you so?"

"*Écoute-moi!* It was the friggin' puppets."

Theo considered his friend, noting for the first time since they had met just how little he knew of him, his background and history. They had formed a friendship out of duress, and while they had spent many hours together, every day for several weeks, swapping stories and sharing in the grief of losing Kay, Theo was not sure, in this moment, of Egon's sanity. Perhaps in the fall from the attic, Egon had landed not on his bottom but on his head. Muybridge had been in a stagecoach accident when he was heading out to California as a young man, hit his head, and was never the same. Shot a man. Stopped time.

"You're skeptical, I don't blame you," Egon said. "But I can only tell you what I heard, what I felt in that toy shop, an overwhelming sensation of another world. I was so scared that I nearly flew that night, but all my things were upstairs in the bedroom, just out of reach of those creatures. So I sat up reading, waiting for the dawn, every page in that book. But what stopped me was the final page. Go ahead."

In his lap, the journal sizzled with sudden menace. The playwright had written his scripts on the right-hand pages, leaving the left side blank for changes, corrections, and small drawings, so Theo came to the end unaware. There were just a few stray lines of dialogue with the word *Finis* in bold letters. But on the reverse of that final flourish, someone had turned the book upside down and penciled in a column of letters under the title *Necromancy.* The first two entries had been crossed out with a single line, but the rest were no less enigmatic. *OC, MC, IC, NT* . . . Initials? At the bottom of the list, he read aloud: *"KH."*

"You see?" Egon asked. "Kay Harper."

A sharp pain spread like a spar of lightning in his brain. There she was. The little man across from him had a manic look in his eyes, daring him to doubt.

"I think the bastards got her. The puppets."

15

She died a second time.

The Quatre Mains brought out the puppet from the bell jar and stood him on a tree stump to oversee the metamorphoses.

First, they deposed the Queen. The Irishman drove a wooden stake through her chest and fastened her to a post. Two farmhands — a lanky teenage girl and a towheaded boy with earnest blue eyes — bent a section of chicken wire into a form about twice the size of a human trunk. Then they began laying down sheets of paper that had been moistened in a thick slurry of paste. As they worked on the new larger-than-life queen, they would often consult the doll pinned like a butterfly, checking to make sure they were creating a facsimile of the original.

The rest of the puppets were similarly fixed to a spot. The Three Sisters hung by their wires on the low branch of a chokecherry tree, and Finch and Stern fashioned copies of each in papier-mâché. The remnants of a lightweight barrel provided the base for a new Mr. Firkin. Striplings and branches were collected to create the full-size Good Fairy. All the others had been lashed or secured into stationary positions while the puppeteers crafted new versions, tall as people with jointed legs and arms. At dusk, the humans quit for the day, heading off to the comfort of the farmhouse, joshing as the cool air settled in, the smell of fresh bread and a bubbling pot of stew filling the air.

Scattered in front of the barn doors, the puppets were left alone, each next to its replica. Unable to move and wary of being heard, they spoke with one another in hushed whispers.

"Is everyone okay?" Mr. Firkin asked.

"I don't like this place," said Noë. "Everything is too big and scary."

"Not to mention this infernal stake straight through my heart," said the Queen. "If I had a heart."

"Ugh," said Nix. "What is happening to us?"

Swinging from the branch like a Salem witch, Olya spoke with a world-weariness. "We are being transformed. Made over to fit in with all the others here. A change will do you good, Nixie."

"These are our bodies," said the Devil. He ogled the shapes on the ground. "Getting ready for our souls. It is not every day that you get to see the next step on life's journey."

Kay stole a peek at the unfinished papier-mâché torso not four feet from where she hung, bound to a fence post with a lash of baling wire. A river of melancholy threaded its way from puppet to puppet. She remembered her first days in the Back Room in Québec and the freedom they enjoyed there during the long, dark nights. "What do you mean about our souls? Are they to inhabit these new forms?"

The Devil's wooden joints creaked in the soft breeze. He was more hideous than usual, captured and trussed like some wild thing ready for the slaughter. "My guess is that they will destroy the old in order to create the new. Not the first time this has happened to me. Once upon a time, I was little more than a horned totem, and over the decades, I cannot begin to tell you how many lives I've led. One more will do no harm. The Original decides, the Quatre Mains does his bidding. Are we not puppets after all, bound to the master's whims?"

"Is there no end to this?" Noë said. "I will go mad."

From the bare limb of the maple, Olya cleared her throat. "There's always the possibility of an ending. How soon you have forgotten our friends, the Judges. The end is always the same for each of us. One ending, and not a heppy one." On each side, her sisters grinned in the starlight.

"Count your blessings," said the Devil.

Over the next four days, the bodies took shape layer by layer, new skin, new limbs, hands and feet, and the heads attached at the end. The Irishman and his two young artisans worked longest on the faces, crafting the features in meticulous detail, the last strokes of the brush articulating the eyes. Some puppets had hinged jaws to give the illusion of speech, while other faces were frozen in a single aspect. Olya, Masha, and Irina wore masks in three shades of melancholia. The Queen's visage was majestic and disdainful. A nearly mad look was plastered on Nix, and the Old Hag had reverted from her time as Marmee into her familiar hundred-years' gaze. From the Québec troupe only the Dog retained his original form, a toy that roamed the barn while the others were bound to their spots. And the Worm had gone missing. Whispers at night intimated that it had been consigned to the old animal pens in the abandoned barn basement. Strange lowings emanated from the bowels of the building in the cramped stalls that led out to a grassy hillside.

On the fourth night, after all the new forms had been completed, the puppeteers were in a festive mood. They built a fire in a ring of stones, the bark from the birch logs popping and hissing and filling the air with thick smoke. Bottles of stout were passed around, and the Irishman regaled the others with stories and songs. Stern and Finch took turns telling long and complicated jokes that ended in dreadful puns and groans and claps of appreciation for the skill of the telling. Even the tall farm girl overcame her shyness and sang a tragic air, and the towheaded boy sat wide-eyed, soaking in the camaraderie of the evening. A million stars filled the cold sky, the constellations slowly spinning away the hours of anticipation.

With a start, the Quatre Mains rose from a log and motioned for quiet. He glanced at the ancient puppet, his face bright from the flames, and announced that the time had come. The Deux Mains held in her hands a pair of long thin spears with sharp, barbed blades strapped to the ends. With a bow, she handed one of the primitive weapons to the Quatre Mains and kept the other for herself. Holding it at eye level, he regarded the sharpness, tapping the point with the pad of his index finger, drawing a dot of blood.

Striding without hesitation, the Quatre Mains confronted the Queen nailed to her post and thrust the spear into her body at the bottom of her rib cage. A sigh escaped from the puppet's mouth, a puff somewhere between shock and satisfaction. With a quick clockwise twist, the Quatre Mains pulled back the spear, a clot of red snagged in the barbs, and the puppet slouched limp and lifeless. He pivoted to the new Queen, a giantess sprawled against the side of the barn, and pierced her chest at the same spot and twisted counterclockwise. When he withdrew the point, the red clot had disappeared into her. Taking turns with the Deux Mains, they repeated the process, piercing the Three Sisters, Nix and Noë, the Good Fairy, the Old Hag, and the Devil, transferring the substance from the old into the new.

Kay was the last to go. She had witnessed the sober reaction of the humans gathered round the fire and seen the terror in her comrades' eyes. They were dying, sacrificed in some bizarre ritual, and she wanted to escape her restraints or cry out, but even in such dire circumstances, she knew it was impossible. Her thoughts raced from the slaughter to memories of her mother, old comforter, young and singing sweetly on her walk from the henhouse, a basket of warm eggs swinging against her hip. And then her husband. She suddenly remembered his name again, Theo, Theo, Theo, but the snap of recognition was wiped away at the approach of the spear. She stole one last look at the ancient puppet she had long adored. Instead of malice, the Quatre Mains wore love and generosity on his face, as though he was presenting her with a gift rather than ending her life. He smiled when he stabbed her, and as the spear twisted where her heart had been, she said "oh," and then the world went dark. Gasping, she regained consciousness in her new body. The hole in her chest closed like a flower.

The Quatre Mains was no longer a giant, but a man of her own size, and at first Kay could not determine whether she had grown or he had shrunk. The others, too, had changed their dimensions, and she felt as if she had gone half mad in dreaming them up. Where had all the giants gone? The Deux Mains was just a woman of ordinary size, no monster. Stern and Finch, the Irishman, the farm girl and the blond boy, they all seemed quite normal to her now, people she would encounter without a second glance. From her spot in the grass, she watched as the puppeteers freed the old lifeless puppets from their fixed places, unpinning the old Queen, untangling the Sisters from the gallows in the maple tree. During the ceremony, the ancient puppet had been spirited away, his tree stump throne now vacant.

One by one, they took the bodies down and threw them in the fire. Old Firkin went first, a whoosh as he hit the blaze, igniting at once, the air in his belly expanding till he burst. Spear in hand, the Quatre Mains left the party and went into the barn, only to emerge moments later with the limp body of the Worm, which he heaved onto the coals. It coiled like a snake and sizzled into black. The Good Fairy lit up like a bundle of kindling. The Devil turned red and then was engulfed by the flames, home at last in his element. They were dead things, miniature creations that burned without a scream or a gasp. Kay watched as Finch unwound the wires holding her old body in place. A look of wistfulness crossed the puppeteer's face as she threw the doll in the bonfire, the hair and clothes catching first, a river of red lacing across the fabric edges, and then the whole went up and burned blue, the body crackling in the October night. Quickly it was little more than ashes and a charred head, barely discernible from an ordinary piece of wood, from all of her comrades. Curious to see one's self disappear that way, curiouser still to be intact and anew.

The mood around the dying fire turned somber. The boy yawned mightily, and the girl gathered the empty bottles. The others began to stretch and shake the cobwebs from their bones. The new puppets were so large that they had to be carried one by one into the barn, and the Queen required both Finch and Stern to hoist her into place in an area that had once served as a tack room. When they had put all of the puppets to bed, the puppeteers left, heading back to the farmhouse, weary and pleased with their night's work. Looking back at the troupe, the Deux Mains paused at the barn door.

"Good night, my lovelies," she said. "Welcome to your new home."

The last lights went out in the house; the puppeteers retired to bed. Exhausted by the ordeal, the puppets stirred briefly, whispering carefully among themselves, making sure they were all present. From the floor below came a great snuffling, the sound of the new Worm readying for sleep. The Dog, who had not undergone the transformation, bounded into the tack room like a windup toy, a miniature pet that went from soul to soul, sniffing and whimpering, puzzled by old friends in new forms. Sometime before dawn, the little toy settled at the Old Hag's feet. He kicked his paws in his sleep, at chase in his dreams.

"They are all naked," Egon said. "Naked as jaybirds, every man and woman. What sort of voyeur was this? What sort of game was afoot?" He flipped through Muybridge's *The Human Figure in Motion,* holding up a spread of images for Theo to see. In the seats across the aisle, a pair of teenage boys glanced his way every time Egon flashed another page. They had been watching with prurient interest ever since the train had crossed the border into Canada.

"They're not naked, they're nude," Theo said. "He was an artist, interested in the body in motion, the way the muscles moved, the shape of the limbs."

Egon was not impressed with the explanation and held up another sequence of two nude men dueling with swords. "Zounds. A fellow could be seriously hurt. So they

254

didn't care — way back when — that this old roué was asking these nubile men and women to strip to their birthday suits so he could take pictures of them throwing a ball or playing leapfrog without a stitch or some chick doing the dance of the seven veils?"

"In the name of science, in the name of art."

Behind his back, the boys whispered to each other and leaned in to take a closer look. The train rocked along the tracks, holding them in its constant rhythm.

In Montreal, Theo and Egon switched from the railway to the road, catching the bus to Québec City in the fading light of late afternoon. For the better part of the week, Egon had been pestering him to make the trip, to see for himself the strange attic in the abandoned toy store, working incessantly his theory of the puppets. Not that he was convinced — Theo went along to shut him up and to put his face in front of the police, remind Thompson and Foucault that he was still hoping.

As soon as the iconic hotel Frontenac appeared like a great birthday cake atop the hill, Theo realized his mistake. Images of Kay flooded his mind. Happy days when they had first arrived in June, her radiant smile, the color of her skin against her dress.

Ducking in the passages under the ramparts into Vieux-Québec, she had grabbed his arm with both hands and looked into his eyes. "It's like a fairy tale." And the excitement bubbling as they raced with their suitcases into the sublet apartment, twirled at the spaciousness of it, bounced from room to room, and threw open the shutters to let in the view of the Saint Lawrence, the cool air taking her breath. And then straight into the bedroom, barely pausing to shed their clothes. *"Baise-moi,"* she said, surprising him with her remembered French, and he was dumbstruck happy, mad with the marvel of her body, the way she hooked her legs behind his back, *my acrobat.* Wild with gymnastics that left him exhausted and panting, he laid his head against the slick of her chest and felt the cannon of her heart in his ear, thought he could die in the moment without another wish. He could picture her moving like a Muybridge sequence, a series of images, the woman as she rocks. And again, she ravished him later that same evening and first thing in the morning as though the novelty of this old place had unleashed a new Kay, abandoning all restraint, and he was helplessly in love.

"We'll go to the toy shop after midnight," Egon said. "We check into our hotel rooms and have a bite. I'm famished."

The sound of his friend's voice broke Theo's reverie, and he tumbled back into the hole of grief. "I shouldn't have come. I'm not ready to face it."

"Buck up. I'll keep you safe."

The little man patted his thigh, and the spell was broken.

Bellies full with rich food and beer, Theo and Egon waddled over to rue Saint-Paul in a thick fog that had settled in the Basse-Ville. The few people about at such a late hour appeared as shadows in the mist, and the ring of their shoes was muffled by the damp and cold. Looking down the street of lost dreams, Theo shivered in the October air. The quiet ate him and he disappeared into the scene, his mind a blank, barely registering his friend by his side or the closed and darkened shops and cafés they passed. Egon grabbed him by the wrist to stop him from walking right by the Quatre Mains toy shop, the painted letters on the sign cracked and faded.

Theo pressed his face against the window, opaque as a television screen. Nothing to be seen, nothing but faint memories of when Kay had delighted in the toys on display. A phantom hand pressed against his back from the times she had to lean into him, holding herself from leaping through the looking glass.

"This way," Egon said, motioning for him to follow. "That's just the surface of things."

Turning sideways, he crabbed his way along a narrow alley, the passage tight and claustrophobic. When they came to the end, Egon shrugged a messenger's bag from his shoulder and produced a small flashlight. Theo turned on the app on his smartphone, which cast a beam and threw into relief the rear entrance, a few sticks of broken furniture littered about like bones. Someone had locked the door. With a crudely fashioned pick, Egon forced the lock and they were quickly in the back room. Dead center sat a table, dark and massive as a tomb, and along the walls rows of shelves and cubbies were coated with dust and debris. They sleuthed their way into the showroom and found the staircase, the treads creaking disconcertingly under their weight. Pale light from the streetlamps shone through the front windows, but they headed for the dark side. Egon crossed himself like a lapsed Catholic at the closed door. A thread of light glowed at the jamb.

"Here goes nothing," he said. "If those puppets come spilling out, make way. My legs may be short, but I'll knock you over like a bowling pin."

The room appeared just as Theo had imagined from Egon's description. A chair lay on its back, two legs in the air, and a tumble of books and boxes were strewn on the floor behind it. A rumpled pillow sat on the unmade bed, and beside it on the night table stood a nearly empty bottle of whiskey. Tacked to the walls were Egon's circus pinups and Victorian postcards. An aroma of fried onions hung in the air. In the ceiling, a rectangle opened to the attic.

"Up there," Egon whispered, shutting off his flashlight. "But I'm sure the hatch was closed when I left. It nearly took off my thumb when I was escaping."

"Well, it is open now, so perhaps your memory is at fault."

"Or perhaps they opened it again. . . ."

"Don't be absurd."

"Just be careful."

"What do you mean be careful? You don't suppose I'm crawling up there by myself?"

"Let's be practical, *mon ami.* First, I could barely reach the attic on the top of a stack of boxes and books on top of the chair. When it all came tumbling down, I nearly killed myself."

The fallen chair and the hole in the ceiling made the room look like a crime scene, a botched suicide without the twisted rope, without the body hanging from the beams. Theo listened for a sign from above, a rustle in the attic, but the room was cold and silent. Beside him, the little man bounced on the balls of his feet.

"Okay, okay, though I'm not sure if this isn't a big mistake." Theo righted the chair and stood on the seat below the opening, finding his reach too short to hoist himself up. Watching from below, Egon found the thickest book nearby and handed it to him, and after an abortive try, Theo finally pulled through the opening and rolled away from the edge across the dirty floor. The diffused light made it impossible to see more than shapes and shadows, so he called for Egon to throw him the flashlight.

He had expected monsters, but they must have been hiding or fled the scene. Here and there, small footprints and handprints appeared in the dust, but these he guessed were Egon's. The long string hanging from the ceiling brushed against him like a spider's silk, and when he tugged on it, the light came on and revealed no puppets, no giraffe with a broken neck, no toys at all.

"There's nothing up here," Theo hollered down. "Just a bunch of boxes and some old books."

"Are you sure? There should be an army of satanic dolls. Heads that can talk. Dummies that can reach out and grab you."

"You want to come up and check for yourself? All this way for nothing."

"I swear they were there. Someone must have come got them. Or maybe they ran away. Check in the boxes at least."

The first carton he opened held scraps of cloth, tiny dresses and miniature coats, a bag of funny small hats, and at the bottom an armory of wooden swords, popguns, and slapsticks. When he cracked the seal on the second box and folded back the lid, he gasped at what was inside — dozens of tiny hands with carved and articulated fingers and thumbs. Another box was filled with eyes, glass and marble and painted ping-pong balls, all staring back at him, the irises gleaming in the light of the bare bulb. A box of wigs, a box of tiny circus props, a wooden hoop, a lion tamer's whip, a juggler's balls and clubs and rings.

"Just bits and bobs packed away," he said. "A bunch of body parts, but no bodies."

"I tell you they were up there. You don't see them? A talking head or two?"

Theo took out his smartphone and snapped some pictures of the contents of the attic. He had wanted to believe in

261

Egon's story and was disappointed in equal measure for himself and for his friend, but it seemed little more than a nightmare, a delirium brought about by too much drink or too little company. "The assembly has disassembled. They were sad to see you go. I'm coming down."

On his way to the hatch, he tripped when his foot struck an object on the floor and kicked it across the room, two pieces parting and skittering in different directions. Theo crawled on his hands and knees to fetch them. Two pale blue shoes, women's heels, one whole and one broken. Kay had worn such a pair. He cupped them in his hands the way he had once held her feet.

16

A half-eaten baguette stuffed with *jambon* and mozzarella sat on Foucault's desk. He set the shoes next to his sandwich and wiped his mouth with a paper napkin. Theo and Egon eased into the chairs facing him, anxious to begin, but they were all waiting for Thompson to arrive. The shoe with the broken heel leaned against the upright shoe. In the stark light of the police office, Theo was more convinced that the pair had belonged to Kay. The policeman regarded them indifferently, as if they were ordinary shoes and not a clue to her disappearance. He seemed more interested in his inter-rupted lunch.

"You must forgive my colleague," Thompson said as he entered the squad room. "If he doesn't get fed by a certain hour, he gets crabby and fickle." He came around the desk to shake hands with his visitors. "What's this I hear about shoes?"

They told him three versions of the story. In the first, innocently enough, they had returned to the toy store, remembering how Kay had loved it so, and seeing it abandoned, they tried the door and rummaged around inside, and came across the discarded pair of shoes. "I am almost certain," Theo told the detectives, "that these are the ones she was wearing the night she vanished. She liked to wear them with her yellow sundress."

"But why would your wife have gone into the toy shop after midnight?" Foucault asked.

"It was on the route between the cirque and our flat. I don't know, perhaps someone was after her and she needed a place to hide. Perhaps that's why she broke a heel, she was running away from him."

"A very distinctive color," Thompson said, picking up the broken-heeled shoe. "If these are hers . . . The right size, I assume?"

"I don't know what size she wore — we had only been married a short time, so it is hard to say."

Foucault finished chewing another bite from his sandwich. "But you don't know for certain. Could be a random pair of lost shoes."

The second version peeled back another

layer to the story. Egon began with a confession — that he had gone back alone and broken into the Quatre Mains well after Theo had left town. That he had found the matchbook with the cryptic SOS. Theo dug the matchbook from his wallet and handed it to Thompson.

" 'Help,' " the detective read aloud. " 'Get me out of here.' Is this your wife's handwriting, Mr. Harper?"

"Hard to say. Normally, she didn't print like that; in fact, I don't think I ever saw her printing."

Thompson handed the matchbook to Foucault, who inspected both sides with mild curiosity. "Have you ever been to this Les Déesses in Montreal? Some sort of gentlemen's club, *monsieur*?"

"Of course that's her handwriting," Egon said. "Just as those are her shoes. I'm telling you, she was at the Quatre Mains."

The sergeant flipped the matchbook next to the shoes. "It could be a clue. Or it could be a joke. A random bit of trash in an abandoned store. Perhaps this is a note from a stripper to one of her customers? *Les liaisons dangereuses.*"

Thompson asserted his authority. "We will look into it, obviously. But unless you could

be sure there is a connection to your wife
—"

"I tell you she was there," Egon insisted. "The place is haunted. I heard them. I seen them."

"Seen whom?" Foucault asked.

"The puppets. The ones who took her."

"He doesn't mean it," Theo said. "Just his imagination running away."

The third version was the true story. Egon told them the whole thing from the beginning. How he had found himself homeless and nipped into the shop for a few nights out of the cold. How he had discovered the broken toys and puppets in the attic. How they had seemed to be alive and threatening, and how he went to New York to fetch Theo to see for himself. "As sure as I'm sitting here, those things were alive. And they have something to do with the disappearance of Kay Harper. There was a book of scripts in the attic, with all their weird plays and so on."

Egon dug out the notebook and opened it to the final page, handing it to Thompson. "Her initials written in the back, plain as day. *KH*. Find the puppets, you find the girl."

Straining to catch every word, Thompson had been listening intently, his elbows on the desk. Now, he leaned back in his chair and switched his attention to Theo, his face fallen with sympathy. "Puppets?"

"Look, I wouldn't have come here if I didn't on some level believe that there's a connection at play. It was her favorite spot in all Québec. Maybe she did venture inside and lost her shoes. Maybe the owners of this Quatre Mains have something to do with it, or could provide some explanation about the notebook, the matchbook, the shoes. Lord knows, it is more than you have been able to find in all this time."

In a loud clear voice, Foucault chided him. "We've turned the Old City upside down. We have spent more time on this case than many, *monsieur.* It's not that we have given up, but puppets —"

"You'll forgive my sergeant," Thompson said. "Of course we will look into the matter. I'm sure we can find something about the proprietors of the Quatre Mains. Track them down, eh, Foucault? Though I must say, the fact that Monsieur Picard was camping out illegally in the building does not help matters."

"Pardon me," Foucault said. "I cannot believe we are talking about these dolls, but I do not want to insinuate anything at all."

As he heard their patronizing apologies,

Theo realized just how far gone he was. Of course, they were humoring him, and he would have felt the same in their place. Puppets. To say it aloud made him realize just how preposterous Egon's theory had been. And just how crazy he was to believe in such fairy tales.

"We will contact you should anything come of our investigation," Thompson said. "In the meantime, let me ask you to leave police work to the police. Under no circumstances are you to go back to the Quatre Mains. Or any other abandoned buildings. Could be dangerous."

Out on the sidewalk in front of the police station, Egon hunched against the wind and lit a smoke. They stood there not speaking to each other, each wondering how such a solid story had produced such disappointing results. A few stray snow flurries danced in the air, and when Thompson came charging through the door, he was bundled for the cold. He grinned when he saw them and hurried over.

"I was hoping to catch you before you left," he said. "I wanted a word in private. My sergeant is something of a natural skeptic."

With a flick of his wrist, Egon tossed the cigar into the street. "So you believe us?"

"Let's take a ride," Thompson said. They drove through the winding streets of the Old City, quieter in late October, free of the summer tourists. Halloween decorations hung from the lampposts, ghosts and witches in colonial garb crowded into the public squares, jack-o'-lanterns dotted the second-story balconies where once had hung baskets of flowers, and in the shop windows, silhouettes of bats and black cats, a few posters advertising special street performances of the *Fantômes.* He parked the car on the corner nearest to the Quatre Mains, and they walked to the shop. The glass rattled when he tried to open the front door.

"Locked tight as a nun's chastity belt," Egon said. "Enter from the rear, like I told you."

Theo looked right and left down the empty street. "Shouldn't we seal off the crime scene? Put up some of that police tape?"

"So far the only crime is breaking and entering. And I don't suppose you'll want me to arrest you for that."

Single file, they slipped down the alley and found the back entrance. With a twist of the knob, the door opened. Stale air pressed down upon them, and the abandoned room

269

looked shabby and desolate in the pale afternoon light.

"This was the workshop," Thompson said, "where they made the dolls and puppets. Where you brought your broken treasures to be fixed."

"You know this place?" Theo asked.

"From when I was a boy. In its heyday, the Quatre Mains was known far and wide, best toys in Québec." He led them through the beaded curtain into the main room and paused, conjuring memories. "Every child loved the Quatre Mains. You could find things here that were nowhere else. My *maman* bought me a set of the Irish Guards here, tin soldiers, I see them clearly as yesterday. Made in England. And my little brother would beg my father on a Saturday morning to come to town for the puppet theater they ran in the tourist season. Punch and Judy most of the time, but every once in a while, something special. Magical." In the dust on the countertop, he wrote the name Nico with one finger.

"They called the puppeteer Quatre Mains because his performances were impossible, as though he had four hands to keep so much in motion. Him and his wife, that's it. Just the two of them hidden from view, and there could be six or eight marionettes on stage at once. I was a devotee, but Nico adored the puppets."

He found a twisted set of sticks and wires and worked an invisible doll. "Halloween was his favorite. This time of year, the puppeteers would do a show filled with ghosts and goblins which would have made you believe. Afterward, late at night lying in bed, Nico would talk about the puppet show and swear to me which ones were just toys and which ones were real. Alive." He walked over to the staircase and stopped on the first step. "Silly boy."

The upper rooms appeared less menacing with Thompson's escort. With no fanfare, he climbed the chair and lifted himself into the attic. Theo followed, leaving Egon in the bedroom below.

"You found the shoes up here? Funny place to leave shoes."

"Nearly broke my neck tripping over them."

Leaning over the edge, Thompson asked Egon where he had found the matchbook.

"In a pile of dust in the workshop. But you must believe me, that place up there was filled with mad puppets and broken toys come to life."

"They seem to have flown the coop." Thompson stood up and gave a desultory look at the open boxes. "I will have Foucault make a full inventory. You never know, something may have turned up. Tell me, Mr. Harper, did you ever finish translating that book of yours? Who was that fella with the strange name?"

"Muybridge? No, I have a little ways to go."

"You must persevere, Mr. Harper, and not give up." He lowered himself from the attic and held the chair for Theo to follow. Clapping the dust from his suit, Thompson cast a quick glance around the room. "This must have been where the puppeteers lived. My brother would have loved to have seen it."

Egon stepped between the two other men. "The notebook was up there as well. With all their plays and scripts. The one with the initials *KH* in the back."

"We'll look into that as well, *monsieur.* Could be something, but we often make clues out of coincidences."

They retreated down the stairs, following the trail to the back room. At the doorway, Theo grabbed him by the arm. "Tell me, Inspector Thompson, what happened to your brother who loved the puppets?"

"Nico? Funny, he's why I became a policeman. He's why your wife's disappearance bedevils me. My brother vanished when he was eight years old. Nicholas."

"Did you ever find him?" Theo asked.

"No," the detective said. He put a steady-ing hand on Theo's shoulder. "Which is not to say that we won't find Kay."

Every puppet needed a person to bring the body to life. A hand would no longer do. Not even the Quatre Mains at the sticks would work, for none of them could be called a marionette. They were giants now. The newness of their size astonished them, as though the whole world had been trans-formed. What was once large was now small, and what had been small was of little accord.

The farm girl lifted Kay from her perch in the barn to carry her to the school bus wait-ing outside. She swayed in the girl's arms, unsteady as a mast in a storm. With a grunt, the girl flipped her to a horizontal position and toted her on board, laying her next to the other puppets in the back of the bus. Most of the seats had been removed and a row of berths had been installed on each side, and the giant puppets rested in the makeshift bunk beds. Kay flinched when the Good Fairy was laid atop her, though she was light as a bird's nest. The people loaded the Queen from the back emergency exit. Her body took up nearly a third of the length of the bus.

Through the Vermont countryside they rambled, along the artery that twisted its way south between the Green Mountains. Kay could just see enough through the window to feel at home, the landscape reminding her of the place where she first fell in love with the world. The trees had dropped their leaves, save a few papery brown stragglers, but the sun shone gloriously, and the crisp air flowed in from open windows. A minivan followed the bus, and behind that, a pickup truck with Nix and Noë resting in the bed. The convoy passed cows lunching in the fields and roadside apple pickers, over hill and dale, and came at last to a crossroads town all done up for Halloween. They parked by a plain white Congregational church with a cemetery adjacent, the rows of gravestones casting long shadows in the slant light. Across the road stood a ruined mansion, weatherworn and gray, and as she was unloaded from the bus, Kay could not help but think of death and decay, all wrapped in the peacefulness of an ordinary day in late October.

He must be wondering where I am.

Some students from the college near town had been recruited to assist in the pageant, girls in dreadlocks, sandals, and skirts. A barefoot boy, a pair of young apostles in matching beards. Gathered around in a half circle, they listened to a quick tutorial from the Quatre Mains and memorized their parts, how to move, where to march. They selected their favorites, fumbling with the puppets as they sought the right balance, testing how to make them move, clapping their great hands together with a swing of the rods. At the head of the line, Deux Mains took on the part of roly-poly Mr. Firkin. The Quatre Mains had the Devil, the college girls the Three Sisters, a boy for Nix, a girl for Noë. The Irishman was beneath the Old Hag, the farm girl was Kay, and the second beard was the Good Fairy. On either side Stern and Finch lifted the colossus of the Queen, and on they marched, at Firkin's whistle, down an easy hill and onto the Main Street proper.

Dressed in their Halloween costumes, schoolchildren from across the county had been bused in for the occasion. They sat on the curbs, wide-eyed. Behind them on the sidewalks their parents, some with babes in arms, and their teachers stood for the procession, mingling with the shopkeepers and the townsfolk gathered for the annual festivities. From the little witches and ghosts, skeletons and monsters rose a bright cheer as the puppets swung into view, and the marching band from the high school broke into "The Teddy Bears' Picnic," heavy on the brass and percussion. Trimmed in black and orange, the whole town pulsed with joy and surprise. Each dog they passed erupted into barks or whimpers, as if they could tell what was behind the still and placid faces. On the corner where the two major roads intersected, a camera crew from WCAX in Burlington jumped into action, and as Kay moved closer, she could hear a blond woman in a jack-o'-lantern sweater report on the proceedings, gushing at the flair of the Good Fairy, her voice rising an octave at the majesty of the Queen.

They came to the end of the parade at the town parking lot, the children in full pursuit. Arms and shoulders aching from the trek, the college kids shed their puppets, but the puppeteers stayed in character, the Devil babbling strange spells, Mr. Firkin twirling like a top, and the Old Hag reaching out with spindly arms to wrap each munchkin in a terrible embrace. Hoofing it with her cameraman, the reporter stopped to interview the Queen.

"Last show of the season," the Irishman told her, as he stepped out from beneath the puppet. "We'll start again in April. Can't have these paper folks out in the winter elements."

Squeals of laughter rang out, and toddlers wandered in crazy circles. Kay sidled over to a clutch of third graders, the girls and boys wary at first, but with the adults' urging, one dared to approach and touch the hem of her paper skirt. The rest of the children, seeing no danger, swarmed over, posing for pictures holding the puppet's oversized hand. One bespectacled girl smiled at her through a mouth of teeth and gaps. "Is she real?" she asked. Kay bent closer to better hear her. "Are you alive?" The farm girl shook Kay's head from side to side and slunk off to another gaggle of children. The thrill of performing and the chaos of strangers filled her with a long-forgotten delight. She felt almost human again.

He is probably looking for me.

As the afternoon began to fade, busloads from the more rural areas left first, and the local parents with small children headed home. The Irishman, Stern, and Finch hiked back to the vehicles, and the college kids piled into a jalopy and headed back to campus up on the hill. A few gawkers kept the puppeteers company, asking questions about how such creatures are made. The Deux Mains passed out flyers for the shows to come next spring after the mud season had passed. Heaped together like corpses for a common grave, the puppets were largely forgotten, remnants of the day's festivities, but of no more consequence than the Halloween decorations.

On the long ride home, Kay watched the sun disappear and reappear as it set over the staggered mountains, the branches of the trees at the crests breaking the red light into shards of fire, until all at once night arrived and the windows of the bus settled into black, and a million stars came out above the sheltered country roads. The old engine huffed and gurgled over the hills, and Finch switched on a classical music station on the radio, and the farm girl and the towheaded boy stretched out sleeping on the pair of long benches behind the driver's seat. With a tilt of her head, Kay could reach the Good Fairy's ear. She chanced a whisper.

"It was good to be out among the people today."

"Not too loud," the Good Fairy said, which Kay found ironic, for her husky voice had deepened after she had grown large and

278

her wooden mouth creaked with each sentence.

"What a lot of kids at the parade. How I've missed seeing children."

"Better to miss them than to have them nearby. I always dread the children. Some of them are too young and know so little that they can instantly guess who we are. Closer to nature, they know our true nature. Children and dogs. Don't get me started on dogs. Try being around dogs when you are made of sticks."

"Still, it was like a memory from another life."

"You should just try to forget that other life."

Noisy springs from the passenger seats alerted them to the stirrings of the humans. The bus had turned onto the dark and bumpy side road to the farm. Lamps had been left on in the house, giving it a cheerful glow like the face of a waiting grandparent. The wheels crunched gravel as the bus slowed to a stop, and the van and the pickup soon followed and parked nearby. The night air was noticeably colder, and the smell of burning birch poured from the chimney. Weary now, the humans were much slower in reversing the day's process, unloading the puppets from the vehicles and toting them back into the barn. The blond boy asked if they could wait till morning, and the Quatre Mains cuffed him softly on the back of the neck. "Never," he said. "Never leave these puppets alone and out of the barn after dark."

Chagrined, the boy went straight to work, hurrying to put the puppets away. He made sure to close the barn door after the last was safely inside. When he threw the bolt through the lock with a shudder, the sound echoed in the stillness, a note of finality to the day. Whistling a few bars of a wistful melody, the boy headed for the farmhouse, the notes trailing behind. The puppets were clustered in three groups, settled into a trough and two stalls, presided over by the Queen, who loomed against an outer wall. No more shows or appearances had been planned for the season, and the prospect of a long winter inside made the mood somber and bound them in the silence of their private thoughts.

He would come find me if only he knew where to look.

17

The red light blinked like a semaphore. Had Egon not taken notice and alerted him to the signal, Theo might have neglected the answering machine altogether. Most people reached him via his cell phone, and he had nearly forgotten about the landline that sat next to his computer. He pressed the button marked Play and flinched at the sound of a voice from the past.

"Theo, this is your mother-in-law. Dolores. Are you home? I saw Katharine on the TV. Kay. Or something like her. Please call when you get this message."

He listened again. Echoes of a ghost.

"Are you going to call her?" Egon asked. "Or should I?"

Their suitcases sat next to the front door, and Theo had just sloughed off his jacket and draped it on the back of his desk chair. Road weary, he wanted nothing more than a long shower and a night's rest. He rubbed the sleep from his eyes. "Maybe in the morning. It's late, and she's probably asleep by now."

Egon threw his hands into the air. "Are you out of your mind? Talk to the woman."

"You don't understand. She doesn't like me. Not to play the mother-in-law card. I think she still secretly suspects me in Kay's disappearance."

"She says she saw Kay on TV. I don't care how crazy —"

"Not crazy," Theo said, picking up the phone.

He pictured her on the other end making her way in the chair to answer the call. After the accident, her husband had installed a phone in every room, but at this late hour, she was probably in bed, watching one of those British mysteries she so adored. Kay had often complained that her mother would not interrupt one of her stories to pick up the phone. It rang and rang. Where could she be at this time of night?

"Hullo." With one word, the memories returned. Her voice was the synthesis of flint and haw, an old-fashioned patrician accent like the distaff child of Cary Grant and Katharine Hepburn.

"Hello, Dolores. I got your call —"

"Theo, dear boy. I have seen the most

peculiar thing. On the television. The six o'clock news last night. They were doing a story about a Halloween parade, what passes for local color these days. Children in costumes lined up on the sidewalks. Would you know, these giant effigies are carried down the middle of the street. Positively Catholic. Like they were carrying icons in a procession. And that's when I saw her. Kay. She was one of those . . ."

"Puppets?"

"Yes, a puppet, a great big puppet. I just caught a glimpse of her, but I would recognize her anywhere. The dead spit. How could they have known what she looks like without seeing her? Mind, it was a very stylized face, but I could tell by her eyes. Like I was looking at my own girl again. You must think me an old fool, but I had to call someone. Where have you been?"

"You miss her," Theo said. "I miss her, too. I see her face everywhere."

"No, no, nothing like that. This was made to look just like her. Have you any news?"

He hesitated a beat, uncertain whether to tell her. "Nothing solid. I just got back from Québec, as a matter of fact. I met with the police, but they are no closer than ever, though there may be a new clue. Do you remember if she had a pair of heels in a kind of robin's-egg blue?"

"Shoes? She had so many shoes. I suppose it is possible."

"They found two shoes, one with a broken heel. I think they might be hers, the pair she was wearing the night she disappeared."

On the other end of the phone, she paused a few beats. Her face would be contorted in that same gesture Kay made whenever she began to cry. Like mother, like daughter. He wanted to reach through the line and hug her by the shoulders, he wanted to tell her the whole story about the Quatre Mains shop, but he dared not raise her hopes. Or confuse her with Egon's half-baked theories.

"I cannot bear to think how she might have lost them."

"They're not entirely sure they are hers, and I can't know —"

"Might I ask you a favor? Could you track them down? The puppet people. Maybe they know her, used her as a model for that giant doll. Uncanny resemblance, took my breath. It was the Vermont station on the television. And the parade was just down the road in Bennington. Yesterday. The television people might be of help in finding who is responsible."

"Dolores, I don't know —"

"Not for me, Theo. For Kay."

"For Kay," he said at last, and with a promise to call again soon, he made his good-byes.

Like a jack-in-the-box, Egon popped up from behind the sofa as soon as the conversation ended. He had been eavesdropping and bore an eager expression on his face, a startling visage since Theo had completely forgotten that he was there. "What gives, *mon ami?*"

"Her mother was watching local news on the TV last night, and she saw a story on a Halloween parade with giant puppets in a little town in Vermont." Theo spoke slowly as if trying to convince himself of the story. "And one of them looked just like Kay."

"That could be her," Egon said.

"But these weren't small, they were big puppets. Giants."

"Yet she swears that one of them looked like Kay? Big or small, you must follow every lead."

Theo ignored his remark. "Dolores wants me to see if I can find the puppet makers. Her theory is that they must have used Kay as a model, but I don't know. Could be that she just imagined the resemblance. She's been subconsciously looking for Kay all this time, and any scant similarity might trigger a reaction. Obviously, she's projecting her grief onto an unrelated situation. I've done it myself, a thousand times. Thought 'there she is.' "

"And you sound ready to disbelieve anything and everything. You think it is a mere coincidence that we find all this evidence in a puppet shop? Maybe your mother-in-law is seeing things, maybe she is, what did you say, projecting? But, if it looks like a puppet and acts like a puppet, then she must be a puppet. Fire up your laptop. Let's do a search."

The video hadn't been uploaded on any of the feeds from the Burlington station, but after watching clip after clip of parades, they chanced upon a homemade version of the Halloween march through Bennington. Ninety seconds of shaky cam, children mostly, the videographer interested in the variety of costumes, and finally a continuous long shot of all the puppets come to town. A barrel-shaped man with a walrus mustache, a devil, three sisters in Victorian costumes, a juggler and a straw-headed girl, an old witch. And for just a few seconds, there she was, the one who looked like Kay, here and gone, and then a creature made out of sticks and branches, and at the end of the procession a queen twice as tall as the rest.

Theo rewound and froze Kay in a single instant, soft focus, bright exposure, but undeniably a stark resemblance. The face turned briefly toward the camera, blank and static features, but the maker had captured her heart-shaped face, the flare of her nose, wide mouth and full lips, the color and texture of her hair, and, just as her mother had seen, a certain life in her eyes. They watched over and over, hoping for another view, a different angle, a close-up that would verify the identity, but it never materialized. Just a fleeting glimpse to study at different resolutions, a few frames to arrest motion.

"Is that her?" Egon asked.

Theo stared at the screen. Nearly six months had passed. Pressing his fingers to the glass, he traced the shape of the paper face. He wanted it to be her. He wanted a way to find her.

Some nights the whole barn seemed alive. The voices in the middle of the night came soft and loud, sudden, or in long slow whispers. Voices from other floors and chambers, places no one dared to go. Most of the time, the sounds were mere gibberish, but on occasion, a stray word or phrase floated in the air. A man would holler "radio" at odd times. An older woman said

287

quite clearly: "I do not care for celery." Footsteps would bend a floorboard now and then, and once the faint melody of a waltz overlaid with many people dancing in a faraway loft.

They were not alone.

The Queen had commanded them to stay out of the other rooms to not risk encountering anyone other than their own. At first, the random noises disconcerted Kay and the other puppets. They had been used to being the only presence moving about in the middle of the night, whether at the toy shop in Québec or the little theater in Montreal, where any sudden sound indicated that humans were nearby and meant they had to return to their places and pretend to be inanimate. Here in the barn, however, the voices suggested that others of their kind prowled the halls and spaces beyond, like strangers in a graveyard. Only, of course, the Quatre Mains puppets were the new arrivals, the real intruders. The others had been here long before, years, perhaps decades. They huddled together in the stalls, afraid of what might be out there. On Halloween, three nights after they had been locked away, the whole place rang with laughter, sometimes joyful and raucous, but sometimes lit with madness.

Noë inched over to Kay, pressed her body close, and sought the comfort of her hand. Bare patches in the straw thatch on her head gave away how she had been pulling at her hair, and dark circles, powdery as charcoal, appeared on the paper skin beneath her eyes. "I don't like this place."

"You're just not used to it," Kay said. "The strange noises."

In the corner, Mr. Firkin rocked back and forth to build the momentum necessary to stand. He was fatter than before, his torso round as a barrel, and it took three tries to get to his feet. Excited by the sudden motion, the little toy dog leapt from the feet of the Old Hag and barked encouragement, and heads turned in the ranks of the sleepy puppets. Waddling across the room, Mr. Firkin deposited himself before the huddled pair, hands on what passed for hips. His great mustache bristled like a porcupine as he chewed on his words before speaking.

"Fear of the unknown is the greatest of fears, and the imagination often makes a tempest out of what proves to be mere drizzle. There is nothing to be afraid of in these squeaks and creaks. Why, those are our kinfolk above and beyond. Actors and performers like us. I am surprised at you girls, jumping at your own shadows, cowering at mere reflections."

Noë squeezed Kay's hand. "This barn is a big place. Who's to say what's in the other rooms?"

"Shall we go investigate? To help assuage the tremblies? If you are reluctant, I could volunteer Nix or the Devil. Everyone's wary of the Devil, and I'm sure they would give him a wide berth."

At the mention of his name, the Devil sauntered over to join the conversation. Like a coquette, he batted his long black eyelashes and affected an unbecoming innocence. "Did someone mention my name?"

"Why yes," Mr. Firkin said. "As a matter of fact, I have an important mission for you. It is high time we get a better sense of the surrounds and introduce ourselves to the neighbors. If you would be so bold, could you scout for us? Find out what or who are on the other floors and chambers and report back to us? You may take Nix if you are at all concerned for your safety."

"Not a problem," said the Devil. "Ever since we came here, I have been curious about those poor souls. And I go by myself. No need for clowns."

From his perch on a water trough, Nix shouted, "I resemble that comment."

A small convex mirror hung on a post by the door, and the Devil went to work, preening. The other puppets milled about, talking in low tones about the idea of sending him to investigate the forbidden rooms. Two camps formed: those who dared and those who fretted. In the end, all deferred to the Queen, who had been silent, content to watch and listen from on high. As a matter of courtesy, the Devil presented himself to her, bowing obsequiously from the waist, and rising with a grin splitting his new face.

"Make our introductions to the others," said the Queen. "Pay our respects to the Original, if he is out there. Play the diplomat with your smiles and sweet words. But find out what you can. Express our hope and desire to be a full part of the community under this one roof, but make sure you uncover any secrets they might hold. Be a good spy and ambassador. We are counting on you."

"The Devil knows how to flatter," he said, and he backed away into the darkness of the hall.

The puppets listened in nervous silence after he left. The Good Fairy thought she heard the click of his cloven feet on the floor above them. Irina claimed she heard him moving below, but then they all realized the noise came from the Worm wriggling in the tightness of the cellar. Bored, Nix picked up three balls and juggled to pass the time, and subdued conversations gave way to general chatter.

"I wonder what is taking him so long," Kay said.

"Dahlink, you mustn't worry," Olya said. "He is a big boy, perfectly capable of taking care of himself in any circumstance —"

A loud scream echoed from faraway. An almost human scream like the wail of a rabbit caught in a snare. A second tortured gargle sifted through the halls. All talk ceased, and the puppets cast worried looks at one another, and nobody spoke. A sudden flurry ensued, crashing and tumbling from the loft, and just as quickly it stopped, and the quiet returned, an emptiness filled with unspeakable dread and malice.

"The dear thing," the Good Fairy said.

They waited until dawn, the light slipping in through the cracks and gaps in the barn walls, the signal for them to return to their places. The light thinned over the course of the morning, and then rain began to fall and continued through the afternoon, a cold rain that spread gloom in the stalls and dampness along the wooden boards, a foretaste of winter. No human entered the barn, and the only sound save the constant patter of the rain was a single moan from the Worm in the dismal cellar. An endless day with nothing to do but wait and think.

At midnight, Mr. Firkin lit a small lamp and announced the amnesty had commenced. Some expected the imminent return of the Devil, freed again from the constraints of the moon. Others pondered the meaning behind the commotion of that night.

"Do you think they got him?" Noë asked, and Kay put a finger to her lips.

The Old Hag twisted a handkerchief into knots. "He should be back home by now. What could be keeping him?" The little dog curled at her feet and whimpered at the melancholic tone of her question.

"Should I go look for him?" Nix asked at last, and the rest rebuked him at once.

"Do you think the Original is with the others?" The Old Hag shuddered. "What a horrible thought. Who knows what he might decide?"

"We will hope a while longer," said the Queen. "There is no sense sending out a search party."

"Or all of us disappearing, one by one," Masha said. She had expressed the unthinkable and cast a pall over the general unease in the room that lasted the whole night. Toward dawn, from the bowels of the building, a strange voice called out and was met with a round of hearty laughter. The puppets took it as a sign that the Devil would not be back.

"He's gone," Mr. Firkin said as he turned off the lamp. "But we must keep the protocols. Places, please, everyone."

The storm had ended. The last of the raindrops dripped from the eaves, the music like a dirge. The Queen sighed and retired from her throne. With a clap and a whistle, the Old Hag called the little dog, who jumped into her arms and fell fast asleep. In the trough, the Three Sisters laid their bodies down, and the jester put away his juggling and bound together the loose twigs and sticks at the Good Fairy's hands and feet.

Disobeying the curfew, Noë spoke to Kay. "Do you think they have killed him? Has he been unmade?"

"Shh. We don't know what happened to the Devil. We don't even know what's out there."

Noë snapped a straw from her head and worried it with her fingers. "Do you think they will come for us? They will kill us, too."

"Nobody's dead. Nobody's killed. Nobody knows."

Mr. Firkin hissed from his spot. "Quiet. Not a word after dawn. Not a word."

18

Nobody came and nobody went. During the daytime, the barn was calm and hushed. Mice scurried along the walls, and in the rafters a mourning dove, reluctant to make the fall migration, cooed and waited for a reply that would never come. From sunrise to sundown, the old boards ticked and moaned as the cold and warmth alternately played off the wood. The people had departed or perhaps stayed inside the farmhouse, nobody could tell, but the familiar sounds of car engines or wheels along the gravel had all but ceased. Nights were quieter still; the bark of a fox, the cough of a deer would startle a soul. And after midnight, when ordinarily they would have had the run of the place, the puppets were too scared to move.

The disappearance of the Devil made them question their faith. Not in the Quatre Mains — they had long ago learned to mistrust him and his seemingly random capacity to dispatch one of their number into the void. But now they feared the others, the unknown lurking just beyond the cramped chamber into which they had been stuffed. Some accepted the close quarters with stoic forbearance. "Make the best of your situation is my motto," Mr. Firkin said more than once. Others could not tolerate the claustrophobia. Noë had pulled out nearly every straw on her head. The sisters looked terrible, too, draping themselves like pashas in the trough. Masha covered her eyes with one mitt and complained of a migraine. Olya wore a path in the sawdust, desperate for a cup of tea. Irina spoke only in sighs.

Kay did not like her new body. She felt like Alice grown ten feet tall, too big to fit into such a small room after tasting from the bottle labeled DRINK ME. "Which would you have liked best," she remembered from her nursery *Wonderland.* "To be a tiny Alice, no larger than a kitten, or a great tall Alice, with your head knocking against the ceiling?" Kay had been small as a kitten, and under the circumstances, given a choice, she preferred that size. She was taller than she had been when she lived in the real world. She was bigger than her husband.

What would he think if he suddenly saw her in the barn? So changed as to be unrecognizable. He would walk right past her as though she were a stranger. Or a stranger still. There was so much she had not told him, sides to her personality kept secret during the months of dating and even after they had moved in together, after the wedding, too. She had always thought there would be time for the whole story. And he, too, hidden by the past, a stranger in many ways, the life he had away from her, the teaching he would be good at, he was a generous and patient man, and she imagined a gaggle of coeds would fall in love with him every semester. The French seduction. A man of words. Muybridge, she recalled suddenly. White beard, animals in motion. She could picture her husband hunched over the pages, moving Muybridge between languages. At the table, his shirtsleeves rolled up, and a serious frown of concentration that sometimes frightened her. Theo.

"What did you say?" the Good Fairy asked.

She would have blushed had blood run beneath her skin. "Theo," she said at last. "Theo was his name. It just came back to me again. Sometimes my mind comes and goes about the way things used to be."

With a creak of wooden bones, the Good Fairy sat beside her and put an arm around her shoulder, a weariness in the motion. A twig snagged on Kay's collar.

"Better you forget all about him," the Good Fairy said, as they untangled.

"I don't think about him much, except to wonder if he misses me. If he is curious about what happened, or if he has forgotten about me yet."

The Good Fairy rubbed her back in wide circles, the rough fingers scratching an itch that had not existed before. "I used to be just like you. When I first came into this world, it was passing strange. Imagine my surprise to find I'd been changed into this scarecrow, this bundle of kindling, where before I was a person just like you and the rest. For the longest time, I ached to be who I once was, to see my people — Lord, how I missed them. But I made my peace with it, took the advice of Mr. Firkin and the Queen and just put the past where it belonged. There is no past, only the right now. Much more appealing to think about what is to come."

"Well, what is to come?" Kay asked. "Are we to be here for long? I heard the Deux Mains say to the people in the village that the next shows will be in the spring. Does that mean we'll be shut inside through the whole winter?"

"You'll learn," the Good Fairy said. "Don't measure the days as you once did, not as something to be endured but as an opportunity to rest. And savor the moments for what they allow."

Behind them came a drumming on the floor, starting out slowly and softly and increasing in speed and volume. Noë stomped her feet and growled, the tantrum intensifying till she threw her hands in the air and howled and caterwauled. "All winter, all winter. I can't stand another minute." Shrieking, she ran across the room and sped around the corner, heading for the barn door. The puppets were too shocked to react immediately, and they stood there, stunned, as her screams bounced off the walls, a spray of curses as she fought the lock.

Nix and Mr. Firkin were the first to move, and the others quickly followed, even the little dog madly barking at the commotion. Kay and the Good Fairy brought up the rear, trailed only by the Queen, who seemed to glide, her robes flowing like a bridal train. They found Noë gnashing her teeth, wailing uncontrollably at the stubborn bar. As soon as she saw them, she banged her skull against the wood. "I'll go mad if I don't get out."

Reaching over the tops of their heads, the Queen grabbed Noë by the scruff of her neck and silenced her. She lifted her as if no more than a rag doll and wrapped her tightly in her arms. Noë sobbed against the Queen's bosom. Trembling, Noë tried to catch her breath, but the attempts to stop herself only exacerbated the emotions. The others watched, wondering whether the Queen would crush her wire and paper body or offer comfort.

"There, there, child," the Queen said. "We must have none of this. You know better. You know there is no way out by yourself."

"I want to go home," Noë said.

The Queen stroked her face, ran her fingers over the bristly stubble on her bald head. They all waited for the sobbing to subside, reluctant witnesses to her despair.

"I want . . . I want . . ." And Noë lost control again and buried herself more deeply in the billowy largeness of the Queen.

Kay could not bear to watch the suffering of her friend. She moved away from the pack, leaned against the wall, and peered through the crack between two boards. Another day approached. In the yellow and lavender light and shadow, she could see the frost coating the grass. In the jagged starlight under the setting moon, the ground sparkled and danced. Theo would have been mesmerized. Gathering her in his arms, he would have stood behind her, holding her until the night gave way. She, too, would go mad if she never saw him again.

Aboard ship on the Atlantic, Muybridge looked back at the United States of America for what would be the last time. Going home at last, back to England, back for good. He was sixty-four, but felt like an old man with a young man's ambition. Turning toward the east, Helios, god of the sun, going back to its rising. The year before, his zoopraxiscope had played motion pictures at the world's fair in Chicago. He had met with Edison and Étienne-Jules Marey, worked in Philadelphia with the painter Thomas Eakins. He had toured the country, gone to and come back from Europe, lecturing to enthusiastic crowds enchanted by his moving images. The foundation had been laid for his two masterworks, *Animal Locomotion* and *The Human Figure in Motion,* but all he could think about on the wild gray sea was his wife and her lover, Harry Larkyns, and the bullet to the heart. And all that might have been.

"Only photography has been able to divide human life into a series of moments, each of them has the value of complete existence," Muybridge once wrote. Each moment part of a series, yet separate and complete somehow, the motion but an illusion, the way to mark time. He could see his wife twist her neck, the realization of what was to happen clearly marked on her face, the recognition in that split second of all that had passed and all that was to come. That scoundrel's eyes bore a permanent regret. All in the space between the smile and the squeeze of a trigger.

New York harbor receded on the horizon. Muybridge rubbed his great white beard and spat into the ocean. He had stopped time, yes, but it could not be unwound, reversed, replayed. There was only one direction: forward.

Theo added the final page to the manuscript and put down his pen. Finished, but for the last revisions. When Kay first disappeared, he had blamed that man from the circus, that seedy old ringmaster, and Theo would have shot that roué had he a gun. But now he was not so sure. Now he had convinced himself that she had made it to the Quatre Mains puppet shop that night and had vanished from there.

She had disappeared once before.

They had been dating three or four months and had arranged to meet at the Central Park Zoo on a Sunday afternoon. She had wanted to see the penguins. He had wanted to see her. So much so that he arrived an hour early and settled in on one of the benches facing the circular pool where the sea lions cavorted on the rocks, the feeding routine drawing in the young families and children like magic. Theo watched the people come and go, idly speculating about his future with Kay, the prospect of bringing their own children to the zoo, to the park. And on the bench in that hour, he decided that one day soon he would ask her to marry him.

When she did not show up at the appointed hour, he wandered over to the iron fence that separated the zoo from the street, and there she was. At first, the sight of Kay amid the crowds of tourists was an early and welcome surprise. But there was something wrong. From the distance, he could see only her animated motions. She gestured to a man who leaned in closer, his face red with anger. They were arguing, he could tell, and unsure of himself, he froze on the bench and watched the show play out with dismay. When Kay tried to break away, the

304

man grabbed her by the arm and would not let go. Theo sprang to his feet and raced toward the fence. He recognized the man from the rooftop party near the Flatiron. Her old boyfriend.

"Get your hands off her," Theo shouted, his face pressed between the bars, and as soon as he spoke, her eyes widened with alarm, and the man reflexively let go of her, and she pivoted on her heels and made her way to Fifth Avenue, running as fast as possible through the clots of people on the sidewalk. By hesitating for one moment, Theo lost the chance to catch her, and by the time he found the exit from the zoo, he could not spot her anywhere. He walked quickly up the avenue, looking for her along the way to see if she had doubled back into the park and was waiting for him, but she would not be found.

She did not answer her cell phone. She did not answer the intercom when he buzzed her apartment building, and he sat on the stoop till nightfall, hoping to intercept her. In those long hours, all he could see was the image of her sprinting crazily through the streets of New York, and his thoughts ran wild with conjecture about the man on the sidewalk and why she had fled rather than simply talk to Theo. Everything that he knew about her seemed to fly away, every dream seemed to curdle. At midnight, he gave up and went home.

Another full day passed before she reappeared on a Tuesday morning in the spy hole in his front door. With a box of rugelach and two coffees, she appeared contrite. The worry that had eaten at him gave way to a gush of relief. He threw his arms around her and led her in.

"What happened to you Sunday? Where have you been? I've been worried sick."

Pulling him close, she kissed him, trembling in his arms till he returned her embrace.

"What is it, Kay? What's wrong?"

Breaking from the embrace, she positioned herself behind an armchair, holding on to the wings for protection. "I can't tell you. If I tell you, you will want nothing to do with me."

Theo remembered that moment as a crossroads, but at the time, his answer was spontaneous and unequivocal. "There's nothing you could say that would make me want to end this. Is it about that man you were arguing with? Your boyfriend?"

She laughed nervously, apprehending his thoughts for the first time. "Barry? Not in the way you are thinking. There's nothing between us, honestly. Not anymore. Nothing romantic, if that's what you are afraid of, if that's what you mean."

"But you were yelling at him, and he would not let go."

"You'll hate me."

"Say anything."

"He's a mistake, a bad influence," she said. "That's not exactly right. He's a guy who can get his hands on drugs. That's what we were arguing about. That's why I ran away from you."

Her confession stunned him.

"I'd needed some speed. There were back-to-back auditions, and I've been feeling run-down and tired. When I saw you there, you were early, you weren't supposed to be so early. I didn't want you to know, so I ran away."

"Are you still using? Are you still seeing him?"

"Lord no," she said. "A little boost to get me through a rough patch. I hadn't seen him in ages, but I knew that he could hook me up. But I've stopped. I'll stop."

"Except for Sunday."

"One time," she said. "Look, he said he was interested, but I'm not. That's why we were fighting. I was trying to end things for good. Untangle the strings."

The moment proved a fulcrum between doubt and trust. He canceled his classes for the day, and they talked all morning, shedding layers of the past. Soon enough they worked their way back to each other, tempered now by the moment. It wasn't the drugs, so much, for he had experimented in his own foolish youth. It was her disappearance, how she did not trust him and instead had run away from him. How Kay had not realized that he would be so frightened. "I do not want to live without you," he told her in bed that afternoon, and she had held on tightly and told him she would not leave. And here he was, living despite her absence.

Tell me where you are, and I will come find you.

The computer chimed when he switched it on, and from the couch, Egon mumbled in his sleep. Just past two in the morning. Careful not to wake him, Theo plugged in his earbuds and clicked on the bookmarked video. He watched the parade again. The video began midstream, a second of shaking as the camera sought its subject. Light fluctuated, too dark, too bright, and then a balanced exposure. Disembodied voices from the crowd, children oohing and aahing as each puppet came into view. "Look at her," some child said clearly when Kay appeared, and he froze the image. She was beautiful as a puppet, her countenance serene, almost peaceful. She looked like an Art Nouveau exaggeration, herself and not herself. The sculptors had captured the heart shape of her face framed by a stylized sweep of hair. And the arc of her cheekbones sharp against the smooth paper skin, the slight overbite that pushed forward her smile, the delicacy of her small ears, the set of her eyes beneath the arch of her brows. He clicked the mouse and set the video in motion, and she was gone as suddenly as she had appeared, and then the children screamed with delight as the giant queen arrived, her handlers struggling to keep her aright and steady, and then she filled the frame before all went suddenly black. The last moment was nearly terrifying in the extreme close-up, as if the taping had suddenly become too intense for the videographer, as if the scene were swallowing the camera. He whispered to the screen, "How could you have gone away?"

Late into the night he typed his corrections to Muybridge, one ear on his snoring friend Egon and one ear attuned to the music of translation. Although the publisher would surely have further questions and corrections, Theo was giddy to be nearly done, the work so long a part of his life. At dawn he put on a pot of coffee and muscled through the transcription of his own spidery handwriting, some pages taking him back to Québec, back to that misery. The morning brightened. There was only one direction: forward.

"I'm finished," he said to Egon as soon as he arose. "Let's find those puppets."

■ ■ ■ ■

BOOK THREE

■ ■ ■ ■

19

Cozied in his office, Mitchell listened to their story from start to finish, surrounded by the artifacts of his passion for the ancient world. From over his shoulder, a bust of Aristotle looked down on Theo and Egon, and the bookshelves were crowded with titles in Greek and Latin. He seemed open and credulous, nodding at certain points as though he recognized elements that mirrored his vast knowledge of mythology. When Theo and Egon had finished, he leaned back in his chair and toyed with a shard of pottery decorated with a chain of fearsome maidens linked in a ritual dance.

"What do I know of puppets? I would like to say it was the Greeks who invented the puppet, but they are older than that by thousands of years. The Egyptians buried clay puppets with the mummified corpses in their tombs. Pull the strings, and their marionettes could knead bread. Even the dead get hungry in the afterlife. In India thousands of years ago, they made a terra-cotta monkey who could be made to climb a stick, and there are puppets mentioned in the Mahabharata and the Kama Sutra."

"Kama Sutra, you don't say," Egon whispered an aside. "I'd like to see that."

"Shadow puppets of ancient China, the Bunraku of Japan, the wayang of Java, still in use to this day. The American aboriginals had their totemic dolls with movable arms and legs, and Cortez, who brought along his own puppeteers, encountered such figures among the Aztecs. They have been with us for millennia all over the world. An ancient impulse."

Theo cleared his throat. "There was one of those primitive aboriginal dolls in the window of the Quatre Mains. Native American. Inuit, maybe? Kay fell in love with it."

"The doll and the puppet are really an expression of our desire to create and control life," Mitchell continued. "We make a little man —"

Egon wriggled in his chair and scowled.

"I beg your pardon," Mitchell said. "Figuratively, hah, in every sense, a simulacrum. A homunculus, a human machine. Like us, but not like us. A stand-in, an actor that can be put in motion, made to speak, and suffer indignities or lift us to transcendence. You see it as well in icons and idols. These effigies that you showed me on the computer."

On the edge of his seat, Egon interjected, "Giant puppets. Life-size. And larger than life."

Setting down the pottery shard, Mitchell leaned across the desk. "Small or large, on the end of a finger or lifted by a dozen men, the idea is the same. What did Horace say? 'Man is nothing but a puppet on a string'?

"You know, when I was about eight years old, I saw a Punch-and-Judy show, and the whole time Punch fought with Judy, the crocodile sneaked up behind him, and the man lifted the slapstick to strike the woman and hit the crocodile on the backswing. Completely by accident. Again and again. We kids shrieked and hollered, 'Look out, look out!' but Punch never bothered to glance over his shoulder. Those jaws would open wide, a mouth filled with sharp teeth, and slap, down he would go. After a few rounds, the croc got wise and sneaked around to the other side. Behind Judy."

"What happened next?" Theo asked.

"He ate her up. First try."

Egon laughed. "There's a lesson there."

"And then Punch started deliberately hit-

315

ting the crocodile with the slapstick, and all the children roared. What the lesson is depends upon your point of view. Turns out all right for Mr. Punch, not so much for Judy and the crocodile. I can remember it like yesterday."

"So you will help us?" Theo asked.

"I had nightmares about that crocodile for months. One bite and she was gone."

Thumping his fist on the desk, Egon said, "Enough of your Greek and crocodiles. Your car, man. We came to ask if we could borrow your car."

"To hunt for puppets?"

"Or at least the puppeteers," Theo said. "To see if we can find out what happened to my wife."

"And you think she is a puppet? She underwent a metamorphosis?"

"Precisely," Egon said.

Theo contradicted him immediately. "Well, no, not exactly. We just need a car. To go to Vermont for a few days. See my mother-in-law and learn what we can about this puppet that looks like my wife."

"Why didn't you say so? Of course you can borrow my car," Mitchell said. "On one condition. I want to help. You let me drive."

"Our bags are packed," Egon said. "We knew you couldn't say no."

"An adventure," Mitchell said. "Boys, I would go to Hades and back for a good quest."

They took the scenic route along the Hudson River shrouded in the gloom of an early November Friday afternoon. Mitchell drove his old Ford station wagon slowly and carefully, regaling his captive passengers with tales from the classical myths. Egon kibitzed from the backseat, pointing out the state police lurking on the shoulders long before the others noticed. They passed into Vermont, almost without realizing the time and the landscape flying by. The mountains rose dramatically from the road on the way to Bennington. Using the map on his smartphone, Theo barked out the directions, and they arrived just north of town at his mother-in-law's farmhouse by dusk.

After all that had happened, he was not prepared to see Dolores again. Now that they were back in touch, he had heard a note of forgiveness and hope over the phone, especially after she had shared the news about the Halloween parade. Still, he could not be sure what she might say or do in person. And certainly not how she might react to his two friends in tow.

Mitchell and Egon walked up the wheelchair ramp to the porch, and Theo took the stairs. Waiting for them at the front door stood Mrs. Mackintosh. He had forgotten about the Scottish next-door neighbor who often looked in on Dolores and helped her with the domestic chores. With a crook of her index finger, she bade them be quiet as they entered the house.

"The poor dear was up to high doh," she said. "Now she's dead tired from all the anticipation ever since you called to say you were coming. I tucked her into bed for a wee nap, and she'll be cracking to see you after a spell."

The travelers settled in the front parlor, and Mrs. Mackintosh went into the kitchen for the tea things. The house held memories of Kay in unexpected places. Dozens of framed photographs on the wall marking Kay's childhood and a few more recent shots. Her father had been the photographer in the family, and it was clear that he had doted on her. Their only child. But the objects held an associate power, a reminder of the world from which she had come. The feel of the doorknob in his hand, the cones of lamplight on the corner tables, the cut-glass dish of hard candies centered on the coffee table. A roast in the oven reminded him of Sunday nights. On the mantel, a

318

great clock ticked, an antique machine with painted oval portraits of Washington and Lincoln said to have once belonged to the latter's son Robert, down at Hildene. The click of nails on the hardwood floors preceded the appearance of a great beast sauntering from the back rooms. Their old bluetick coonhound named Sal, a last connection to Kay's father, recognized Theo at once with a look from her mournful brown eyes. Her tail spun in circles as she trotted to his side and buried her head in his lap, and when he reached down to greet her, she drank in the scent of him and rolled onto her back, begging for attention.

"Get on offa that," Mrs. Mackintosh scolded the dog. She set down a pot of tea and the service, complete with a plate of shortbread, and the men fell to it, pushing aside the dog's curious nose.

"I want you to know, Theo, just how sorry I am for your loss. Miss Kay was a fine young woman, much loved, and sorely missed."

Theo looked up from the dog. "Missing, yes. But not yet gone."

The smile melted from her face. "Dolores says as much. She has been going on about those puppets ever since they showed up on the telly, but I'm afraid there'll be no good

319

of it. You mustn't get her hopes too high."

Mitchell and Egon munched their cookies, staying out of the way.

"It could be a wild goose chase," Theo said, "but we aim to find those people who made that puppet that looks like Kay. You have to admit the resemblance. I've reason to believe they might tell me something."

"Aye, but it's a lang road that's no goat a turnin'."

"Inscrutable as ever, my dear." Dolores had rolled silently into the parlor. The dog left Theo's side and loped over to greet her. Looking older now, and careworn, she lifted her arms to Theo, and as he embraced her, he fought back tears. She was a ghost. He had forgotten how much she looked like her daughter, a resemblance that pierced him yet again and opened the hole in his heart.

They put Noë in a corner and wrapped her in a musty old horse blanket, and for the next three nights, someone always sat beside her, holding her hand and telling her everything was going to be all right. She pulled at the paper skin of her scalp, peeling back layers, so Firkin and Nix forcibly bound her hands in gloves crafted from twine. The hardest moments were just after midnight when everyone woke, groggy from slumber, and just before dawn when everyone had to return to their places and forgo control. Noë yelled upon waking and cursed before sleeping, always the same plea to be allowed to go home, and at first they reminded her just how impossible that was, and how she would survive in any case, as a puppet in the wind and the rain, not to mention the coming ice and snow. Such bitter foreshadowings of winter only made matters worse.

On the fourth night, Kay took her turn to watch over Noë. She sang to her, tunes her mother used to sing, lullabies and nonsense songs, and the music seemed to ease her troubled mind. They nestled in the corner of the stall, warm against the chilly night. "You're the only one who cares," Noë said. "The only one who understands. There is something inside my head. Please untie my hands."

"You know I can't do that," Kay said. "The Queen would have my head."

"You must let me be free. Pay no attention to the Queen."

"But Mr. Firkin would catch us."

"Surely you jest. He's nothing more than a tub of hot air."

"I can't, Noë, I wish I could."

She let out a drawn-out hiss. "Listen, then, and tell me if you hear it, too, and perhaps once you hear the noises in my brain, you'll change your mind." Opening her mouth wide, Noë pressed her lips against Kay's ear and held still. All Kay could hear was breathing, and she shook her head. So Noë shifted and pressed her ear against Kay's ear, and they sat cheek to cheek for some time until the hum, faint and distant, began. An electric current going up and down in volume like an oscillating fan.

Alarmed, Kay faced her. "There *is* something in your head besides thoughts and ideas."

"And I can't very well do anything about it like this." Noë held up her twine-bound hands, useless as mittens. "My brain is going to explode. I'll go mad."

"I can't untie you."

"Poke a hole in it," Noë said. "It doesn't have to be big. A little puncture, just enough to let out the pressure, or I'll just burst."

The thought of stabbing her friend in the head mortified Kay, but she could see the agony and need in her eyes. Making sure the others were occupied, she searched for a sharp object. When she dropped to her hands and knees, Kay had to fight off the advances of the little dog, who thought she was playing a game. On the floor, she spied wedged in a corner an old horseshoe nail, a bit rusted but keen enough. She pricked a hole in her thumb, surprised by how little pain she felt, and returning to Noë's side, she double-checked on the weird noise by pressing ear to ear. "I don't want to hurt you."

"It won't. Just a small incision, somewhere no one will notice." Noë turned and bowed her head, exposing the base of her skull.

The nail punctured the varnished paper with ease, but Noë jerked at the sensation, and a two-inch vertical cut opened. Kay gasped at what she had done.

A pearl of amber liquid formed at the bottom of the wound and oozed in a long strand that dripped to Kay's lap. Noë groaned with relief as the buzzing grew louder, and from the slit emerged an orange and black honeybee, which perched on the fold of paper skin, tasting the air and testing its wings before flying away. A second bee followed quickly, likewise departing from her head, and then all at once, dozens of angry bees emerged, their buzz grinding louder and louder. Nix was the first to notice the swarm. Dropping a hoop, the clown shouted a warning, and the stalls were suddenly busy with flailing arms and shouts as the bees poured forth, swirling pell-mell around the puppets' heads, alighting and taking flight again. Mr. Firkin rolled about, calling for order. The Sisters screamed with fright, and the Old Hag cradled the Dog against her chest as it yapped at the insects, desperate to bite and swallow these bizarre toys.

The honey flowed freely and pooled on the floor behind Noë, who had crumpled to her knees and thrown back her head, and some of the bees raced to the spot to collect their spilled food. As soon as her head emptied, Noë fainted, and a few bees crawled on her resting body, buzzing angrily as they looked for a way back inside. Squeezing the nail in her hand, Kay crouched next to her, wondering if she had killed her. When she tried to brush them away, she felt a bee land on her hand and plunge its stinger into the web of skin between her thumb and index finger. She watched in fascination as it took flight, ripping the weapon from its abdomen, and stumbled in the air and plunged to its death. They were dying all around her. Those that hadn't sacrificed their stingers fell victim to Mr. Firkin's ingenious trap. He had spaded the honey from the floor into a gunnysack and lured them to it, tying the end with twine when most of the hive had gathered. The few bees that had avoided either fate eventually found their way out of the room and flew off to parts unknown.

While the bees were herded away, the Good Fairy attended to Noë. She cleaned her best as she could of the sticky honey, and taking the horseshoe nail from Kay and a length of twine, she sutured together the ragged ends of the paper wound. The whole time Noë said not a word, the expression on her face as blank as a doll's. Kay watched the operation, torn between guilt and hope, and when order was finally restored, she was held for an accounting. The puppets arranged themselves in two rows along the stalls, and the Queen paced back and forth between the troops, boiling her thoughts.

"And just whose brilliant idea was this? To plague us with this swarm?"

"Mine, Your Highness," Kay volunteered. "Though I had no idea about the bees —"

"You don't think. You hear a sound inside a head, so you cut a hole? What on earth gave you the idea that it was allowed?"

Noë spoke for the first time. "I asked her to, Your Majesty. I was going mad and needed some relief."

"And you thought that poking a hole in your brain would help? Did you not consider that if you open your mind, you will release everything it holds?"

Kay pondered the question and thought it most unfair. "She had bees in her brain."

"And that gives you the right to let them out where they might attack the rest of us? Have you not heard of keeping your thoughts to yourself? Had Mr. Firkin here not been as clever, those nasty things might have flown up my nose or into your ear, and then where would we all be? Mad as hatters. Mad as March hares. Mad as your friend there, missy."

"I beg your pardon, but I was only trying to help."

Noë stepped up to her own defense. "I feel much better now, I do. No more racket in my mind."

"Have you stopped to consider," the Queen asked, "that these bees were not the cause of her problems but a symptom of them? I didn't think so. There will be no more poking of holes in anyone's head, do you understand? No more fraternizing at all between the two of you plotters."

The heartbreak showing in her eyes, Noë could not bear to look at Kay. The Queen stepped before her and with a wave of her hand demanded that she bow down. "You are to no longer complain of bees in the brain. I command you to give up this nonsense of madness and the desire to escape. You are a puppet of the Quatre Mains, and it is high time you started behaving like one."

Her robes sweeping the air, the Queen quickly turned to Kay. "And as for you, learn your place and like it. Or I shall lump you till you do. I want you to go to the corner and stay there, until I say you may be excused. You are hereby charged with ensuring that no bees will come near our person . . . not one, you understand? And you will clean up the bodies. Well, what are you waiting for?"

Kay felt like a little schoolgirl, sitting by herself in the corner, but she was glad that she had tried to help Noë, who seemed better already, the madness drained, a pleasing dullness in the way she moved. As for the petty tyrant who ruled their world, the Queen must be obeyed, but loyalty is best earned and never coerced. Kay would bide her time. She would find a way to show that hearts trump the Queen.

20

They gathered around the television set like a nuclear family. Theo, Egon, and Mitchell on the sofa, Mrs. Mackintosh perched on an ottoman, and Dolores in her wheelchair, the dog dozing at her feet. The Yankee pot roast had disappeared, the apple tart as well, and night had settled into the restive hours between supper and bedtime. Through sheer persistence, Dolores had been able to track down a copy of the video recording from the TV station in Burlington, and they were all ready for another point of view on the Halloween parade.

The biggest difference between the recordings was the quality and higher resolution. The whole piece had been constructed like a story and not merely a series of images marching across the screen. However, one did not see as much of the puppets on the news as they had on the home movie. More intercuts of the children and parents watching the parade go by, and a cute ten seconds of a little girl telling the reporter which puppet was her favorite. "The sticks one," she had said. Kay had appeared twice in the story, both times fleetingly — in the parade and in the aftermath in the parking lot.

"I'm surprised you spotted her," Theo said.

"She's sharper than you think," Mrs. Mackintosh said.

"Quiet, the both of you," Dolores said. "I badgered them to send the B roll as well."

Mitchell leaned forward. "B roll?"

"All the background stuff they shoot and then splice into the main story. Just watch."

The cameraman had started with a panorama of the decorated streets of the small town, the children gathered at the edge of the sidewalk, sitting on the curb, waiting for the show. The footage jumped to the actual parade, three full minutes, with good shots of each of the puppets, from the tubby barrel man at the head to the giant queen at the end. Kay appeared from a different angle than in the home movie. She was clear and crisp and the shot stayed with her longer as her handler wobbled her forward. At the moment the puppet's face was closest to the lens, Dolores froze the picture.

"That's her. I would know my own daughter anywhere."

Mrs. Mackintosh swiveled on the ottoman to face the three men. "I nearly fainted when I saw her. Whoever made that doll surely knew Miss Kay."

Theo stared at the image on the screen. So much time had passed since he had last seen her. Lately he had been wondering just how true the face he conjured in his imagination was, between the idealized and the real, the desire to see her again so great that he had forgotten precisely what she looked like. Sometimes he could not picture her at all, and other times, he could close his eyes and re-create all the colors of her eyes, a rough patch of skin on her hand, a beauty mark behind her left ear. The paradox fell apart as he stared at the face on the TV. He, too, was certain that the puppet had been copied from his wife's face.

Dolores pressed Play, and Kay walked out of the frame. There was the fantastical creature made of sticks and the titanic queen, and then the scene shifted to the parking lots, interviews with children not quite charming enough to air. The puppets moved about in the background, and now and then, he caught a glimpse of Kay. Toward the end, a few of the handlers unburdened themselves of the effigies. They were just college kids, the same as his own charges. A few seconds of the puppets leaning against light poles and walls like a gang of hooligans, and then the tape suddenly scrambled and another story picked up, something about a moose, that had been recorded over. Just as the original B roll would have been by now. Theo was grateful for Dolores's quick thinking and tenacity in securing a copy before it was too late. They had proof. But of what?

"I know who they are," Dolores said. "I've tracked them down."

"She's a Sherlock on the Internet," said Mrs. Mackintosh.

Dolores reached for a folder on the end table and triumphantly held up the evidence. "The Northeast Kingdom Puppet Company, established in 1973. Right here in Vermont. 'Making street art and political theater to reenchant and reclaim the world.' Whatever that might mean."

Mitchell cleared his throat. "So how did your daughter come to be a puppet?"

Nobody seemed to notice that he had misspoken.

"That, my friend, is what I expect you to find out and report back to me. Could be someone remembers her when she lived here, but that hasn't been for years, and,

331

besides, why does she show up now? If there's a connection, maybe we can find out what's happened to Kay."

From his spot in the middle of the sofa, Egon jumped into action. "Let's go, if we are to find this place."

"Not tonight," Dolores said. "It's a three-hour drive on some mighty windy back roads, almost to Canada, and you boys need your beauty sleep. Mackintosh here has made up beds for you all. Get a fresh start in the morning."

Mrs. Mackintosh showed Egon and Mitchell to their bedroom on the upper floor, cleaned and aired out for their stay, leaving Dolores and Theo alone in the parlor. They watched the tape again, stopping it whenever Kay appeared, moving ahead frame by frame, until they could bear it no longer. She flicked the switch, and silence pressed down like a stone.

"I blamed you," Dolores said. "Thought you should have taken better care of her."

"Not just that. You held me responsible. You seemed suspicious that I had something to do with her disappearance. As if I could ever hurt her."

"I don't know you, Theo. Not really. Just a man, the older man who took my daughter away. So, yes, I thought that maybe you had grown tired of her, that some foul play was the reason you kept your distance when I was trying to help. I thought you were protecting yourself, but I was wrong. I can see how much you loved Kay."

"I am heartbroken."

She motioned for him to come closer and reached out her hand for him to take. They sat for a few minutes, not speaking, looking for some accommodation for each other. Dolores patted him and told him he could sleep in Kay's old bedroom, and then she wheeled off to her room at the back of the house, the hound trailing her in devotion.

Nothing had changed since the last time he had stayed in Kay's room. Her mother had not kept it as a shrine exactly, for most of the childhood mementos had long ago been put away, and the new furnishings were simple, almost austere. Yet the mere fact that Kay had long inhabited the space gave him the sense that she had just recently departed. Her essence lingered. On the nightstand beneath a lamp stood a photo-graph taken no more than two or three years before, Kay at her finest, togged out in ski clothes in some northern chalet, snow on the trees outside the window, cheeks red with blood. The dresser, which once held her clothes, stood empty, but in the closet were the formal gown she wore to her high school prom and her wedding dress. Their wedding. A row of childhood books stood on a birch shelf. He ran his fingers along the spines, looked for her name hand-printed on the endpapers.

He crawled into her bed and fought for sleep against the spirits that roamed the house and slipped into the room. Midway through the night, as he dreamt of Kay dangling from a set of marionette strings, he was awakened by someone wandering in the darkness. Not Mitchell or Egon prowling for leftovers, the sound was not right. When he poked his head out of the doorway, he heard the chair being pushed across the floor. Dolores was startled to see him as well, her white hair loose for sleeping, her brown eyes wide in the darkness. She put a finger to her lips and bade him follow.

Mugs in hand they sat at the kitchen table, the clock ticking away the time. She was a firm believer in the soporific power of warm milk, and he had not had such a treat since boyhood. He drank it quickly, as if downing a potion. They spoke in whispers, the quiet of the country night unnerving and insistent. "You're not the only one with a broken heart."

"I am so sorry, Dolores."

"I haven't slept in months, and now this is my first real hope in ages. You have to find her. Or find out whatever happened to her."

"Do you think that after all this time we might? That she might —"

She smiled at him. "She is an independent girl. And strong. If something has happened to her, if she's just lost. Let's think she is just lost. She will survive and you will find her."

"But we can't know for sure."

The smile faded. She finished her milk and let him take the two empty mugs to the sink. "I know what Mackintosh really thinks, and maybe that Dr. Mitchell you brought along. The puppets are just a coincidence. Maybe, maybe not. The mind sees what it wants to see, but all I know is that you will not find her if you do not look. I'm off to bed now, if I'm to be up making breakfast for the lot of you in the morning." He nodded from his chair, and as she wheeled behind him, she laid a hand upon his shoulder to say good night, a kind and simple gesture, but he felt the weight long after she departed, conjuring complexities of emotion, memories of the last time Kay had touched him so. He wondered for the millionth time if he would ever see her again.

The barn door swung open and the late afternoon sunshine blasted the shadows, bits of old straw and dust swirling in the light. A calico cat slunk in and trotted over to where the puppets rested, rubbing its head and body against the legs of the Three Sisters and stopping to scratch its back on the Good Fairy. Behind the cat tromped the Quatre Mains, dressed like a country squire in long boots and a field jacket, and the Deux Mains in a hunter-green flannel and new blue jeans. He carried a small bag of tools. She was eating an apple, the snap of each bite sharp as a gunshot. A crow, curious about the visitors, flew in and paced in the yard. Together the puppeteers inspected their creations, straightening a crooked limb, folding the hem of the Queen's robes, wiping a line of frass from Nix's shoulders.

"Where is the Devil?" the Deux Mains asked. "Did you put away the Devil?"

"I don't see him. Maybe the boy misplaced him in one of the other rooms. We'll have to ask." Pausing before Noë, the Quatre Mains stared at the patches of broken straw upon her head. "What do we have here?"

"The poor dear."

He looked confused at the puppet's

changed condition, and with the gentleness of a father, he cradled and set her down upon the ground. The Deux Mains, who had been attending to the Good Fairy's branches, hurried over for a closer look.

"Do you think this happened when we last had them out? At the parade? Or has someone not been behaving herself?"

"The latter," the Quatre Mains said, and he flipped Noë to her side to reveal the crude stitches at the base of her skull. Working quickly, he popped off her head and set it atop a post.

The Deux Mains disappeared into the maze of back rooms and brought back a length of muslin and a sheath of broomcorn straw, brightly colored, some of the stalks with panicles intact, delicate as oats. In the meantime, The Quatre Mains picked the broken follicles from the top of Noë's head and removed the twine sutures. He fashioned a patch from the muslin and cemented it in place with a dab of wood glue, and together they wove her a bright new hairpiece strand by strand.

"What on earth got into her?" the Deux Mains wondered as they worked.

The Quatre Mains stopped, picked up the head, and gave it a few good shakes. From the neck hole, the dried husks of two honeybees fell into his open palm. He blew and they drifted to the floor like snowflakes. They finished the hairdo, and while his wife held the head in place, he sewed it back onto the body. Satisfied with their handiwork, they put her back in the stall, jostling Kay in the process. She would have fallen over had not the Quatre Mains caught her. The feel of his hands on her was electric.

"We'll have no more funny business," he said to them all. "Winter is a-comin', and I don't want to have to be traipsing through the snow drifts to check on you, and I surely do not want to find more trouble next spring after the hibernation."

The puppets stood impassive but listening. Slipping her arm into the crook of his, the Deux Mains rested by his side and faced Mr. Firkin and the Queen. "It is a long wait, I know, but not forever. Keep your wits. You may go anywhere you like as long as you do not try to leave the barn. Be well, my pets. And where has that cat gone off to?"

They stood still and listened. A low rumbling came from the belly of the barn, and the Deux Mains called "Mimi, Mimi," but when the cat did not come, a note of panic rose in her voice. "Come, *ma minette,* time for dinner." From below came another grumble, louder still, and she unhooked her arm from her husband and ran out of the room.

"The Worm," the Quatre Mains said. "Oh, that stupid fearless cat."

The floorboards lifted and gave a sudden lurch, and the Quatre Mains moved quickly down the stairs to aid his wife. Something long and large was squirming in the basement, moist earth moving, and banging into the side walls. The cat hissed and screamed. The Deux Mains shouted a warning in French, and the Quatre Mains bellowed for everything to just stop. An animal mewed deeply as a cello. More commands were issued — stop, drop it — and then the Worm went quiet.

Moments later, the cat reappeared in the stalls, no worse for wear. It roped its way through Kay's legs and meandered to the front door. Huffing from the climb, the Quatre Mains rested in the doorway. "Go anywhere you like. Except down in the cellar. That one has gotten away from us a bit. And for heaven's sake, keep an eye out for the Devil."

"Have a nice long rest," the Deux Mains said. She laid her hand briefly against Kay's papery cheek. *"Bonne nuit, mon chouchou."*

After they shut and locked the door a soft whimper came from below. A sigh of missed opportunity.

At midnight, they exploded with talk. Nix went down on his hands and knees searching the floorboards for cracks or chinks through which he might locate the Worm, but at that late hour, all he could see was the dark basement and perhaps, he reported, the bare outline of a form that took up most of the space. He whispered "Worm, Worm," but the thing did not respond. Curious, the little dog sniffed for clues, pawing at the sawdust whenever Nix spied through a hole. The Three Sisters parried the notion that the Devil had been misplaced somehow, while the Old Hag insisted that he was dead, killed by the others lurking in the other rooms. On the whim of the Original. The Queen and Mr. Firkin were engaged in a dialectic over the new rules and restrictions imposed by the Quatre Mains and how best to maintain law and order.

Gathering together the scraps of muslin and sorghum straw, the ball of twine, and scissors the Deux Mains left behind, the Good Fairy sat on the corncrib making puppets. Primitive little marionettes who could dangle from the ends of her twiggy hands. By her side, Noë, resplendent with her full head of new hair, played idly with each doll as it was finished. Kay found herself drawn to their game, and the three sat in a triangle pursuing the goal of one puppet to tie to each finger.

Kay watched her friend for signs of disturbance. "I was afraid when they took off your head that they were not going to put it back on."

Noë wiggled the doll back and forth. "I call this one Pinkie because she fits just fine on my littlest finger."

"And I was afraid about what might happen to that cat when it went to the cellar."

"Cats have nine lives," the Good Fairy said. "Perhaps it had one to spare."

"Your feet," Noë said. "It would be terrible to lose your feet. Or your hands, how would you play with a puppet? No, I guess the worst would be to lose your body. No, I take that back. Your mind! Maybe it is the head after all?"

"They've done a good job with your new hair."

"Do you like it? I feel much better with no more bees. I call this one Tom Thumbkin. He is in love with Pinkie on the other hand. Were you ever in love, Kay?"

"Yes, of course. My husband."

"Theo."

"That's right, Theo. I was in love with

Theo. Back in the other world."

"What other world?"

Leaning in close to Kay's ear, the Good Fairy whispered, "There are worse things to lose than your heart, poor dear."

"The real world," Kay insisted. "The world of the living. Where you come from, the real people, don't you remember?"

Noë looked up with a mad glint in her eyes and showed them a puppet mounted on her middle finger. "This one's name is too rude to say."

With a laugh they went back to their craft, making puppets, putting on a show in the wee hours of the night.

21

The dog wanted to follow them out to the car, but she was afraid of the rain. Instead the travelers said their good-byes on the porch, Sal bouncing among the three of them, and Dolores stoic in her chair with Mrs. Mackintosh faithfully stationed behind her. They had made a late start to the expedition, dawdling over their pancakes with maple syrup. All discussion of their mission was put off until the last moments.

"You'll keep in touch," Dolores said. "And let me know the minute you find out anything. Call as soon as you get cellular service. It's miles from nowhere, so I'll understand."

"Don't forget — we'll be by the phone," said Mrs. Mackintosh.

Theo promised and kissed his mother-in-law. "You have my word."

With a disconcerting swiftness, she grabbed his hand in hers and held it close, silently imploring and wishing him success. Mitchell and Egon jogged through the raindrops to the car.

"You know the way?" she asked.

"I have my trusty guides. Listen, if she can be found . . ."

He looked over his shoulder as they rolled down the driveway, and the tableau had not shifted. The dog wagged her tail, considering whether to chase the car. The women raised their hands, offering a final salute.

They got lost along the way, stopped for lunch, stopped again for directions, and reached the farm in the shank of the afternoon. Rain had given way to a misty drizzle shrouding the red barn in gray. A pair of wet chickens foraged in the grass before a yellow farmhouse. A handmade arrow, inset with the word Museum, pointed to the barn. A ramshackle school bus — Northeast Kingdom Puppet Co. painted on the side — stood in the driveway, but no other vehicles were about, and no lights shone in the windows against the gloom.

"Nobody home," Mitchell said from behind the wheel.

"Looks abandoned," Egon said. "Like a graveyard after the last funeral of the day."

"Knock and it shall be opened," Theo said.

Nobody answered when they banged on

the storm door. Egon went to the window and peered into the front room, which was dark and empty. "Maybe we should have called first."

"Try again," said Mitchell.

Theo hammered on the door.

A teenage boy with a crown of white-blond hair appeared, framed in the window of the storm door. He stared blankly, surprised to have visitors and uncertain what to do next. For a few moments, a standoff ensued.

"Good afternoon, young man." Mitchell broke the silence. "Is this the Northeast Kingdom Puppet Company?"

The boy nodded and gestured toward the barn and the bus.

"We've come a long way," Mitchell said. "Do you think we might see the puppets?"

The boy looked confused and did not say a word.

Egon stepped closer. "Is there a grown-up around? Someone in charge we might speak with?"

The boy shook his head.

"Would you mind opening the door?" Theo asked. "Could I bother you for a glass of water? A chance to use your bathroom? We mean no harm, we've just come to see the puppets."

With a push of his hip, the boy opened the storm door and made way for them to enter. Hanging on the walls of the foyer were posters from past shows. The puppet adaptation of Kafka's *The Trial,* with a sad effigy behind bars. *I, Claudius,* with the puppet emperor raising a bloody fist. *One Day in the Life of Ivan Denisovich,* a tortured line of puppets marching through the snow. The boy led them into the living room, where even the furniture appeared handmade and primitive, and bade them sit.

Theo made the introductions. "I'm Theo Harper. These are my friends Egon and . . . Dr. Mitchell. We've come from New York City to see the puppets."

The boy nervously shifted his glance from side to side.

"How about you, boy?" Egon asked. "Got a name?"

"Drew," he said at last. "We're closed."

"Hello, Drew," said Mitchell. "Are your parents around? You're not here all alone?"

He snapped his fingers, hiding his hands behind his back. "She's here. But she don't like to be disturbed during the day, not while reading."

"Your mother?"

"Don't have no mother. No father neither. They took me in."

"I'm so sorry," Mitchell said. "Who took you in?"

"The puppet makers."

From the upper floor, a door opened and then slammed shut. Heavy footsteps in the hall. Drew looked toward the staircase. "Now you done it. She's gonna be mad. Watch yourself."

A lanky young woman with long red hair hanging in a single braid came stomping down the stairs and stormed into the living room. When Mitchell rose out of habit, Theo and Egon aped his etiquette.

"Sit down," she said. "This isn't 1893. What can I do for you gentlemen? I am sure Drew has told you — like I asked him to — that the museum is closed for the season, so if you come to see the puppets, you'll have to come back in six months, sorry to say. And if you're here for something else — I can't imagine what that something might be — out with it. I was trying to read."

Mitchell dared to speak. "We were just telling your brother —"

"Not my brother." She laughed.

"Drew, here. We came all the way from New York just to visit the puppet museum."

"You should have read up about us on the Internet, then you'd have known we are closed November first to April first. Cold

347

up here in Vermont. Would have saved a lot of trouble."

Egon picked up the case. "We're with a big talent agency in Manhattan and have heard great things about your work."

The girl looked down upon him with disdain. "No exceptions."

"Is there someone else we could talk to?" Egon asked.

"You could talk to the puppet master. His farm, his puppets. But he isn't here."

"When will he be back? Later this evening?"

"Can't say."

"Does he have a cell phone?" Egon asked. "We could make an appointment."

"No phone," she said.

From the rocking chair, Mitchell said, "Surely you could just let us have a quick peek, and then we'll be out of your hair."

She tugged her hand along her braid. "Barn's locked. Don't have the key."

Behind his fist, Drew snickered a wet guffaw.

Through the picture window, the red barn glowed softly in the late afternoon mist. She would not be persuaded, and they would have to find another way. Theo stood suddenly and announced they were leaving. "We'll check back tomorrow after we've had a good night's sleep. And if you see this puppet master, could you please tell him we are in the area and are very much interested in his work?"

"I'll tell him about you New York people when I see him, but we really aren't interested in that sort of thing."

"Thank you for your hospitality. We'll see ourselves out."

They drove around a bend until the farmhouse was just out of sight, and then Theo had Mitchell pull over and shut off the engine. In the gloaming, they backtracked down the country lane, sneaked in behind the bus, and made their way to the barn. Egon tried the handle to the front door, but it was locked as the girl had said.

"There's got to be another way in," he said softly, and they walked along the perimeter, the grass wet and spongy under their feet.

A wooden fence abutted the silo standing at the barn's western end, and behind it the grass had been worn away and a few slabs of granite jutted forward to make a ledge. Enclosed by the fencing, a pasture gradually sloped fifty yards to a small stream that marked the end of the property. Beyond the stream, the land rose through a forest of birch and pines that led to the road at the base of another mountain.

"I'll just hop over into the meadow," Egon said, "and see if there's a back entrance. See that ledge there? I'll bet you that's where the sheeps or goats used to sit and watch the day go by. Some of these old barns on a hillside like this have a cote built into the lower floor. The sheeps go in and out through the basement door, so to speak."

"Too dangerous," Mitchell said. "You'd break your neck if you fell down that hill."

From inside the barn came a muffled barking that sounded like a mechanical yap from a windup toy. With a wave, Theo herded them toward the front entrance, and the barking intensified and changed directions. From the direction of the farmhouse, a black mastiff charged straight at them, ears pinned back, teeth bared. They froze in place, and the dog stopped a few feet away, tense and ready to spring if they took another step. It moved its snapping jaws on a swivel among the three of them so quickly as to appear to have three heads at once. The storm door slapped shut, and the redheaded girl hurried across the yard followed by the boy. She ran like a Muybridge series, a jerky stop-motion sequence that made her look like a puppet, and the boy's timing, too, was just a fraction out of sync. The boy grabbed the dog by the collar, and it relaxed under his grip.

"I thought I told you we were closed," the girl said. "I told you it was locked. Now, I think you better get and don't come snooping round here no more."

"Did you hear it?" Kay asked.

Olya stretched and yawned mightily. Just after midnight, and they were the first ones astir. "Such a reckit. Who can sleep with such a reckit?"

Her sisters grumbled at the disturbance and rolled away from the lamp that Mr. Firkin had lit before going to see to the Queen. Nix woke up beside them and immediately reached for his juggling. One by one the puppets roused themselves.

"There was the dog," Kay said. "Did you not hear it barking outside? And strange voices. Someone trying to break the lock."

"Dahlink, I can see trying to get out of this drafty old place, but why would anyone try to break in?"

"Didn't anyone else hear it?" Kay asked again. "Three voices."

The Old Hag lifted a hand to her ear. "What's that you say?"

Over in their corner, the Good Fairy and

351

Noë were hanging their finger puppets on strands of twine from a crossbeam above the stall. With the brush of her hand, the Good Fairy called her close. "I heard it, too. Late in the day after the sun had dropped behind the mountains. Noë heard them, didn't you?"

"The men. Three new ones, and then the girl who lives in the house, and the boy, and the big black dog."

The tiny puppets spun on their ropes like witches on the gallows. The Queen was passing, and the prodigious train of her gown stirred the air. Because of her great size, she commanded the tight quarters, and they were ever watchful and aware of her presence. The three of them huddled closer so as to not be overheard, but secrets were difficult to keep from one whose ears were twice as big as theirs. From their crouched positions, they waited till she was safely gone.

"I do not trust the Queen," the Good Fairy said. "Or that she always has our best interests at heart."

For the first time in ages, Kay felt relief and a sense of camaraderie with another puppet. Noë had long been her ally, but she may well have gone mad. Or was maddening everyone with her pretense. To have the

Good Fairy admit to treason, an impulse she shared, made Kay near delirious with happiness. "I quite agree with you about the Queen. She has gotten too big for her own good."

Eyes gleaming with mischief, Noë drew a finger across her throat. "Off with her head."

Covering the hole of her mouth, the Good Fairy held back a laugh. "Shh, not so loud."

"I wonder what would be inside her head," Noë said. "Delusions of grandeur and notions of power."

"You must be quiet and more circumspect," the Good Fairy said. "Kay, what do you make of the noises at the door this afternoon?"

"The girl and the boy were angry. Why else would they let loose the black dog? I think the men were trying to come inside, but they were stopped at the door."

"Who were they?" Noë asked. "I bet they were here to rescue us. We just need a person to come along — any person will do — as long as they are willing to lead the way."

Kay stroked her arm and smiled at her. "You don't suppose they made it inside before they were caught?"

"Could be. There is only one way to be sure that it is still locked," the Good Fairy said. "But we must get by the Queen and Mr. Firkin."

"We'll need a diversion," Kay said. "Something that will keep their attention while we slip off and check the front door."

"If I had a match," Noë said, "I could start a fire —"

"Don't even joke," the Good Fairy said, holding up the kindling of her arms. "It doesn't have to be serious, just enough so they won't notice we are missing. We'll be there and back in two shakes of a lamb's tail."

A new idea hatched in Noë's addled brain. Fetching a length of rope coiled on the floor beside the corncrib, she twisted a noose in one end and measured out the remaining length. With a quick toss, she flung it over the crossbeam and tied it off to a rail on the stall. Masha and Irina watched silently, wallowing too deep in their own ennui to stop her or utter a warning. Climbing into position, Noë balanced on the rail. Taking care not to muss her new straw hair, she slipped the noose over her head and tightened the knot against her neck. Nodding once to Kay and the Good Fairy, she sighed as loudly as she could. When no one took notice, she cleared her throat and clapped her hands three times.

"If in this world I cannot be free, then I cannot stay in this world," she announced.

"Get down from there at once," Mr. Firkin hollered as soon as he had spotted her. "No, wait . . ."

The Russians shook off their slumber and got to their feet. Nix dropped a ball, which rolled across the room, setting the little dog in motion, which startled the Old Hag. The Queen, anxious over this unscheduled execution, charged to confront her. Seeing their chance, Kay and the Good Fairy darted out of the room in the commotion. Noë had launched into a political diatribe, venting her long frustration in a fit of oratory.

They rounded the corner into a small vestibule that served as the entrance to the museum. The room was brightened by moonlight streaming in through an octagonal porthole inset above the outer doors. Atop a rickety table stood a tin coffee can with "Donations Welcome" taped to the surface. Next to the can was a guest book with handwritten entries: The Millers from Woodstock found it "spooky." Andi *und* Christian Ludwig from Ulm, Germany, wrote *"fantastisch"* and "never seens anything like it." Along the opposite wall, bins filled with silk-screened posters from past shows were available for a few dollars each. The room as a whole produced an odd stereophonic effect. The stray voices in the other rooms were louder, but they could also hear the Worm crawling about in the chamber below, grumbling to itself, as well as their comrades in the stalls raising a ruckus over Noë's admonitions.

"You don't think she'd really go through with it?" Kay mimed the pulling of the noose, the snap of the neck, the loll of the tongue.

"I doubt it. But what if she did? The worst that could happen is that her stitches give and her head pops off. We'd simply have to sew it on again."

Offset from the center of the room, the great doors loomed. A wooden bar laid horizontally across the frame was braced against a metal clip, and they knew at once that nobody could have entered past that barrier. Whoever had locked it must have used a separate exit, perhaps the subterranean one guarded by the Worm. Directly opposite was a stairway that led to the basement, but the door to it, too, was shut tight. The visitors from that afternoon must have gone home disappointed.

The temptation proved too great. Kay asked, "Shall we?"

She grabbed one end of the bar and pulled while the Good Fairy pushed from the other end, and it slipped away easily. A beam of moonlight shone through the slim space between the double doors, and the handles were cold to the touch. With all their might, they pulled and the doors swung free.

The night air crackled. The open yard stood before them, the frost glistening on the grass, the farmhouse dark and silent. Mere steps away, they hesitated on the threshold, listening and watching, studying the suddenness and impossibility of the world that looked as false as a painting on a curtain. Like her first time at the circus, holding on to one of each parent's hands, and all at once burst forth the spectacle, the color, the sound, the motion hadn't seemed real. Just as the world outside the barn challenged her sense of what was artificial and impenetrable. Yet there was no denying the chill breeze rushing into the barn, the stars fanning out into the endless sky. An owl hooted from a faraway tree, and they found themselves laughing at the staging. Kay wanted to leap through the surface but was afraid. She closed her eyes and watched a film of images flash by from a thousand different memories, each moment distinct but combining to make a whole picture of all that she had held dear and left behind. Her father, mother. Theo. Just out there, just beyond reach.

"You cannot leave," the Good Fairy said, laying a hand upon her shoulder. "You can only be rescued from this place by someone from the other side. Someone who will agree to lead you away."

"But they were here," Kay said. "I know it. I can feel it."

Out in the yard, the cat mewed, the strange yellow light reflected in its eyes as it walked toward the barn. The cat stepped closer, growing bigger, until it was nearly at the edge, and then it penetrated the landscape as though stepping out of a two-dimensional picture of the night. It headed straight for the darkened alcove that held the cellar door. A light went on in the farmhouse, and a window flew open, the farm girl crying out in the night for her cat.

A voice came from behind them.

"You better shut those doors."

Startled, they spun around together, and there in a weak circle of light, grinning despite his best efforts, was the Devil himself.

22

The Devil bowed his head slightly, introducing himself again to his friends who thought him dead and gone. Kay and the Good Fairy rushed over and mashed their arms around him with joy. Had he the power to blush, he would have colored from scarlet to crimson. With an awkward shrug, he freed himself and picked up the cat nuzzling at his cloven feet and petted its fur with his sharp-nailed hands. Setting it gingerly on the floor, he whispered "scat" and the cat pranced through the doorway, holding its tail in the air like a question mark before running back to the yellow house.

"The doors, my friends, shut the doors before we are caught."

Kay and the Good Fairy rushed to the doors and swung them shut, careful not to put the locking bar back into place. From the corner by the cellar, the Devil produced a kerosene lantern and, striking a match on his thigh, lit it, and the Good Fairy gasped at the flame.

"Please, don't worry," the Devil said, with a diabolical smile. "If I cannot manage a little bit of fire, who can?"

"We thought you were unmade," said Kay. "We thought you were dead."

"What happened to you?" the Good Fairy asked.

"Dead? Not dead. Come with me and I will show you what happened, but you must not be afraid."

His hooves clopped on the wooden floor like a billy goat crossing a bridge, and they followed his horns into the adjoining room. A dozen puppets stood frozen in a line. Blue from head to toe, they were dressed in tattered rags and wore rough beards and wild hair of tangled curled paper. Each man had an arm on the shoulder of the man in front of him save the leader of the gang, who bent forward as they trudged grimly toward a primitive cell with real iron bars, and around their broken shoes an excelsior snow had fallen. They looked cold and miserable and forlorn.

"I don't think I've seen a sadder bunch of creatures," the Good Fairy said.

The Devil held the lantern close to the

leader's face. He bore a frozen expression of utter despair in his eyes. "These comrades are headed for the gulag. Some Russian play — the Three Sisters might know the name. Perhaps one day soon we can arrange a rendezvous between these lonesome souls and those charming young ladies."

The first prisoner cracked a smile, and a chuckle ran the length of the chain, intensifying man to man until the final prisoner burst into a hearty laugh.

"The Devil puts a spoon of honey into another man's wife," the leader said. "We have been waiting for you for ages."

The line broke apart as the puppets roared to life, laughing and clapping one another on the back. A pair of the prisoners broke into a chorus of a drinking song, and the leader embraced the Devil and pumped his hand in congratulations. One of the men winked at the Good Fairy and mimed his appreciation for the cleverness of her unusual wooden construction.

"Follow me, comrades," the Devil said. "More wonders to behold."

In the next room, more puppets cheered their arrival. They were dizzying in their variety, long and short, fat and thin, bright and somber in design. Three giant disembodied heads — long-forgotten buffoons

361

made for a political satire — propelled themselves forward by chomping their jaws. A quartet of skeletons shook their bones and danced a mazurka. Old familiars from children's stories sang out: the Three Little Pigs pink as hams, a Dish and a Spoon with the glow of the recently eloped, and a little old lady who sat by a giant shoe, eight tiny heads peering through the eyelets and another young one sliding down the tongue. All the people were happy to see the new arrivals and clamored for their attention.

"No wonder we heard voices from our room," Kay said.

"Wait," the Devil said. "You ain't seen nothin' yet."

Some of the gulag refugees stayed behind in the impromptu celebration, but the Devil and his entourage crowded into the narrow hallway and proceeded toward the next room. Stopping suddenly and holding his hand for silence, he motioned for Kay and the Good Fairy to join him. The space was dark and cool, and a small circle of light appeared and expanded from the size of a dime to the size of a dinner plate. Delicate notes from a koto set the tone, and a Bunraku puppet took the stage, a beautiful Japanese woman in a marvelous embroidered kimono whose movements harmonized with the music for six measures. Then a switch in her head was thrown, and she rolled back her eyes to a hideous yellow, horns popped out of the front of her skull, and she grimaced to reveal two rows of sharp teeth. Kay yelped at the sudden transformation, and the demon quickly changed back into the young woman and began laughing hysterically at her own joke. A deranged monkey clapped its hands against a gong. Two samurai drew their swords and waved them in a blur, and a braggart waggled his bushy eyebrows.

Introductions followed all around, and bowing low, the ningyō proved gracious and begged forgiveness for having scared the visitors. The Devil took delight in the machinations set in place but could barely contain his enthusiasm to show them the next chamber. He led them into a tableau which Kay recognized at once from *A Midsummer Night's Dream.* Fairy marionettes hung from the ceiling and spun slowly, the light reflecting off their silken wings — Cobweb, Peaseblossom, Mustardseed, Moth, and the rest surrounding a lifesize Oberon and Titania reclining on a mountain of pillows brocaded with gold and silver threads. The changeling boy, an Indian prince, done as a rod puppet, nestled in the bed between the fairy king and queen, and off to one side lolled the rude mechanical Bottom in his ass's head crowned with a garland of paper hibiscus. The four youthful lovers were shadow puppets flat against the wall, and perched on a cider barrel, Puck awaited his cue.

"My people," the Good Fairy exclaimed.

"Lord, what fools these mortals be!" Puck shouted, and all at once, the puppets danced to life, shouting their huzzahs. Bottom brayed. The lovers swapped places and swapped back. Oberon joked, "Ill met by moonlight" to Kay, and the fairies swam in the air on invisible wires. Kay felt as though she was back in the cirque and stretched her limbs, wondering if she might ever be so fluid as to tumble and balance again. The others from the other rooms jammed into the scene till it nearly burst with puppets exuberant with performing before a new audience.

"I had no idea you were so many," Kay said to Puck.

"This is but the floor below. Wait till he takes you to the loft. Wait till you see the Original." He pointed to the wooden staircase leading up.

"The Original?"

"The man in the glass jar." Puck clapped

his hand to his mouth, suddenly aware that he had let out a secret.

Intrigued by the prospect, Kay pestered the Devil, pulling on his tail to get his attention. "Will you take us there? To the upper floor."

In the din, he pretended not to hear her question. The Russians were singing about vodka, the Bunraku witch played a surfing song on the koto, and Puck ran amok, spreading mischief. Even the Good Fairy had joined the party, branches thrown into the air, allowing the children from the shoe to have a good climb.

"I want to see more," Kay said.

The Devil took her hand. "All in good time. We should be getting back. We can't leave Noë swinging from a rope all night long."

"How did you know about what we were doing in the stalls?"

"This barn is at least a century old and is filled with cracks and chinks and holes through which one might easily spy. You don't think I would just up and abandon my old friends without keeping an eye on you. We've covered the whole perimeter of the bottom floor and are nearly back where we started. Take a look. . . ."

Through a sliver in the wall, Kay could

see the stalls and the trough, the backside of the Queen obscuring most of the view, but she glimpsed Noë on the beam, the noose around her neck, continuing her fili-buster.

"Before we go any farther, we should rescue our old comrades. Let them know that this is everyone's barn and that they have nothing to fear from these so-called others. There are no others, only us, all the same. One big happy family."

"And then you'll take us all to the loft?" Kay asked. "To see the Original?"

"If you hadn't come to investigate the noises at the door, I would have come back to you in any case. There's a great celebration to be held tonight in our honor, for the puppets of the Quatre Mains. All we need do is convince old Firkin and the Queen to let our people go. Now, go fetch our bosky friend. We have an entrance to make. Not every day one comes back from the dead."

"Good-bye, good-bye," the fairies cried in their twinkling voices.

"Hurry back," the samurai said. "Don't miss the shindig." A Russian dissident blew a kiss and winked as they passed. They wound their way back through the maze, astonished a second time at the new worlds just around each corner.

366

■ ■ ■ ■

They were lost. Driving around rural Vermont in the dark looking for a place to eat,
they were not only hopelessly off course but
shaken by the events back at the farm. That
dog had been all teeth, and those two
children of the corn had given them the
creeps. At one point, Mitchell suggested
that they head back toward Bennington for
the night or better yet to forget the whole
thing and go home to New York, but with
the help of the GPS, they found an inn still
serving supper.

Over onion rings and ales, they hatched a
new plot. On the back page of the menu,
Theo drew a crude map of the property,
the position of the farmhouse, the bus, and
the barn. He penciled in the meadow and
the stream and the small wood. With his
friends' assistance, he added the road that
curved past the property.

"We'll go back when they are asleep. Dr.
Mitchell, you will let us out here on the road
behind the barn and then circle round past
the farmhouse and park just out of sight.
We will hike through the woods, across the
stream, over the fence, and up the hill.
Egon, are you certain there will be an

entrance at the back?"

Raising his tipsy head, Egon wobbled. "*Mon ami,* one is never certain of a theory until confronted by proof, and even then I am not sure about anything having to do with these puppets and the crazies back at that place. Before I met you, life was a simple thing: a warm bed, a cold beer, now and then a hot woman. But let us leave that all aside. We are here now and must see it through. What was your question?"

"Another way into the barn?"

"Yes, that's where the sheeps and the goats would go in and out. A cote. Why would they lock the back door? Perhaps there is no door at all, merely a hole in the wall."

Theo stared at his friend, trying to judge his sobriety. "Good, then we sneak in, look for this puppet —"

"How will you see in the dark?" Mitchell asked.

"Flashlights." Egon rubbed his hands together. "I never travel without them. And I know what to do if we meet up with that hound from hell." Glancing around to make sure none of the waitstaff was watching, he wrapped a piece of steak in a napkin and crammed it into his jacket pocket.

"This is more complicated than I

thought," Mitchell said. "And more dangerous."

Theo offered him a way out. "Let us take
your car, then. You could spend the night at
the inn, and we'll be back in the morning."

"I wouldn't dream of it. All of my life I
have been reading about gods and monsters,
the great quests, and I have gotten no
further than a book in the armchair. Count
me in, Harper. I am honored to be one of
the Argonauts."

Flush with drink and food, the route well
mapped, they set out and arrived at the
farm just after midnight. A light appeared
in one upstairs window, but no new vehicles
were parked in the drive. The girl would be
reading in her room, the boy would be
asleep, hopefully next to the dog. Mitchell
continued on as planned and drove around
the bend to the spot on the road at the edge
of the woods.

"How long should I wait?" Mitchell asked.
"Before I get worried?"

Egon calculated the distance. "Fifteen
minutes' walk, twenty if we run into trouble."

"Give us another half hour or so in the
barn to find the puppets," Theo said. "There
were what . . . a dozen in the Halloween
parade? We might not find Kay at first. Wait

two hours, just to be safe. If we are not at the rendezvous, drive up to the house, and we'll meet you there."

As they stepped out of the car, Mitchell called out from the driver's seat. "What should I do if something happens to you?"

Theo popped his head through the open window. "Make sure my book gets published. And tell Kay's mother that we tried."

"No," Mitchell said. "Nothing quite so . . . final. I meant, what do I do if you don't show up at the house?"

"Knock on the door and wake that harridan and that half-wit," Egon said. "Tell them the truth and pray that dog is asleep."

"Audentes Fortuna iuvat," Mitchell said. He waved good-bye as they climbed over the guardrail and disappeared into the woods.

"Forward," Theo said.

With no path to follow, Theo and Egon had to pick their way down the incline through the trees, alert for any roots or ditches buried beneath the shag of fallen leaves. Up on the road, Mitchell started the car and drove away to the meeting spot. They had decided beforehand to walk blind through the forest without using their flashlights until they were actually in the barn, so as to not give themselves away. But

370

that meant being alone in the forest in the dark and subject to its bewitchments. The pines brushed against their faces and arms and the white birch glowed like skeletons. The slightest noise became a fox or black bear. Stirring in the undergrowth meant a snake. Every breath escaped in a small cloud. Theo could feel the beating of his heart, hear the suddenness of his gasps. They stumbled and stopped to a rest at the bottom of the hill.

The stream was dead ahead, shards of moonlight breaking on the gliding water. They were nearly upon it before realizing how wide it was, and of course, there was no way to tell just how deep it might be. Huffing from exertion, Egon put his hands on his knees when they reached the banks of the stream. Theo turned on his flashlight and played the beam across the surface, a few stones hunched against black water.

"Looks like we could use a boat," Egon said.

"A ferry across the Styx, Mitchell would say."

"We could turn back now. Or I could try to find a way stone by stone." Egon hopped from the bank to the first stone, and Theo followed him, conscious of the music of the water against the rocks. They forded the

371

stream until the very last stone. Egon gauged the leap incorrectly and landed on the edge with a splash. "Christ!" he shouted and hopped to the bank. "Cold as a grave."

With his longer legs, Theo jumped onto the soft shore. "Are you all right?"

"Mes souliers sont chiés," Egon said. "And my socks are sopping, too. But here we are."

Running along the edge of the pasture was a wooden fence topped by a thin strand of wire.

Theo flicked on his light and studied the obstacle. "You don't think it's electrified, do you? I wouldn't want you getting zapped, wet as you are."

"Fortune favors the brave," Egon said, and without hesitation, he climbed up and over to the other side, with Theo fast behind him. At the top of the meadow, the barn loomed in the darkness, blotting out the moon and stars.

An owl, white as a ghost, screeched as it passed overhead. Beating its wings soft as a whisper, it flew to the cupola atop the roof. Faint notes from a mandolin reverberated as it landed, and a round of laughter came from the upper loft of the barn.

"What the hell is that?" Egon whispered.

"Music."

"I'll be damned."

"Coming from the barn or from the house? You don't suppose they're dancing in there?"

"It's the puppets."

"Are you sure about this?"

Egon said, "I am certain she is one of them somehow. A puppet. Black magic. Two kinds of people come to the supernatural: some who don't believe and some who approach the world in all its inexplicable dread and wonder. There's only one way to know if I am right or wrong. If I'm wrong, what harm to us? And if I'm right, then there is a chance we've found your Kay."

"Ridiculous, can't be . . ."

"Don't let doubt be your enemy, *mon ami.* Trust what you hear and see, and let your heart be your guide."

Following the old goat trails, they zigzagged up the hillside. Halfway to the barn, they could see the light seeping through the cracks between the boards and hear stray voices and the clomp of dancing feet coming from the loft. The whole building seemed strangely pulsing and alive. Atop the rocky ledge by the cote, they stopped and found a small doorway just the right size for a goat or a sheep.

"That's my entrance," Egon said. "No use you crawling in on hands and knees through

373

the muck. You go round to the front, and I'll make my way through and unlock it and let you in, unless I get caught up in the polka. Just be careful if you hear that hellhound. Go on, then. *Bonne chance.*"

23

Noë screamed and struggled for her balance when she saw them return with the Devil in tow, quite nearly hanging herself by accident. The Quatre Mains puppets turned as one to witness the Devil's entrance, a demonic grin across his face, his forked tail wagging like a hound's. They forgot all about Noë's threatened suicide and rushed to welcome him home with astonished embraces. Wrapping his arms around the Devil's belly, Mr. Firkin lifted him atop the corncrib to be more easily applauded and admired. During the homecoming, Noë stepped out from under the noose and cornered her friends.

"So he's been hiding this whole time?"

"Not hiding," the Good Fairy said. "Playing the diplomat. Winning us new friends. You'll be so happy when you meet them all."

Turning her back on the celebrations, Noë was determined to find answers. "What about the front door? Was it locked? Did someone come for us?"

"In all the excitement, I nearly forgot," the Good Fairy said. "There was nobody at the door."

Kay whispered in her friend's ear. "But we left it unlocked. Just in case."

To stop the little dog from whimpering and pestering, the Devil scooped him up in one hand, and for his troubles, he was nearly licked to death. He handed the beast over to Nix as the puppets gathered round for the sermon.

"Ladies and gentlemen" — he bowed to the Queen — "Your Majesty. I come back from the dead with great news. The others are us. Or should I say we are the others. Or there are no others, only us."

"But they tried to kill you," said the Old Hag. "We all heard the screams that night. It was a most horrible noise, and you were surely unmade or near death throes."

"Nothing of the sort, madam."

"Was so, was so," Nix insisted. "Never heard nothing like it in my life."

"What you heard were shouts of joy and astonishment. There are great wonders and enchantments in other rooms. Ask your friends the Good Fairy and Kay."

Commanding silence, the Queen rose to

her full height and paced back and forth, casting a pall over the whole room, everyone anxious over her reaction to the Devil's story. She was thinking, never a good sign. Tucking his hands behind his back, Mr. Firkin trailed her footsteps, a look of great consternation on his face, as the little dog bounced along at their feet.

"We are not amused," the Queen said at last. "Not amused in the slightest. First, Devil, you left our person without permission, without so much as a by-your-leave, and made yourself absent these several nights, bringing grief and consternation to us all. We thought you had perished, my dear friend, at the hands of the others. But rather, you were on a spree. And were discourteous enough not to let us know your whereabouts or of your general health and well-being."

The Devil hung his head contritely.

"Second, and I see now what rogues you are, the three of you — Noë and Kay I understand, but you, too, Good Fairy? The three of you conspired and colluded to fashion this most distasteful ruse. That you would concoct a hanging, not even as a mere public execution but as a diversion so that you conspirators could sneak away to search for the Devil here —"

"That's not what happened," Kay interrupted. "We heard a noise at the door and —"

"Silence!" The Queen stomped her foot. From the cellar came a horrible yawn, a growling lip-smacking groan as the Worm awoke from its sleep and slithered in its tight compartment, banging its body on the side walls. Nix dropped to his knees and looked through the cracks.

"Now you've gone and done it," he said. "The thing's awake."

Mr. Firkin reached for an old shovel and banged the blunt end three times on the floor. "You needn't worry about the Worm. Just restless. He's totally harmless and can be trained like a dog if you show him who is boss."

Pressing her hand to her brow, the Queen shook her head. "Enough of these constant interruptions. What, pray tell, am I to do with the lot of you?"

"Begging your pardon," said the Devil. "We have been invited to a fête tonight. In our honor, up in the loft. You will have the chance to meet the other puppets and see for yourself that we have absolutely nothing to fear. Why, the Original himself extended the invitation —"

"Enough!" cried the Queen. "No more.

There will be no celebration, and I forbid each and all to leave this room without my express permission."

"But I assure Your Majesty, I assure you all. You have my word. This is but a kindness, a way to meet the neighbors and join the company of puppets in the museum."

"How do we know this is not some other plot and fancy? No, I say, I forbid it. And I'll not have another word on the subject."

The Good Fairy stood up to speak, and Mr. Firkin lifted the shovel over his head. "One more word out of you," he said, "and you'll be kindling. You heard the Queen. It is forbidden."

The threat of violence chastened them all, and they returned to their places. Nix picked up three balls and commenced juggling. The Three Sisters retired to the trough and swooned. Visibly shaken, the Queen sought the counsel of Mr. Firkin in a private spot.

Under the miniature puppets dangling from the crossbeams, the conspirators huddled together as far away as possible, given the tiny confines. The Devil sat on his tail and wrenched it from under his legs. Noë fought the temptation to play with her new hair, but the Good Fairy was stolid as a tree. They said nothing at first, pretending

to sulk, but Kay could see in her friends'
eyes the determination to thwart the royal
edict.

"The Queen has gone too far this time,"
the Devil said. "Does the power reside in
the monarch or in the people?"

"Ever since you've come to Vermont," the
Good Fairy said, "you've become a regular
socialist."

"When in Rome . . ." He smiled and
stroked his beard. "We must convince the
others to stand up to them, to go with us,
then old Firkin won't be able to use his
scare tactics."

Kay pointed to the Queen on her throne
and Firkin whispering in her ear. "You
won't persuade those two. Or Nix, either —
he does what the fat man asks. And I don't
think the Old Hag is brave enough to join
the cause. That makes four for them, and
four for us."

"What about the Three Sisters?" the Good
Fairy asked. "They seem too dissolute to
care about politics one way or another."

The Devil tapped his horny nails together.
"You must give the voters a reason to vote.
Leave it to me."

World-weary, trapped in their sense of life
as a gray and dismal condition which must
be endured, the Sisters lay in deep and list-

less indolence. The Devil crept into their boudoir.

"Old *chort.*" Olya barely lifted her head. "So heppy to see you again, dahlink."

"*Mesdames,* you are looking well. Beautiful Olya, elegant Masha, and ravishing Irina."

Sighing, they sat up to hear his flattery.

"We are planning a revolution. Join the masses and we'll be seven to four. Five if you count the Dog, though I'm not sure he is a radical. I want to take you out of this place. Some music, some dancing. A little romance, perhaps?"

Fluffing her cottony hair, Irina sat up straighter.

"There's a bunch of Russian dissidents. Refuseniks. They haven't seen one of their countrywomen in ages."

While the younger two responded with interest to the news, Olya frowned.

"There are others, darling," said the Devil. "A samurai, perhaps? A pair of young and foolish men who like to swap lovers. And there are many more puppets besides, up in the loft."

"I will go," Olya said. "Not for some man but for the sake of freedom and revolution."

The conspiracy of puppets marched to the other side of the room to confront the

Queen. She wobbled and nearly fainted when they told her they were going to the loft and that they would not, could not be stopped. When Mr. Firkin reached for his shovel, he was stopped by the iron grip of the Devil's left hand.

"This is treason. Unhand me, imp."

The Queen waved him aside with an imperial flutter. She shook her head sadly. "I suppose this day was inevitable, what with such sedition all around. But you should know that I act only in the interests of my people. Yes, it may seem a perfectly charming invitation, and we ourselves have been yearning for some new company, new conversation, for some time. But the rules are made for your protection. You will remember that we did not consort with the Original back at the toy shop. He in the Front Room, and we in the Back Room. It was better that way. Safer from his unpredictable nature."

The puppets gathered at the door into the dark.

The Queen abdicated her power. "Go, if you must, but take heed you are not tempted to lose your place or forget your roles. We are as we are and have been long before we came to this . . . barn. Always behave with your integrity and pedigree intact. As puppets of the Quatre Mains."

Nix set down his juggling balls and groveled at her feet. "I should like to go as well, Your Highness."

"Where are we going?" the Old Hag hollered and lifted the fan of her hand to her ear.

As the Queen and her lackey Mr. Firkin sat together forlornly in the empty halls, the others set off for the celebration. Even the Dog joined the Devil's entourage. They had just rounded the corner to the vestibule on their way to the stairs when a loud croaking sigh seeped through the floorboards, followed by a bang on the walls below as the Worm twitched in its lair.

Egon picked the constellations from the sky, remembering his childhood in Québec and his father naming the stars to him. Nights had been their time together. Under the cover of darkness and away from inquisitive strangers, they would escape in its thrall, their differences diminished when they were alone. He lit a cheroot and blew smoke at the heavens, wondering what had become of the old bastard. He enjoyed his little cigar down to the end.

How did I get caught up in such a strange plot? he thought. One day running the back of the house for the cirque, a good steady gig, the next hunting for missing girls and finding puppets. On a rescue mission with that egghead Mitchell with his history and mythology, and that other egghead Harper with his philosophy and obsession with that dirty old photographer. The world spins in crazy circles. His feet were wet, and he was cold and tired and not so eager to discover what might be inside the barn. Puppets gave him the willies.

The small entrance into the cote was fronted by a swinging gate, and he imagined those long-ago sheep and goats lowering their heads and butting it open. With one good push, it gave way and he stepped inside. The ripe smell of ammonia filled his sinuses and made him cover his nose. He trained the flashlight to the crossbeams dappled with swifts' nests, and he nearly tripped over a bag of quicklime resting near the door. Running the length of the cellar, a black mass swelled from floor to ceiling, nearly taking up the entire available space. His instinct was to hurry out of that place as quickly as possible, but he was drawn toward the strange object. Metallic red and gold shimmered in the circle of light. Scales like snakeskin, but the size of dinner plates, were arranged in perfect symmetry. As he drew closer, he could see each one was decorated in delicate bands of green along the borders. Unable to resist, he ran his fingers along the scales, relieved to discover that they were made of paper covered with foil. Along the bottom and running down the spine was a jagged feathery plume. A dragon, like the ones he had seen in street performances for Chinese New Year, a long wormlike thing that took several men hiding under its skin to maneuver. A taloned foot rested under its belly two yards away and another one further along, and he realized that he was at the tail end of the beast.

"Maudite marde," he muttered to himself. "That is a big feckin' worm."

Small clawed feet scrabbled on the wooden floor, and he worried about encountering a mouse or, worse, a rat. Nothing worse than a rat. He swept the light around the room and saw the stairway near where the dragon's head must be. Between the monster and the row of goat stalls lay a passage barely wide enough to squeeze by. One hand on its side for balance, Egon inched along the walkway. Each step was made with trepidation, for the side of the dragon undulated under pressure. Egon stopped, pressed his ear against the shiny scales, wondering if it was breathing or if he was merely hearing the pulse of his own blood in his ear. From the floor above, muted voices rose and fell like the end of an argument. He wanted another smoke to calm the hell down.

The back of the dragon's head looked like a flower. Ornate flames resembled bright yellow petals, and on the very top, two stylized horns curved like parabolas. Egon peeked around the fearsome head and saw at once the bright green eye, dead as marble, the long whiskered muzzle with nostrils widened to spray fire, two rows of dagger-like fangs, and a blistering red and yellow tongue.

"Fortune favors," he said and wrapped his fingers around one pointed tooth. Cardboard and hollow.

The dragon sighed, a sudden intake of air and then a croaking exhalation that caused Egon to pull back his hand and reconsider. From head to tail, the beast's body rippled and then repeated the motion tail to head. The jaws opened wide. It seemed a trick, a toy automaton sprung into action by some hidden lever or button that he had accidentally touched. He shone the light down the dragon's throat, paint and paper, real and not real. Curiosity overruled common sense. Egon stepped inside the dragon's mouth. The jaws snapped shut, and he was gone.

Bloodred in the night, the barn hulked against the sky, nearly blotting out the stars. Theo craned his neck to catch their faint light. At his feet, dried pokeweed and witchgrass clung to the ground along the building's perimeter, and he came across a rusty gear abandoned in the weeds. The owl in the cupola screeched once and took flight in pursuit of something rustling in the dead leaves. Theo was in no hurry to make his way around to the front, not with the fresh memory of that vicious dog. Cigar smoke curled around from the sheepcote entrance, and he toyed with the notion of going back to his friend to find some courage there.

Across the road, the farmhouse was silent, the girl, the boy, and the dog hopefully asleep for the night. He walked to the barn door and waited for it to open, expecting Egon with good news. From deep inside the building came a mechanical croak and the crash of something heavy against the walls. Things that go bump in the night. He tried the doors, certain that they would be locked, but was surprised when they swung open. Faced with the opportunity to find some clue about Kay, he hesitated. In his darkest moments, he thought she must be dead. There had been no sign of her for months, and if not for the chase after these puppets, no connection or clues at all. He had no reason to think it might be otherwise without any actual proof or evidence, but part of him would not relinquish hope, however scant, that she might be alive. Love is the madness which allows us to believe in magic.

He stepped into the barn, and when his eyes had adjusted to the darkness, he realized the entrance fronted a small gift shop of sorts. Silk-screened posters and pamphlets on how to make your own puppets were for sale. Donations were accepted in an old coffee can. Fishing coins from his pockets, he dropped them through the slot and they clattered to the bottom, a startling noise in that quiet space. He noticed that a light was on in the room around the corner, and he went to it like a moth.

At the back wall, perpendicular to two rows of old stalls, rested two puppets. Sitting on the floor was the giant queen, ten feet tall, swathed in her regal robes, and standing beside her was a life-size effigy of a man in a bowler hat and a walrus mustache and a barrel-shaped body. Their presence startled him at first, but they were as still as mannequins. Theo recognized them from the video of the Halloween parade and wondered where the other puppets might be. Where was the one made of sticks? Where was the juggling clown? The old crone? Where was the one who looked like Kay?

Here and there on the floor and the wooden partitions lay the husks of dead bees, dry and light when he held them in his hand. Above the stall farthest from him, tiny figures floated from strings hanging from a beam. Primitive dolls in muslin gowns that looked like the work of a young child, the girl from the house perhaps. Drawing close, he saw each had a crude face that had been fashioned out of pins and buttons, marks of a pencil to create a mouth. One of the tiny marionettes reminded him of Sarant, that contortionist acrobat from the cirque, and another had hand-drawn goggles like Reance, the man who had followed Kay. He stood beneath the flying dolls, wondering about their connection to her days in Québec. Egon would know. Where has he gotten to? Theo wasn't sure he could inspect the other rooms without him.

Dominating the room, the two effigies leaning against the wall had an uncanny lifelike quality that put him on edge, even though he could tell they were made of paper and wire, decorated with paint and dressed in old clothing. He drew close to study their faces. The queen stared at a spot near the ceiling, but the barrel man's eyes were closed, though ready, it seemed, to blink awake at any moment. His mustache appeared to be made of the trimmings from a broom. Curious, Theo touched one finger to the whiskers, and the puppet flinched and sneezed.

24

Giddy as schoolchildren, they took the stairs as if walking on air. The Devil led the way, and a great roar from the mob of puppets in the loft resounded when his horned head appeared. One by one, the others, too, were welcomed with cheers and hooting, shouts and whistles, a great cacophony that made them feel like stars.

Kay stopped at the top of the stairs, astonished by the sheer number of puppets in the great loft. Crammed into the space like a Manhattan cocktail party, dozens milled about. Tall as the Queen herself, the four Rushmore presidents — Washington, Jefferson, Lincoln, and Teddy Roosevelt — were engaged in a political colloquy. The Children from the Shoe played hide-and-seek, laughing and chattering in squeaky tones. The Bunraku witch was frightening the Three Little Pigs with her demonic transformation, and they squealed in mock horror. Oberon was chatting up a young Juliet as Romeo flirted with Titania. Four ghostly figures on sleek black horses fumbled with the fairy marionettes, tangling crossed wires and laughing through ruined mouths. Hanging from the rafters a giant moon rolled his eyes from scene to scene and smiled at the new Quatre Mains puppets, and underneath the moon, a cat played folk songs on a fiddle accompanied by a tall white man with long black curls, who strummed on a ukulele and sang falsetto.

The Devil took Kay by the elbow. "See, they are just like us."

"Opa!" a deep voice hollered jubilantly from the middle of the room, and the musicians responded with a quicker tempo. Along the walls, the puppets crowed together and started a rhythmic clapping that started slowly and rose to a crescendo. In a grand entrance, emerging from a hole in the wall near the silo, six young women burst forth and set the partygoers into ecstasy.

Ravishing in their primitive costumes, the young women glimmered with bare limbs and feet, long wild hair, and a look of madness in their eyes. Two held spears in their hands, much like the ones Kay recognized from her metamorphosis from doll-size into her current form. Two were robed in animal-skin tunics, and two had wineskins bando-liered across their chests. They waved to the audience, and the music slowed as they began to tumble and somersault and cart-wheel in the space carved out in the center of the floor. Wild cheers met every leap and canter. Kay thought back to her fellow acrobats in the cirque and was mesmerized by the kaleidoscope of color and the power of their dancing.

"Who are those women?" she asked the Devil.

He stroked his beard to the point. "They are the maenads. Don't get too close."

From behind them came the clatter of footsteps on the stairs, and the Quatre Mains puppets parted to allow another six creatures to come bounding in, bare chested and shouting with lusty throats. They danced across the room on cloven feet, the lower half of their bodies fur covered, the hooves beating against the wooden floor. The satyrs chased the maenads, grabbing at their costumes, snatching at the wineskins to drink and spill dark red wine. Embold-ened by the bacchanal, three of the gulag dissidents sauntered over to the Three Sisters and pulled them onto the dance floor. Nix took the cue and picked up three of the shoe children and juggled them in the air, the babies laughing with abandon. The little dog bounded to the cat with the fiddle and howled at his spot in the chorus. The skeletons played their bones like xylophones, beating a tattoo on their ribs. Scooping up the Old Hag in his giant hands, Teddy Roosevelt swung her round to his back and trotted about on all fours like a great moose while she cried "Bully, bully!" The Devil grabbed the Good Fairy in his arms and they fox-trotted into the mob. Pockets of laughter erupted. Shouts of feigned protest were met with delight and surrender.

A hand slid into Kay's hand and squeezed tightly, and she sensed at once Noë's plaintive gesture. She allowed herself to be led away into a somewhat quiet corner where the two wallflowers could be alone, but they had to shout to be heard above the din.

"Looks like we're not the only ones after all," Kay said.

"There are too many. Where did they come from?"

"Same place as us, I suppose. You must be relieved to see so many others like us."

"A relief?" Noë looked at the wild party unspooling all around them. "If anything, it makes things worse."

"But look at all the fun they're having."

"I don't belong with these puppets." She bowed her head to avoid having to see them.

Kay bent down so she could face her friend eye to eye. "Why would you say such a thing?"

"Have you forgotten who you are?" She seemed more bewildered than ever, the madness returned.

"Noë." Kay brushed her hand against the doll's painted cheek. "Just who is that anymore?"

As the song stopped, the Devil and the Good Fairy rounded the dance floor and broke off to rest before them. His face was redder than ever, though the Good Fairy showed no signs of exertion. The band paused, and the noise diminished enough for regular conversation.

"Ah, you party poopers," the Devil teased. "Join the fun. Won't you come with me, Kay? There's someone dying to say hello."

Dragged away, Kay looked back at Noë, dejected against the wall, the Good Fairy wrapping a branchy arm around her shoulders. The Devil elbowed through the mobbed floor, the painted faces leering as he and Kay passed. The other puppets seemed to know a secret.

A very fat and hairy satyr with horse's ears

stopped them with two outstretched arms. "Don't take another step," he said with a hiccup. He wobbled unsteadily and blinked his red-rimmed eyes. "Don't mess with them dames, turn away. The maenads are nothing but heartache and violence. Go back to your life of ignorance and delight."

"Silenus," the Devil said. "Move aside, uncle. We just want a word with the Original. My friend here knew him once, you see. Before she became one of us."

"Better to keep the past in the past," the old drunk said. "People are always chasing chimeras, trying to make things as they once were, but let me tell you a secret, Bub. That's a fool's game. The past isn't there any longer, and it never was. Not as we remember it, not as we remake it over long years soaked by our imaginations. Let go, let go, I say. Better to keep it up here." He tapped a finger on his skull and nearly knocked himself over. "Keep the past in the old noggin where it belongs."

"Your brother Bottom has been looking for you," the Devil said. "Making a complete ass of himself, but he has a full flagon of new wine. . . ."

Silenus nickered and trotted off, but he was quickly replaced on the spot by two maenads, one fierce in a leopard skin, one clad in ivy vines and carrying a wicked-looking spear. They blocked the path with crossed arms and deep frowns.

"Ladies," the Devil said. "Looking lovely as ever —"

"No visitors," the ivied guard said.

"But he sent for this dear child himself. She's one of the Quatre Mains come to pay her respects."

The two women conferred, and after some discussion they stepped aside. Kay passed between them, nervously aware of their barely contained fury, as if they might explode when triggered by a false move.

The noise in the room fell away when she saw him again. The man in the glass jar, the *poupée ancienne* from the toy shop window in Québec, now free and alive like the rest of them. He had not changed a bit. Made neither smaller nor taller, he was the puppet with whom she had fallen in love — how long ago was it now? Forever it seemed. He moved slowly and carefully, stepping toward her in the staccato walk of the stringed ones.

"You are the one I knew," she said.

"And I knew you," he said. "You would visit me in the window almost every day."

"I wanted you for myself."

The Devil whispered behind her ear. "He is very old, the oldest of us all. He is the

Original."

"Are you the first one?" she asked.

"Some say." The puppet's black eyes blazed to life, and he cast his gaze around the loft swarming with familiars. "I see you've brought almost everyone else from the Quatre Mains to our welcoming party, though I am sad to see that Mr. Firkin did not make it."

"Oh, he's here," Kay said. "Down below. He chose not to come tonight. Out of loyalty to the Queen."

The ancient puppet sighed heavily and looked distraught. "And she would not come. My old friend and foe."

"She said to beware of the others. Beware of you."

Around them the maenads began their frenzied dancing and somersaults. The satyrs whooped it up and were chasing any female in the room. The women screamed and the men bellowed. The music grew louder, and spirits emboldened by the celebration lifted and soared. He trembled where he stood. Kay could not believe they were meeting face-to-face at last, someone she was sure she would never see again. And yet, there he was right in front of her, at the center of the world.

■ ■ ■ ■

When the man with the walrus mustache sneezed, Theo pressed his hand to his chest, certain that he was having a heart attack. He wanted to run away, to retch, to believe anything but what he could see right in front of him. The puppet brushed one finger under its nose and opened its eyes, dumbly staring at him with a sheepish grin, surprised to be caught doing what he ought not to have done.

"What strange place is this?" Theo asked. "What the hell kind of thing are you?"

The barrel-shaped man dropped his hand to his side and looked off into the distance, pretending that nothing had happened.

"I saw you," Theo said. "I heard you sneeze. What on earth is going on?"

Unable to resist, the puppet snapped open his eyes and waggled his great mustache. Pressing a hidden lever, he magically lifted the derby from his head in greeting. "Mr. Firkin," he said. "At your service. And who, may I ask, are you?"

"You can talk. . . ."

"Of course I can talk," Firkin said. "So can you. Let me re-pose my original query and ask for your name."

"Theo Harper. But you are a puppet."

"How do you do, Theo Harper? A performer, really."

"Made of papier-mâché."

"We prefer to be called actors. It's what we do."

"How is it that you can talk and move about without a man inside? Is there someone at the controls?"

Firkin raised his brows quizzically and looked down at his enormous belly to check his hollowness. "What time do you have?"

Theo checked his phone. "It's after midnight. Nearly one o'clock in the morning."

"After midnight and before dawn, we are free to move about here in our home. As long as we are alone." His voice sounded as if it was being thrown into his mouth, like a ventriloquist's dummy, slightly false and off-key.

The giant queen rested inertly against the wall. Theo pointed toward her with his thumb. "Just you? Or is that one alive, too?"

Like a windup doll, Firkin chirred into motion, and with a guiding arm, he escorted Theo to the farthest stall, looking back over his shoulder to check. "Do not trifle with the Queen."

"Holy shit, so she's alive, too? Just resting her eyes?"

400

With a jerk of his arms, Firkin tamped down the loose talk. He whispered, "If you know what is good for you, you'll not wake her. Best to let sleeping monarchs lie. Why have you come, Theo Harper? Are you a puppeteer?"

He brushed aside the question. "Are there others here? Others like you who can walk and talk like they're alive?"

"Others? There are many others."

"I've come about just one. My wife, Kay."

At the mention of the name, the Queen opened her plate-sized eyes and looked directly at him. She drew in her knees and pushed up off the ground, rising slowly to her full ten feet. The top of her head nearly grazed the ceiling as she lurched forward. Each step of her stiff-legged gait required considerable effort, and Theo saw her walk like the stop time of a Muybridge sequence, a series of still images, fluid and static simultaneously. He could outrun her if need be, if she meant him some harm, but her face displayed curiosity rather than fear or malice. Firkin laid a heavy hand on Theo's shoulder, encouraging him to stay put. Just steps away, she stopped, towering over them and swaying like a tree in the wind.

"There is no Kay Harper here," she said. "And you should not be here either. Get out while you can."

"But I saw her," he said. "In the Halloween parade. And I saw you and this rolypoly man and several others besides. So you won't mind if I have a look around for her?"

The Queen squared her shoulders and flared out her robes to make herself as large as possible. "I most certainly do mind. You have no business in this place. Be gone, and forget what you have seen here."

"You heard her, friend," Firkin said. "There'll be no second chances. Go, and say nothing of what you witnessed in this place."

"You don't scare me. My friends will soon be here. Matter of fact, there's a man coming right now through the cellar."

"Oh dear," Mr. Firkin said. "I wonder how he'll pass the Worm. He may well be detained longer than any of us expect."

From the floor above came the sound of music and dancing, so raucous that the miniature puppets above their head began to swing in the air, revealing the old faces from Québec. He knew Kay must be upstairs and took a step toward the exit.

"What do you think you are doing?" the Queen asked. "Let's say she is here, for the sake of argument. Let's say you can find her somehow. Do you think you can just waltz in and take her away? And what would you do anyway with a puppet? She would not be who you remembered. She would not be as she was before. No, go home while you have the chance. If you persist in this folly, there is nothing I can do for you."

"But I love her," Theo said. "I miss her. She is the other voice in my head. Blood in my heart, song in my brain. You have no right to take her away. I've looked for her every day, and now that I am so close to finding her, I won't be stopped. Not even if she has become someone else. Even a puppet."

Mr. Firkin shuffled his feet in the sawdust. "You had better forget her, chum. Nothing to be done. So sorry for your loss."

The Queen fell to her knees and sat back on her heels to face Theo. Her shoulders slumped and she folded her hands in her lap. "Am I growing soft? Have I lost the iron will I once enjoyed when we few were in the Back Room? My size, I fear, has only heightened my sympathy. Much better for a queen to have a cold heart. Is there nothing I can say to you, dear man, to convince you otherwise? The world, if given time, will break your heart, but the heart will heal with time to be in the world again." The Queen lifted her hands to hold his face. She felt like a mother, he felt like a child.

"I need to find her and, if possible, to take her back with me. My wife is a real person, a human being. If there is a way to make her whole again, please tell me."

"Kay is here, but first, you'll have to find her. The way is not that difficult, just keep turning to the right till you find the stairs. But I cannot say what, if anything, lurks in the rooms along the way. There are puppets about, strange creatures over whom I hold no influence. And then you will have to get past all the others who have no wish to see Kay go. They would recognize you, of course, in your current form, as a man. So a costume is in order, though even the best mask will not hide your true identity for long."

She brushed the ghostly puppets hanging on their strings. "Simple is best, under the circumstances. You will need to act quickly. They are distracted by their revels, so you may be able to fool them as a ghost."

Mr. Firkin interjected, "There may be some spare muslin about, and you'll need a cloak over those clothes."

"If," the Queen said, "if you can manage to avoid detection, you will have to be cunning and not alarm her. Convince her who you are, and, even so, she may not wish to leave. There are others who may want to go with you."

"Noë, for one —"

"Thank you, Firkin. Others who would be more than happy to attempt escape. But you may need to assure Kay of your love and get her to believe that life — her old life — is possible beyond these walls."

Theo brightened. "I have faith enough for both of us."

"You may need it," said the Queen. "There are two exits. You could try to retrace your steps to the front door, but the others will surely notice and you may not get very far. The better choice is through a hole in the wall, up by the silo somewhere, I reckon. I'm afraid I cannot be more specific, as I've not seen it from the inside for myself. But I know it is there. I saw it from the outside when we arrived, and the wind blows through it on certain nights. You'll have to plan your route before you go. Speed will be of the essence. Once they notice you are trying to flee, the others will come after you and quickly."

"You'll have the one chance only," Mr. Firkin said.

"Manage it before dawn, and she will return to her human form once you are outside. Don't underestimate the other pup-

405

pets. They are strong and fierce and are not likely to allow you to escape. Once you are outside, you must run away as fast as you can, and do not under any circumstance tell a soul about what happens here."

"That's it?" Theo asked.

"Provided you don't look back as you are passing through the exit," the Queen said. "If she loves you, she will follow. If not, you may lose her for good. But you have to trust her."

Above them, someone was tumbling across the floor. "Mr. Firkin," Theo said, "I'm ready to become a puppet. Let's make that disguise."

25

They cut the head out of stiff muslin, stitched it together like a bag, and stuffed it with rags. When they had finished, the false head appeared three times larger than his own, and he had to work to find the balance to keep it on straight. Behind the table in the vestibule where the silk-screened posters were sold, Mr. Firkin found a pot of black ink, and they daubed a crooked mouth and two crude eyes, piercing them so Theo could see through small holes at the center. Over his body, he wore a simple floor-length sheet, also made of muslin, tied at the neck with the noose that Noë had fashioned. He looked like a giant version of the marionettes strung up in the rafters.

"Keep your hands hidden once you are in the loft, and nobody will notice. You make a nearly acceptable ghost."

"Turn around," said the Queen. "Let me see. Hmm, it will do. Nobody will know you, Ghost. And our timing might be advantageous. The others will think you are one of us, and the Quatre Mains puppets will assume you are one of the others. Be wary of the Devil, however, for he knows everyone."

"The Devil, you say?"

"Red suit, horns, pointy beard. Watch out for him. Try to glide as best you can and make yourself inconspicuous. Think like a puppet, move like a puppet. When the time comes to escape, hasten to the passage."

Firkin trimmed away the frayed end of the noose. "And if all else fails, run like hell. You're ready now, so get going. Through the rooms to the stairs. Can't miss them."

"I can't thank you enough —"

The Queen raised her hand. "No thanks are necessary. If you manage your escape, you will forget all you have seen and learned here and the secret life of puppets. Go, find your beloved. But beware of the primitive wooden puppet at the center of it all, a plain and unassuming doll who will do the unspeakable if he catches you."

Theo walked away through the darkness. The first room he came to was empty but for a few bare branches and white excelsior on the floor, a deserted set to a forgotten winter's tale. A giant empty shoe dominated the second room, and he did not want to imagine the size of the puppet whose foot belonged inside it. In the center of the third room was a single shōji with a delicate painting of a plum tree in blossom. After inspecting the screen for any puppets hiding behind it, he hurried into the adjoining chamber, a set right out of a fairy tale. Resting in a bower was a full-sized man, gently snoring next to an empty jug. He clutched a swag of purple grapes in one chubby hand, and the other hand rested upon a small sleeping black donkey, worn by its toils.

"What ho, spirit?" The puppet sat up, a fat and hairy satyr wearing nothing but a laurel garland encircling his head, an unkempt beard, and horse's ears. "Whither wander you?"

If I remain still, Theo thought, he will think he is dreaming and fall back asleep.

The fat man burped and chuckled to himself. "Will you not speak, ghost, and tell me why you are here? Have you come at last for me? Have my wanton ways finally bested me? One hopes. Ah, well, he lives with the least worry who knows not his misfortune. Come and sit with me awhile and tell me what it is like to be dead. Whether or no it is wiser to have never been born at all."

Theo put on a false voice, deeper than his own, his cadence slowed by half. "Had you not been born, you would not know what it is like to be alive, and without life, death is impossible to understand."

Raising a fist to his forehead, the fat man appeared to be in pain. "You are a strange spirit with a strange philosophy, and you are giving me a headache. I am called Silenus, friend. What name did they give you while you were upon this earth? Or are the names we keep but hollow things? Come have a drink, whoever you are, and we shall celebrate your escape from melancholy reason." Silenus gently slapped the donkey on the rump, and it hawed once and rolled over to sleep on the next pillow.

Theo shuffled up the mountain of cushions, and folding his legs to keep his shoes hidden, he sat next to the drowsy old drunk. When offered a tipple from the jug, he politely demurred.

"What need of wine has a ghost, eh? When one is dead, the crass appetites disappear, but if one is immortal, appetite is all, I am sad to say." Silenus patted his enormous belly. "Tell me who you have come for, friend, so I may drink to your good fortune."

"I came for my beloved —"

"Ha! 'Tis an old story. The oldest. Love."

"Do you know a puppet named Kay?"

"Again with the names. I am lucky to remember my own. Or my brother's name, Bottom, is it? Are you looking for Bottom?"

Theo shook his great ghostly head. "I am looking for Kay."

Silenus scratched his head, dislodging the laurel garland from his head, but he took no notice that it had slid to cover one eye. "They are all above in Elysium. I had to take my leave of their giddy-paced shindig. Too much for me. But ask the Original, he knows everyone. Before you go, take a holiday, Old Haunt. I have no one else to talk to but this little ass."

The donkey brayed its complaints.

"I must go," Theo said. "I have an appointment to keep before dawn."

"Yonder love awaits," the old drunk said. "Chase her if you must, but remember you must keep what you catch." He flopped back suddenly and was asleep again before his head hit the pillow. The little donkey shifted till they were side by side like spooning lovers.

Rising carefully, Theo straightened his costume and rehearsed how to appear to be floating as he headed for the stairway. The music swelled as he climbed each step, the conversations rising and falling in symphony and dissonance. Through the small holes in his mask, Theo saw flashes of light and color till all at once he reached the top and the room exploded into cacophony. A mad attic full of nightmares. Puppets everywhere, so many that he was frightened enough to consider retreating to the peace and quiet of the bower. Wait for Egon — where the hell was he? But Theo pressed on, lifting himself across the threshold, and stepping away from the opening, finding a shadow near the wall to soak it all in.

Small and tall, little fairies twirling on wires and giants walking as if on stilts. Fat and bone thin, a tree person, flat shadows propelled by sticks, effigies, dogs and cats and the Four Horsemen of the Apocalypse on cardboard horses dark as molasses. Three little pigs and nine little babies. Huge heads bouncing along on their jaws. A carnival on acid, a mad costume party with the empty costumes walking, talking, dancing, singing. A couple of marionettes locked in an embrace. A juggler spinning a bird on the end of a string in an infinite loop.

Hot in his overstuffed head, Theo breathed in the aroma of paper and paste, balsa and coiled wire. His mouth tasted of sawdust and ink. With no holes for his ears, Theo could not easily make out the directions of the sounds which seemed to come from everywhere and nowhere at all.

A little dog, no bigger than a toy, found him out at once. It sniffed around the hem of his costume and whimpered at the alien scent, and Theo tried to nudge it away with his toe. A beautiful Japanese woman in a luminous kimono rushed to his rescue, but she stopped short when she apprehended his costume.

"A g-g-g-ghost!" she screeched, and her eyes rolled back to an awful yellow, and red horns stuck out of her forehead, and her smile became a rictus of horrible pointed teeth. Theo blanched and thought this must be the devil the others had warned him about, but just as he started to speak to her, a samurai crept up behind her and with one swift stroke chopped off her head. It rolled across the floor, laughing. Yapping and snarling, the little dog chased after her noggin in a macabre game of fetch. Arms extended, the headless body took off blindly to try to find it first.

"Do not worry," the samurai said. "She will trip over it soon enough, and we will patch her up before dawn."

Theo floated away from the racket to find a quiet vantage to pick through the crowd,

413

trying to distinguish the familiar from the strange. Looking for those from the Halloween parade, he spotted the Three Sisters at once. In a line with men in Russian costumes, the tallest sister had hitched up her skirts to dance the kazotsky, her hinged legs kicking out like a Cossack's, a broad smile striping her face. Two children were climbing on the shoulders of the puppet made from twigs and branches, and he saw as well the old woman asleep in a rocking chair, oblivious to the chaos all around her. The Devil was in hiding.

His first glimpse was fleeting and from behind her, a flash of hair, the curve of a bare arm. The woman with the straw hair was facing him, directly opposite, deep in a corner of the room. Even from a distance, she looked bereft, and another woman reached out to offer what seemed to be a gesture of consolation. Half-hidden by the crowd, she turned toward him slowly, a series of still images that coalesced into a whole motion. He saw her face again. Kay. Alive. In the form of a puppet, but Kay at last. He broke and crumbled. At last, at last, at last.

The Original could not rein in his anger. While all around him the maenads and satyrs cavorted, he paced creaky and stiff legged, muttering to himself. "Beware of me? The Queen said to beware of me. Of the so-called others. That's a fine irony, coming from her. Beware the Queen is more like it. She is a monster, a tyrant, the very bitch of power and duplicity."

Kay cowered in front of the little wooden doll, uncertain what to say to cool his temper.

"I make the overture," he said. "I extend the olive branch and what answer has she? I cannot come to your party. She warns you and all my friends from the Quatre Mains of me? I ask you, who is in the wrong here? That minx, that trollop, that petty husk of paper and glue." He scratched the scar line that bisected his chest, and his eyeholes glowed with ire.

"To be fair, sir, she gave us permission to attend, and we were concerned that you had taken our friend, that you may have unmade the Devil."

"Murdered the Devil, is that what she'd have you believe? And I suppose her fat friend is in on this, too. Firkin, hah. Why would we want to get rid of the Devil? Why would we want to lose anyone at all? The Queen is under a misguided impression if that's the story she bruits about. I am all for harmony among the toys. Every puppet in his place, follow the rules, and you will find happiness. And peace, order, freedom."

"Freedom, is it?" Kay asked. Through the whirl of the dancers, she looked for Noë and saw her standing alone and anxious despite the jolliness around her. "So we are free?"

Stopped by her question, the Original slowly turned to face her. She saw just how old and worn he was. Cracks along the poplar grain had deepened, and the holes on his arms and notch atop his skull where ropes had gone were dark with the grime of centuries. "We are all free," the old doll said. "Free as destiny allows."

"Then you will hear out my friend Noë?" She pointed to the forlorn figure on the other side of the room. "She is slowly going mad from this puppet life and wants her old self back. Can you grant her that freedom?"

A shadow of disappointment crossed his face, and the hinges at his neck groaned as he bowed his heavy wooden head. "Child, you mistake me for something I am not. Long ago the shamans made me who I am, just as I had the Quatre Mains make you into what you have become. You ask for a free will beyond my power to grant. The puppeteers can take her away if they please, as has been done before at times. Though I do not know what fate awaits those who are cast out. But, we are free in the night hours, free within this space —"

"That's no freedom at all."

Livid, she turned away and pushed aside a scowling maenad in her path, deaf to the entreaties of the ancient doll calling her back. She stormed away in long strides till the Devil caught up with her. Grabbing her by the arm, he spun her around with brute force. "What in the hell are you doing? What did you say to him? Have you lost your senses?"

"Once upon a time, I thought he was a god," she said. "But he is nothing more than one of us. Grown old and tired by the centuries."

"You must have respect for your elders. He's seen things and done things that you and I can only dream of."

"Nothing more than a puppet on a string."

The Devil laughed at her and loosed his grip. "Come now, my dear Kay. It's not as bad as all that. You may think this is some kind of hell, but think again of all that you have forsaken and all that you now enjoy. We have no hunger, no real thirst. Our day-to-day anxieties vanish. There is no need for heartbreak or sadness or tears. We do not tire or grow older than the age we were made. No hate, no jealousy, no crime if we so choose. All we are asked to do is what we love. To perform. To make people laugh or cry or feel the heart's tug in the dark for an hour or two. We are immortal, eternal, and loved as long as there is an audience for our few antics."

For the first time since her arrival, Kay wanted to slap someone in the face. "And what if we do not want to be puppets anymore?"

Time slowed, and she spun on her toes to take in the spectacle all around her. The comedy of the damned, oblivious to her exasperation, continued. She heard Olya's deep laughter as a dissident bellowed, "Catch me if you can." Puck tiptoed around the four lovers sleeping it off, squeezing nectar onto their drowsy eyes. Good old Nix was entertaining the children from the shoe with another from his bag of tricks. A ghost she had not seen before hovered at the staircase. Such a life was filled with novelty and fun, loud as a carnival, happy as a circus, but she could not reconcile her desires. She searched the crowd for Noë, the Devil watching every move.

"She has always been a little crazy, our

418

Noë," the Devil said. "Touched since the day she arrived. Never heard her not going on about how she cannot stand one more moment, but I ask you, who is better in a show? Don't let the madness rub off on you. Enjoy the party, and don't waste your time with sadness. It's a long, cold, dark winter ahead, baby, and we don't want you to be so blue. A little sin will do you good."

"Get thee behind me," she said and walked away from the Devil. She fought her way to Noë, stuck alone in a corner, idly playing with the straw on her head.

"Men," Kay said. "I had such high hopes for the Original, but he turned out to be no better than the rest of them, all talk and no action. And to think I used to adore him, back in the toy shop window in Québec. I remember passing by the Quatre Mains on my way to rehearsals each day, and there he was in all his antique glory. A wooden man trapped in a jar. My husband was jealous of him, can you imagine, but I never coveted a thing so much in all my life. He seemed alive, and I was such a fool for him."

"Love makes such happy delusions."

"The old man offered no way out, I'm afraid. I asked for you."

Noë sighed. "I would give anything to feel that way again."

Kay rested her hand on Noë's shoulder. "We could try the front door. Sneak away from the party, nobody will notice, and try our luck. Just because they say it is impossible doesn't mean we shouldn't try."

"But what about the Queen and Mr. Firkin? They're still down below."

"If they are in the stalls, they will not notice. And if they are guarding the door, we could always slip by the Worm in the sheepcote through the cellar door."

With a nod of her head, Noë gestured at a figure over Kay's shoulder. "Don't look now, but I think you have a secret admirer."

"Never mind all that —"

"He's staring a hole through me. I have not seen him before, have you? What's that strange puppet supposed to be, a ghost?"

Feigning nonchalance, Kay snuck a peek at the creature. He was the poorest excuse for a ghost that she had ever seen. Little more than a sheet and an oversized lumpy head. Slathered in mismatched ovals of black ink, his eyes appeared to have been painted by a child, and the mouth was but a slapdash brushstroke in the same dark ink. Holding it all together was a thick rope wound around the neck. Kay looked back to Noë and laughed. "You see the type who's interested in me."

"Shall we run away?" Noë asked. "Before he says boo and tries to scare us? Where has this darling fellow been all night?"

Kay looked at him again, astonished to find him shaking as if he were afraid of her. The Ghost lurched forward awkwardly, unsteady on his feet, and then he looked right and left to make sure nobody was watching him. With a more measured pace, he seemed to float toward them, but halfway across, the woman in the leopard skin tunic, one of the maenads, stepped into his path.

She sniffed the air and held her spear across her chest. "I've not noticed you before, ghoul. Are you one of the Quatre Mains puppets?"

The Ghost nodded.

"And you are after that girl over there? The one who loved the Original?"

More tentatively, the Ghost nodded again, and the maenad huffed and stepped aside reluctantly. As he drew near, he grew more familiar, his strange costume and demeanor giving him away.

"Who is that? Isn't he one of those small puppets that we hung in the stalls?" Kay asked. "How did he come to grow so large? What strange magic is this?"

Cocking her head, Noë studied him more intently. "He wears my noose around his neck. Perhaps we should be frightened of this ghost."

Theo floated to Kay's side and hesitated, awestruck for an eternal moment. Reaching out to hold her hand through the cloth, he bent to whisper in her ear. "It's Theo. I've come to take you home, Kay."

26

His voice in her head stunned Kay. Impossible, yet unmistakable. A voice out of the past, from another world, a dream sound. She pulled away and stared at the Ghost. A make-believe doll made of scraps with a drawn-on face. He was not real, he could not be her Theo, he was little more than idle imagination. A cruel trick conjured by some prankster. The Devil's plaything. A hoax.

"Kay," the Ghost said. His great head shook uncontrollably, the muslin sheet quaked.

"Go away," Noë said. "Don't bother her. What kind of creature are you, anyways? Who made you, Ghost? You look like old Firkin's handiwork. Did he send you? He can't even paint a straight line."

"Kay," the Ghost implored. "It is me under this costume." He stepped forward as if to embrace her, but she backed out of reach.

"You heard her," Kay said. "We want no part of your twisted game. I think it is quite mean of you to pretend to be someone you are not."

Stomping her foot, Noë shouted, "Boo! Leave us alone, you handkerchief!"

From beneath the sheet, he held out his hands, and she saw his skin and bones, the wedding ring on his finger. "You are Kay Harper," the Ghost said. "Your mother is Dolores Bird, who lives alone on a farm in Vermont. You and I met in New York, and we were married earlier this year, and I lost you in Québec. I am Theo Harper. *Tu ne te souviens pas de moi?* I love you."

Drawing her paper face close to him, she saw in the center of the painted ovals his blue eyes peering through the small holes cut into the cloth. Kay pulled him toward her, holding him tightly enough to feel the beating of his heart against the hollow chamber of her chest. "It's you? Have they made you one of us? Are you dead? Have they turned you into a ghost?"

She kissed the streak of black smeared across his face.

Behind them, the makeshift orchestra played the first bars of an antic melody. The assembly sorted itself into two groups facing each other across the floor.

"I'm not a ghost," Theo said. "And I'm not dead. This is a disguise so that I won't get caught. I am not a puppet, I am a man."

Unable to contain herself any longer, Noë tapped Kay on the shoulder. "The others will notice the two of you together. Take heed."

Kay remembered who she was and separated from Theo. "This is my friend Noë. She is all right. She won't give you away."

Seizing the opportunity, Noë grabbed Theo's hands and nose to nose peered closely into his eyes. Like an infant entranced by a new face, she scrutinized with a rapt intensity. "So you are a real person hiding under there?"

With a laugh of delight, he squeezed her hands. "I'm Theo, and a real person, last I checked."

"Really real? From the other world."

"Come from the outside world."

"How did you find us?" Kay asked.

"How did you get here?"

Theo told the story as quickly as he could, beginning with the toy shop in Québec and ending with the journey of his friends Egon and Mitchell and their plan to break into the barn to look for her. "We were to

425

rendezvous at the car with some evidence, but that was before I met the Queen and her consort. That was before I saw the puppets were . . . alive."

The puppets began a line dance, one from each row matching with another and promenading down the middle of the two clapping rows, making for some unusual combinations: Puck and the Good Fairy; the Bunraku demon, head in hand, with Teddy Roosevelt; the Three Sisters escorted by the Three Little Pigs. Each pair showed off their best steps and moves.

Breathless, Nix ran over and planted himself in the middle of Theo's story. "Join the fun. Have a go. The Devil wants to know why you aren't dancing."

Noë tried to shoo him away. "Some of us prefer not to make spectacles of ourselves. Go to the Devil and tell him leave us be."

Bouncing like a restless child, Nix would not be so easily deterred. "And he wants to know who you are, Ghostie. He says he never set eyes on you around here before. Where'd you come from?"

"He's the ghost in the attic," Kay said. "Ordinarily invisible, but he makes himself known when there's a-haunting to be done. Go tell him that, Nix, and stop pestering us so."

Nix pulled at the sheet. "You don't scare me. Can you pass through walls, Ghost?"

Fearful that he would be unmasked, Theo stepped away, but the clown kept coming for him until Noë stepped to his rescue. "We can't have you misbehaving, Nix. It's not polite to ask so many questions. How about I take you to the dance, and if I promise to take a turn with you, we can leave these poor folks alone for a moment." She took the juggler by the hand and led him off, glancing back at Kay. "You owe me one."

Theo and Kay watched till they were safely out of earshot, and he risked taking her hand in his. The paper crinkled slightly under pressure, and it did not warm to his touch. She was two things at once, her true self and simulacrum. To reconcile the conflict in his mind, he stared at her, trying to scrape away the facade and see whether she existed apart from her form. Or whether form mattered at all. He was thrilled to be so close at last.

"What has happened to you? How did they change you into this?"

"I do not know how I changed."

"I missed you, Kay. And nearly went mad when you disappeared. I searched for you, looked every day, and saw you everywhere.

The police thought you had drowned, but that was another woman. Dead, she came to me in my dreams. I couldn't eat, couldn't sleep, couldn't work. I was so lonesome for you."

Kay leaned her shoulder against him. "I wondered where you had gone. Do you remember the old toy shop on the rue Saint-Paul? I was afraid someone was after me, and I went inside. When I woke up, I was in the Back Room with the puppets. I had become one myself."

The passage out of the labyrinth of her story became clear to him. "The Queen, she said that there is only one chance to have you back as you were. We must escape this place tonight, before dawn."

"As I was? Not a puppet?" The possibility seemed to momentarily disconcert her. She lifted her hand to eye level and considered its shape and substance, and then she looked at the rows of dancing friends, Nix and Noë making their procession down the center aisle. "I don't remember how I was."

"You were real. A person, alive just like me."

Her shoulders drooped, like a marionette whose strings have been unbound.

"We need a plan," he said. "We could try to sneak away downstairs, but we would have to make it through the crowd un-noticed. And if we were not caught, we could try the front door which was —"

"Unlocked," she said. "We heard voices outside earlier. I didn't know it was you who was coming, but we left it unlocked."

"Or if someone is guarding the door, we could slip out through the cellar. My friend Egon is waiting for us, and there is a third man, Mitchell, with a car out on the road."

"Dangerous. They might see us try to leave."

"That's why I think it better to go through the hole in the wall up there." He pointed to the spot a few feet off the ground where the silo joined the barn. A few boards were missing, and the opening looked wide enough to squeeze through. He stared at the spot, wondering how to sneak by the puppets and make their escape. "We'll need a diversion. Perhaps your friend could help us? The one with the straw hair."

He looked for her in the crowd. The puppets strolled down the line, their movements out of rhythm with the music, and he realized that their timing was off. In other respects, they seemed quite human, their size, the sophistication of their forms and features, but they could not fully disguise the time signature of their motions. Like a film played at the wrong speed, they could not quite trick the eye. Theo felt like Muybridge at his spinning-wheel camera. If he could just turn the crank with the correct rotation, he could make them appear more lifelike.

"I had not thought of Noë," said Kay. "She has helped me before. And when we were in the Back Room, she was punished for trying to escape. But she is going crazy in this place."

"Perhaps there is someone else you could ask. That fellow she is dancing with. Or that creature made out of branches —"

Kay laughed. "The Good Fairy? I suppose I could, but what do we do about Noë? Can we take her with us, Theo?"

The music stopped abruptly, and the lines dissolved, the puppets laughing and clapping and nearly falling over with fatigue. The Cat played a melancholy air on the fiddle, the strain reflecting the change of energy in the room. Quiet conversations took over. Romeo wrapped his arms around a sleepy Juliet. The ningyō monkey pulled its tail and in a slow whirr of gears curled up into a ball the size of a melon. Even the little Children of the Shoe were tired and one by one nestled against their old mother for their naps. An interlude in which to rest and find a second wind.

The perfect moment for their getaway, Theo thought, but the tap of a sharp nail on his shoulder pinned him to the spot. The Devil had materialized in the silence, and his other hand held Nix by one ear.

"Mr. Ghost," he said, "my minions have been watching you, and I have been told that you have been here in the barn all along. Hiding in the attic. Can you imagine such a thing? There is no attic to a loft, so dear Nix must be mistaken."

"I'm afraid that's all my fault," said Kay. "I said attic when I meant to say . . . the silo. Isn't that right?"

Theo nodded.

The Devil let go of Nix with a snap of his fingers. "You must listen more carefully, Nix. But tell me, does Mr. Ghost not speak for himself?"

"He is a creature of few words," said Kay.

"I'm hoarse," Theo said in his best falsetto. "From talking philosophy with Silenus."

"Silenus? You know Silenus? I've been wondering where he has gotten to."

"Down below," Theo said, pointing through the cloth.

"I'm obliged to you, old spook," the Devil said. "The Original has been looking for Silenus this past hour to settle a conundrum.

You and I shall have to continue our discourse later." His tail wagged like a dog's as he hurried to the stairs.

Checking to make sure they were alone, Theo whispered to Kay, "We must go."

"Not without Noë."

"There's too much risk."

"I cannot leave without her."

He blew out a long breath, settling the matter. "Fetch her, but be quick, while the Devil is away. And see if the Good Fairy would be willing to create some distraction."

"You are out of your mind," the Good Fairy said. "You will never make it. And, besides, what proof do you have that he is who he says he is? Have you even seen his face?"

All around them the others rested, sleeping on the bare floor, bodies twined around bodies or slouching against the walls. A stupor had befallen the party, too much wine and song. Kay glanced across the room at the Ghost, trying to remain inconspicuous near the hole by the silo. "I don't need to see his face to know my own Theo. He's been to see the Queen, and she granted him permission to try, but we need you to cause a commotion when we go through. Something that will capture their attention."

Jittery as a hummingbird, Noë bounced

on her toes. "Please, please, please. We would ask you to come with us, but your head would never fit through the hole."

The Good Fairy felt the broad crown of sticks jutting from her head, ruefully gauging the circumference. "I suppose you're right. Big-headedness is the curse of a broad intelligence and wide learning. Are you sure you want to leave us? Could you not instead ask the man if he would stay? I'm sure it could be arranged if broached delicately."

"I will lose my mind if I don't get out of here," Noë said.

"And you, Kay? Much to gain, but much to lose as well."

For a moment, she considered her life among the puppets. She thought back to the week of shows in Montreal with the Quatre Mains, the thrill of being out of the chorus and made the storyteller to perform in front of cheering audiences. And she thought of the friendships she had made, and how sad she would be to leave the Good Fairy, the Sisters, and all the others. "He is not suited to this life. And I love him. Surely you understand."

With a sharp yap, the little dog made himself known at their feet, looking anxious for a game. Noë shook her finger and told him to be quiet or go away.

"I do not understand," the Good Fairy said. "I am afraid I will never understand love, or how you allow emotion to better reason. But you are my friend, and I will help you. You'll need to be quick when the time comes. Don't delay, fast as you can."

The Dog whimpered at Kay's feet, and she bent to pet it one last time. "What will you do to keep everyone's eyes away from us?"

The Good Fairy picked up the little dog and held it close and quiet. "Leave that to me, best you don't know. Now, go, tell your man to get in position. As soon as you hear me shout, be on your way. Good-bye and good luck."

"Thank you, thank you," Noë said.

"You are the best of us," said Kay. She rested her hand on the tangled branches of the Good Fairy's face, and with that good-bye, she led Noë through the drowsy puppets to Theo at the silo's edge. The passageway was just wide enough for them to squeeze through one by one.

"Are you ready?" he asked.

"Everything is set. We are to go when we hear the Good Fairy shout and everyone is distracted."

"You'll go first," Theo said. "And then Noë, and I'll bring up the rear."

"Noë goes first," Kay said. "We have to take care of her, make sure she gets away. Then you go, so you can pull me up."

"I'll push you next, after her."

"No, Theo. I'll take your hand, I'll follow. Trust me." She hugged him so hard, her chin left an impression on his forehead. "We'll need that rope from around your neck. In case there is a drop on the other side, we don't know how high up we are from the ground. If she changes into a girl again, she could get hurt."

He loosened the noose around his neck and pulled it over his head to hand to Noë. She unraveled its full length and tied a knot around an iron hook screwed into the floorboard.

Kay looked into his eyes. "I want to see your face before we go."

"It's too dangerous."

"The Good Fairy wants to be sure you are who you say you are. It's the least we can do."

The three of them turned as one and signaled to the Good Fairy. Grabbing the hem of his muslin head, Theo lifted gently. The rag stuffing spilled to the floor. Gasping for air, like breaking the surface from under water, he pulled off the disguise completely. She saw his disheveled hair and

435

bright eyes. She kissed him and remembered. Noë grabbed the rope, ready to climb.

Across the room, the Good Fairy snapped a stick from the lattice of her forearm and tossed it toward the spot where the Original lay surrounded by his entourage. The little dog jumped to chase the stick, and the Good Fairy shouted, "My arm, my arm, the Dog has stolen my arm." Barking and snarling, the Dog charged around and over the sleeping bodies, heedless of where it stepped, surprising them from their slumber. The stick landed with a clatter at the Original's feet. The Good Fairy saw the others were distracted and signaled to the escapees.

"Here we go," Theo said, and taking her by the hips, he hoisted Noë up to the slit in the wall. Teetering on the ragged boards, she turned sideways, framed by the black night, and tossed the length of the rope through the exit, testing it once to see if the knot would hold. Quickly shinnying up the side, Noë pulled herself through and disappeared over the edge.

"You go," Kay said. "I'm right behind you."

In the loft, the clamor rose, shouts of dismay over the intrusion of the little dog, the puppets stirring, waking. Barking, laughing, a sudden scream. Theo lifted himself to the threshold. Outside, the night sky glistened with stars, and six feet below, he could see Noë let go of the rope and land on firm ground. "Are you there, Kay?" he shouted over his shoulder, but he heard no reply. He forced himself to keep facing the darkness. The puppets were shouting for him to stop.

The Original hollered, "No!"

He looked back to see if she had followed.

Her face was beautiful. Wide-eyed, startled. He could imagine her whole again, real and alive. She was mouthing something he could not hear, only see the movements of her lips, "I love you" or "All I knew" or . . . and they were right upon her, the satyrs pulling her away from the wall, as if she were drowning and swept out to sea. A great tide of puppets swelled forward, holding her back, and Theo knew at once his mistake.

The point of the spear pierced a spot just below his sternum and took his breath away. The metamorphosis began at once. His hands went first, turning from flesh to paper, his head emptied into a husk, and he felt the transformation jolt through his body, as he lost all sense of himself. He became instead a hollow man, a puppet.

The awful puppets were crowding around him now, their language indecipherable, a primitive guttural chanting, and the little wooden man, the one she had loved through the shop window, withdrew the spear, and Theo collapsed to the wooden floor.

Like a little tyrant god, the ancient doll held up the spear to show to the assembly. The devil was there. The sisters forlorn. A fairy made of sticks. He tried to find Kay in the crowd, to tell her that he was sorry, but he could not speak, could not remember how to raise himself from the ground, lift his head, or move at all. He had a vague recollection of his life, a series of images in stop time. The Original sought a response from the crowd. He was asking a question, looking for their affirmation of his judgment, and the mob roared in reply.

The maenads leapt upon Theo at once and tore him to pieces. They were at him in a fury, rending cloth and cardboard and twisted wire, unmaking the puppet body. A woman in a leopard skin severed his head with a single blow, others split apart his limbs at the seams, and where his heart once had been they left nothing but paper tatters.

27

Muybridge intuited that in order to record motion, one must break it into components.

A single second of film requires 24 images to make the motion seem fluid, natural, lifelike.

Persistence of vision depends upon our physiological ability to see both the image and the afterimage at the same time. Try spinning a sparkler in the dark.

A puppet cannot fully replicate human movement because it cannot move at the proper and constant time signature.

Do I love her, or the after her?

Mitchell closed the notebook and settled back in Theo's chair. Random notes in the margins of his translation, the vagrant thoughts of a troubled mind. Outside his office window, snow was falling, a February snow thick and heavy. The weather report showed the storm's path wide and long, snow in Québec, snow in Vermont.

The doctor advised him to go slow and easy, not to try to do everything at once when he came back to work, and of course, the college understood fully, granting Mitchell a semester's sabbatical, considering. If only they knew the whole story. But whom could he tell now? They might think he was still mad.

Love or, as he saw it now, infatuation had made him say and do things out of character. The night nurse, a pretty young woman with whom he was hopelessly smitten, would sit with him after the nightmares those first few weeks. Mitchell would sit up with a start, drenched with sweat, and the nurse would answer his terrors, calm him, while she held his hand as he told bits and pieces of the story.

"I should have gone in right away. Maybe I could have saved him. One or the other."

"Not your fault," the nurse said. "You mustn't blame yourself."

"They had taken so long, you see. I fell asleep in the car, we'd been driving around all day, and it was two in the morning. They said to wait two hours, but I couldn't stay awake. I should have knocked on the farmhouse and fetched those two kids. De-

440

manded that they unlock the doors. Or gone into the barn myself."

"You were tired. The hour was late. What finally woke you up?"

"I don't know, I don't know. My memory is shot. It could be that I saw her, I think so. There was a light on in the barn streaming out through a hole in the wall by the silo, and a rope hanging down nearly to the ground. That's when the puppet appeared."

The nurse did not judge him but squeezed his hand and brushed the hair out of his eyes.

"A silhouette, really, but it could have been, I think it was one of them. But then I must have been dreaming. I closed my eyes and fell back asleep until the fist beat against the car window."

"That's when you first saw the girl?"

"Unless she and the puppet are one and the same. But how can that be? She was a real girl, as real as you are."

"You need to rest," the nurse said. "I'll get you something to help you sleep."

"No, wait. There was no puppet. They're not alive. She was a runaway. . . ."

The girl banged on the glass, pleading for his help. Straw-colored hair, a simple dress but no shoes, no coat on that frozen night. Instinct took over, the chance to be a hero.

He rolled down the window and saw the panic in her eyes, the clouds of condensation with every word. "Help me," she said. "They're after me. We've got to run."

"Who is after you?"

"The Original must have found them out. Help me."

"Who is the Original?"

"He will not let me go."

"Get in the car," Mitchell had said, and she walked stiff legged to the other side and bent awkwardly into the passenger seat.

She looked over her shoulder at the barn, light streaming through a hole in the wall near the silo. And then she turned to face him, terror in her eyes. "They will kill us. Go, go now."

He started the engine, turned on the lights, and drove away recklessly down that lonesome road. The girl was hysterical at first, alternating between tears and laughter, at then she started to shiver, her teeth chattering, so he turned on the heat and she was fascinated by the blowing air. Intensely curious about the car, as if she was seeing one for the first time. She seemed to regard him with that same disbelief. Mitchell asked her name, but she said she did not remember, only that she had to get away, far away.

"They will kill him," she said. "And then

442

come to unmake us."

Mitchell sobbed and looked into the nurse's accepting eyes. "I should have stopped the car right then, turned around, seen to my friends. But the only thing that seemed to matter was that poor woman's safety."

"She was scared and traumatized. You did the right thing in bringing her to the hospital." The nurse laid a hand against his chest until he fell asleep.

On that snowy afternoon in Theo's office, he felt the remembered weight of that hand over his heart and wondered anew what leads some to love and others to miss it altogether. The runaway girl snuck out of the hospital before dawn without a trace, her name an alias, her destination unknown.

One of the policemen told him so. It had taken hours to convince them that his friends had gone missing in the night, but they finally agreed to accompany him back to the farm the following morning to take a look around, ask a few questions.

An older man answered the door, and one of the policemen introduced himself and Dr. Mitchell and explained the reason for their visit. When they shook hands, Mitchell felt the tensile strength in his grip, the rough calluses in his palm. The fellow spoke with a Quebecois accent and seemed put out by the intrusion on his privacy. "You mean to say that your friends actually broke into the barn to see the puppets? Whatever for? You can come by anytime and have a look around for yourself."

"Did you notice anything unusual last night?" the policeman asked. "Any signs of disturbance?"

A booming bark came from the back of the house. "*Tais-toi!* Quiet! That dog, he sees and hears everything," the Québec man said. "If your friends were here, he would have howled his fool head off."

The policeman looked anxiously around the edge of the door for the dog. "And you were here all alone last night?"

"My wife, just the two of us. She is out shopping at the moment."

Mitchell asked, "Not a blond-haired boy and a tall redheaded girl?"

"Ah, we have some help in the summer, but we are closed for the season. I can show you around if you like, but it is dead as can be."

The man fetched his coat, and they walked toward the puppet museum. He asked Mitchell, "So, you are a doctor?"

"A Ph.D. in the classics. I teach Latin and Greek."

"The great myths," the Quebecois said. "I have a treat in store for you."

They went into the barn and turned left, past the stalls, and went room by room with the quiet and uncanny dolls, neat and undiminished. Some looked as if they had been positioned and forgotten about for years. Dust covered their paper heads and gathered in the seams and wrinkles of their painted faces and hands. He led them past exhibits from children's shows, Japanese Bunraku, and fairy tales to a short flight of stairs into the barn's great loft. Puppets crowded every available space, standing shoulder to shoulder and arranged to the rafters, great giant effigies intermixed with tiny marionettes. The puppeteer led Mitchell to the wall adjoining the silo where two new boards had been nailed in place next to the weathered gray wood.

"Ah, here is what I wanted to show you, Dr. Mitchell." With a showman's flourish, he pulled back a purple scrim. Stacked in two rows were a half-dozen goat-footed men and six women girded for battle.

"Satyrs and maenads," Mitchell said.

"We used to do a spring bacchanal in my younger days. Not so often anymore. *Sic transit gloria mundi.*"

"And that must be old Silenus." Mitchell

pointed to the fat philosopher, silent as a stoic. A little black donkey looked like it was sleeping at his feet.

A worn and ancient puppet stood beneath a bell jar on a pedestal. The puppeteer lifted the glass. "I call him the Original. He taught me everything I know."

Mitchell stared at the primitive puppet, wondering how the girl could be afraid of a mere toy, a little god whose time had long since passed.

From the loft, they traveled down two flights to the sheepcote at the back of the barn to see the beautiful Chinese dragon ready for the New Year, and they finished their tour by walking through the stalls. They found no trace of a break-in, no sign at all that anyone had been there the night before. "Everything in order, gentlemen?" the puppeteer asked.

Mitchell recognized the Quatre Mains puppets from the video, the giant queen, the roly-poly man with the walrus mustache. He asked the policeman to take a photograph on his phone of the puppet who looked like Kay. The one who had reminded Theo and Egon and Dolores of the missing woman. He dared to touch her once, lightly, on her cheek, but she was only paper. She was as beautiful as Theo had described.

The terrors began that night for Mitchell, the twisted nightmares and delirium. Just before he checked himself into the hospital, he received an e-mail from an Inspector Thompson from Québec. "Thank you for the photograph of the puppet. Sgt. Foucault says he cannot see the resemblance, but I find it looks very much like Kay Harper, and I have included it in her file. There was another puppet in the background. A juggler? Reminded me of my brother. Funny how our sorrows play such tricks on our memories."

Files and forms. Mitchell put Theo's notebook on top of the manuscript in the box. The department had long ago closed the files from his classes, the materials related to his employment. All that remained fit in a simple cardboard box, a few personal effects, a dog-eared manuscript of his Muybridge translation, a photograph from their wedding day, and from Québec, a fleur-de-lis paperweight etched with the motto *Je me souviens*. He thought of the woman who had nursed him through the worst nightmares. When they discharged him from long-term care, Mitchell was too distraught to tell her how he felt. Perhaps he could try to find her. How difficult would it be? Maybe she could tell him what happened to

Theo and Egon. Outside the snow covered the grounds, gathered in the branches of the trees, making everything new again. "I am better," Mitchell told himself. "I will forget all this in time and start again."

The puppet theater, fashioned out of an old wooden nail box, stood atop the corncrib. The Queen had to slouch to view the action, but the others were seated comfortably. Resting on his elbows, Nix stretched out on the floor to keep the little dog company. Recruited out of their ennui, Masha and Irina had designed the set, drawing on the back of a silk-screened broadside the ruined mansion and the weeping willows drooping with Spanish moss. Clouds obscured a pale moon, and a bat flew in a fixed spot in the sky.

Hiding as best they could, the three puppeteers crouched behind the box. Olya and the Good Fairy were in charge of two puppets each, and Kay controlled all the others, sometimes two in hand, sometimes four, or even six, pulling the strings wrapped around her fingertips. They had taken the tiny dolls from the ceiling, re-creating them into new characters, and making other puppets besides in the long months that had passed. Filling the winter hours with their craft, attentive to every detail, more elaborate with each new story.

She called her play *Bayou Gothick,* and the scenario was always the same. In the old house on the outskirts of the Vieux Carré in New Orleans, two faded southern belles were beset by some sort of nightmare visitors — spirits, imps, hobgoblins, zombies, or voodoo witches, as the mood determined. Once they found the dried exoskeletons of Noë's honeybees and fastened strings around their middles and flew them around the mansion, but the show so frightened the others that Kay banished it from their repertoire.

Trapped inside, the two belles fled from room to room, pursued by the monsters and demons, until they reached the attic, where the resident ghost kept watch. Sometimes the ghost would help them, and together the three gallants would fight off the undead intruders. Sometimes one or both of the Sisters managed to escape, but the ghost was always left behind. Alone on the stage. For he could never leave the place he haunted, the muslin ghost with the ink-stained eyes and crooked mouth. *"Je me souviens!"* he would cry as the Sisters ran to safety, looking back, always looking back at what they left behind. Every night the other puppets watched a different version of the show, and even though they knew how it must end, they were wrapped up in the story and clapped vigorously at the curtain call.

"Next time!" Nix shouted from the floor. "He will get away next time."

When the cheering ended, Kay would take the strings from her fingers one by one, wind them into coils, and gently put the dolls to rest. At the conclusion of the performance, the Queen rose first and held out her arm for Mr. Firkin to escort her to her usual position. The Old Hag retired with the pup snuggling in her lap. Chastened by his soured relationship with the others, the Devil kept mostly to himself, and Nix, being Nix, whiled away the interval till dawn juggling hoops and balls.

"Listen," Kay said as the others settled in their places.

"Snowing again." Olya sighed. "We will be buried alive till spring."

Her sisters feigned sympathetic looks and flopped onto the railings of the stalls.

"I think it is a beautiful sound," said the Good Fairy. "Makes everything quieter than usual somehow. Peaceful."

The old barn groaned under the weight of the accumulating snow. Outside the white world was cold and empty. Kay put her ear against a crack in the wall to listen. The wind picked up from the west, whistling in the gaps, howling now and again. She thought of Theo in the storm, in the woods where the others had discarded the pieces of him. Caught in the branches of the trees, the tattered clothes snapped and rippled like ruined flags when the wind blew, and the paper limbs and hollow head made a kind of music. Kay could hear him singing, always singing for her.

ACKNOWLEDGMENTS

Thank you to all of the magical puppet companies that inspired this story: Basil Twist, the Old Trout Puppet Workshop, Pointless Theatre Co., and the Bread and Puppet Theater. Thank you as well to my agent, Peter Steinberg; to my editor, Anna deVries; and to all of the wonderful people at Picador. And, as always, thank you to Melanie, for making a better book.

ABOUT THE AUTHOR

Keith Donohue is an American novelist, the author of the national bestseller *The Stolen Child, Angels of Destruction, Centuries of June,* and most recently *The Boy Who Drew Monsters.* He also writes reviews for *The Washington Post.* Donohue has a PhD in English with a specialization in modern Irish literature and wrote the introduction to *Flann O'Brien: The Complete Novels.* He lives in Maryland.

The employees of Thorndike Press hope you have enjoyed this Large Print book. All our Thorndike, Wheeler, and Kennebec Large Print titles are designed for easy reading, and all our books are made to last. Other Thorndike Press Large Print books are available at your library, through selected bookstores, or directly from us.

For information about titles, please call:
(800) 223-1244

or visit our Web site at:
http://gale.cengage.com/thorndike

To share your comments, please write:
Publisher
Thorndike Press
10 Water St., Suite 310
Waterville, ME 04901